The New Girl

M. I. Hattersley

Dark Corridor Books

Read my books for free...

To show my appreciation to you for buying this book I'd like to invite you to join my exclusive Readers Club where you'll get the chance to read all my upcoming books for free, and before anyone else.

To join the club please click below:

www.mihattersley.com/readers

1

The large steel and glass building at the Marble Arch end of London's famous Oxford Street was certainly impressive. But as Jade Fisher's gaze wandered up the glass façade, up towards the third floor, an icy shudder ran down her back. So, perhaps impressive was the wrong word. Imposing was nearer the mark. Ominous, even. Yet she also knew that the head office of Beautiful You! Incorporated was no more scary-looking a place than the Tres Chic offices in Manhattan, where she'd spent the last six years. So maybe it wasn't the building that was making her stomach flutter and sending her mind down dark and unhelpful passageways of thought. Because she also knew what was inside the building. She knew what it represented. And what she was here to do.

Lifting her phone from where she had it clasped to her chest, she could see it was almost nine. Time to get in there. Pushing through the large glass door she found herself in an expansive lobby area made entirely of white marble with the steel doors of an elevator (lift, now she was back in England) on the back wall, next to a high reception desk. To her immediate left was a waiting area, comprising two white-leather sofas and a round coffee table, on top of which was a stack of the new Beautiful You! magazine. Beyond the seating area stood a strange futuristic-looking device that she only knew was a water cooler because they'd had the same one in New York. Large plants had been distributed around the perimeter of the space, each one taller than her and with leaves bigger than her head.

As the main door sucked closed behind her, she walked across the space, her new Prada sling-back kitten heels click-clacking across the hard marble floor and announcing her arrival to the smiley young woman on the desk.

"Good morning," the woman said. "Can I help you?"

"Yes, hi there. My name's Jade Fisher. I'm starting here today. As the new intern."

The woman's smile faltered for a second, but she caught herself just as quickly and flashed her eyes at Jade. She was attractive, with sparkling green eyes and thick, wavy hair dyed dark copper. "Of course," she replied. "If you wouldn't mind taking a seat, I'll let Marsha know you're here."

"Thank you," Jade said, click-clacking over to the waiting area where she perched on the edge of the nearest sofa, facing the lift.

Marsha was head of HR here at Beautiful You! and had interviewed Jade for the position via Zoom. Jade had still been in New York at the time and what with the time difference and a pesky delay on the line, she'd worried she hadn't presented herself that well. Yet two months later, here she was. Back in London, her hometown, scared and uncertain and slightly discombobulated, but ready to do whatever she had to do to make this work.

In front of her, the lift doors slid open and a slim, bordering on skinny, woman with jet-black hair cut into a sharp bob stepped out. Marsha. She was taller than Jade had imagined and more angular than she appeared on the internet. But even if

Jade didn't know she was head of HR, she'd have guessed it. There was something about the way she held herself, the tension in her jaw. It was like she was carrying the entire weight of the world on her shoulders. This, despite being painfully aware that no one in her charge cared one jot about the things that concerned her. That was probably the life of any Human Resources officer in any company. But Beautiful You! - and similarly Tres Chic - were companies run by mavericks and fashionistas, dreamers and artists. These were people who didn't concern themselves with protocol and policies.

"Jade," Marsha cooed as she got closer. "So good to see you again. Did you find us okay?"

Jade got to her feet. "Yes, no problem. I used to work on Oxford Street when I was a teenager – a shop assistant at Miss Selfridge. I'd walk past this building every day on my way home."

Marsha pulled her face. "We all have to start somewhere, I suppose."

"Absolutely," Jade replied, not sure if it was the correct response. Her insides were churning, and she wondered if Marsha could tell how nervous she was.

She breathed in deeply through her nose, filling her lungs and holding it there for a few seconds before exhaling. This wasn't like her. She wasn't nervy. She was forthright and confident. The same girl who'd upped sticks and moved to New York City on her own at just twenty-six, landing a job as a fashion assistant at one of the newest and most influential wellness and lifestyle brands in America.

But there was more riding on this job.

The stakes were higher.

"Do you want to follow me?" Marsha said. "I'll show you around and you can get settled in."

She led Jade over to the lift, which was still on the ground floor. The doors glided open without a sound and Marsha gestured for Jade to enter first, stepping in behind her and pressing the button for the third floor. Her nails were perfectly manicured, with exquisite French tips and Jade made a mental note to book herself in to get her own done as soon as possible. It was important to look one's best. To fit in.

"I'm afraid it's a bit of a madhouse around here at the moment," Marsha said, as they stood shoulder to shoulder, watching the numbers above the door illuminate in turn. "We've got assignments coming out of our ears and with the recent launch of the magazine, we're still chasing our tails, as it were." As she spoke, Jade detected a hint of a Birmingham accent in her voice, which she hadn't noticed before.

"That's fine," Jade replied. "I like to be busy. I like to be amongst the action."

"Good, because there's going to be a lot of that over the coming weeks. I'm not one hundred percent sure what you'll be working on initially, but I'm sure Rebecca will have something she needs you to do. Pronto."

At the name, Jade stiffened. "Is Rebecca in the office today?"

The lift shuddered as they reached their destination and came to a gentle stop. "Not yet," Marsha said. "But she's expected at some point. Are you keen to meet her?"

Jade gasped. "Well, you know, Rebecca Burton-Webb. *The* Rebecca Burton-Webb. I still can't believe I'm going to be working for her."

As the lift doors opened, they revealed a wide landing with polished hardwood floors that stretched out in front of them towards a glass-fronted office space. The walls were white with prints running down each side, displaying some of the most iconic items from the Beautiful You! range over the years. The famous bamboo-cotton overshirt, the crocodile-effect hessian tote bag, the yak's milk candle. As they got up to the glass doors of the office the last picture showed the front cover of issue one of Beautiful You! magazine. The company's most recent venture.

"Well, believe it," Marsha said, snaking her long fingers around the door handle. "You've earned your place here, and I think you're going to fit in perfectly."

She opened the office door, releasing a dull hum of noise as she did. The open-plan room was immense, taking up at least two-thirds of the building's footprint. Glass panels, floor-to-ceiling, spanned both sides of the space and at the far end, one corner was partitioned off by more glass. Desks had been placed around the room at right angles to each other, each with the most recent model of iMac sitting on top. Most of the staff had yet to arrive, but those already in were young and beautiful. They were mainly women, but Jade noticed one or two men, equally beautiful. Most were sitting around talking or leaning into their screens, symmetrical features twisted slightly as they concentrated on whatever they were working on.

"Well, this is it," Marsha said, raising her arms dramatically. "Beautiful You! in all its rebellious, ramshackle glory." She turned back to Jade and tilted her head to one side. "What do you think?"

Jade smiled. "I think it's wonderful," she replied. "I can't wait to get started."

And despite her trepidation, despite the nerves tickling at her throat, she was telling the truth. She'd been waiting a long time for this moment. After months of planning and preparation, of doubts and fears and second-guessing herself, she was finally here. She was going to meet Rebecca Burton-Webb. What's more, she was going to be working for her.

2

The air in the room was cool and stale as if no one had been in the space for some time. Despite this, Jade made herself comfortable, settling in the middle row of the company's small in-house cinema to take in the short film Marsha had tasked her with watching. The film told the story of Beautiful You! and its founder, Rebecca Burton-Webb, from her humble beginnings in Brixton to becoming the influential and respected figure she was today, worth well over sixty-seven million dollars. The screen showed Rebecca as a young woman of twenty-nine, the age she was when she first started the company. She looked so vibrant and full of energy, laughing with Richard Branson at some industry party in the early nineties before the film shifted to footage of her meeting the Queen and getting her OBE.

To watch the promo film, you would think Rebecca had single-handedly built the company from nothing. But Jade knew the unofficial story behind Beautiful You! which was very different from the one presented here. She knew there were other people involved in the inception of the company. Yet, much like the photos of the beautiful models in the window displays of their one hundred and forty-three stores across the world, or in the pages of the new magazine, the narrative had been airbrushed to paint Rebecca as the sole founder. The brains, brawn and power behind the brand. But why wouldn't it? She was the last woman standing. History wasn't recorded by those who the conquerors stepped on to get to the top.

The film told how Rebecca had been blessed with both a business head and a creative soul. She was a dreamer, but also a doer. As a child of the eighties, she'd been a regular at The Wag Club and was already making her own clothes and accessories when she enrolled to study fashion at Saint Martins. It was here that she had a revelation, that the next big movement had to be in direct contrast to everything going on around her. After leaving university with a 2:1 honours degree in Fashion Design with Marketing, she spent the next 4 years focusing all her efforts in setting up Beautiful You! Her vision for the company then was the same as today. To be pure, ethical, ecologically sound. An antithesis to the extravagance of the eighties.

She opened her first store on a side street in Covent Garden in nineteen-eighty-nine and Beautiful You! was an instant success. It was the first of its kind, a clothing and lifestyle brand, specialising in ethically sourced eco-friendly products: bamboo clothing; eco-friendly cosmetics and homeware; naturally sourced vitamins and supplements. The film ended by talking about the brand's vision for the future - to embrace and revolutionise the health and wellness industry. To this end, there was the new magazine, plus mindfulness and productivity apps and a new website planned for the new year.

The film finished with a message from Rebecca herself, looking straight down the camera lens and welcoming her to the Beautiful You! family.

"Glad to be here," she replied under her breath, then sat upright as the lights flickered on.

She glanced around, wondering what she should do. Marsha had said she'd return before the end of the film. Getting to her feet, Jade headed for the door. It swung open before she got there.

"Shit. Sorry," Marsha said, as Jade jumped back. "I got waylaid. Are you all right? I didn't mean to startle you."

"No. It's fine. I'm just a bit anxious this morning. First day in the new job and all that."

Marsha raised her eyebrows. "I've just heard Rebecca is coming in this morning at some stage, so you'll meet her sooner rather than later. Don't worry, she's a pussycat. Most of the time."

Jade nodded, surreptitiously rubbing her palms on the side of her blazer.

"How did you find the film?" Marsha asked.

"Great. She's quite a woman. I did know most of the story."

"Oh, good. It pays to be well-informed, doesn't it?"

"I've always thought so."

Jade smiled, and Marsha did too, but an awkwardness bristled in the air between them.

"Why don't I show you around?" Marsha said, spinning on her heels. "Follow me."

Jade trailed along in Marsha's wake as she paraded through the large office space pointing out areas of interest – the kitchen, the 'chill out' zone, the mindfulness and meditation room. These were all things Jade had expected to find here, but it was still rather impressive and if things were different, she'd have been excited to be working in such a positive and forward-thinking environment. As it was, she still had a flutter in her belly and was doing her best to ignore the nagging voice telling her she was going to be found out at any moment.

"We'll set you up here for now," Marsha said, stopping next to a bank of four desks, three of which were already occupied.

Two women in their mid-twenties and an extremely good-looking black man looked up from their computer screens. "Meet Thomas, Lauren and Anita. They're our junior designers here at Beautiful You! Guys, this is Jade. She's the new intern. Will you make her feel welcome?"

"Erm, of course we will," Thomas exclaimed, holding his hand to his chest dramatically. He met Jade's gaze and winked. "Good to meet you, sweetie. I love that top, by the way. Where's it from?"

Jade tugged at the front of the silk button-down shirt. "It's a Gabriela Hearst," she said. "I picked it up from Bergdorf Goodman last fall."

"Last fall, hey?" Thomas frowned, perhaps working out whether she was as pretentious as she sounded.

Jade realised what she'd said and tutted. "Sorry. Habits. I mean last autumn. I've been working in New York for the last six years. I've only just got back to the UK."

She was still going in strong with this statement. But her boldness seemed to pay off as Thomas and the two women glanced at each other and then looked back at her with impressed expressions.

"Wow! Humble brag much?" Thomas said, but there was warmth in his voice. "I bloody love it. You'll fit in here."

The two women chuckled and Marsha placed her hand on the small of Jade's back, guiding her towards the empty desk. "I'll leave you to get acquainted," she whispered. "Jade, I am going to need some paperwork from you, but that can wait until later."

Not for the first time that morning, Jade tensed. "Yes. Sure," she said. "No problem."

"And once Rebecca arrives, I'll come and get you and introduce you. Don't be worried." She wandered off, and Jade watched her go before turning back to find the trio staring at her. Pulling the chair out, she sat and hunched up her shoulders.

"Nice to meet you all," she said, waving a finger between the two women. "Sorry, can you remind me again which one is Lauren and which is Anita?"

"I'm Lauren and that's Anita," the blonde-haired one said. "Don't worry, we're very different, so you won't get mixed up."

"Yeah, I'm nice and she's a vicious slut," Anita cut in.

"How dare you!" Lauren hissed. "Vicious slut indeed! A hot mess, yeah. But I'm not vicious. Jesus!"

They all laughed, and Jade did too, despite it being the last thing she felt like doing. But hot mess was probably a decent description. Lauren's full lips were thick with what Jade presumed to be the company's famous Heartbreak Red lipstick, and her balayage hair looked like it hadn't seen a hairbrush this side of the pandemic. But she was beautiful all the same, with a faint smattering of freckles across her face. She caught Jade taking her in and wrinkled her nose at her.

"So, what brings you back to the UK?" Anita asked. "It sounds like you were doing all right in New York if you can afford Gabriela Hearst tops." Anita, too, was beautiful. She looked to have East Asian blood somewhere in her lineage. Her straight black hair was styled in a short pixie cut and her eyes were so dark you couldn't see where the iris ended and the pupil began. A silver ring through her septum finished the look, giving her an air of alternative beauty. The goth diva, to Lauren's party girl chic.

"It was in the sale," Jade said, clawing back her initial boast. "And it's the only piece of hers that I own. But I like it." It was a black shirt with white flowers, and she'd picked it out especially for today. She hoped it might empower her. "And in answer to your other question, I suppose I missed London. New York is great, as I'm sure you know. But you can't beat home, can you?"

Lauren snorted at this. "What were you doing over there?"

"I was a fashion assistant at Tres Chic magazine."

The words practically fell onto the desk in front of her with a thud. Thomas, Anita and Lauren exchanged more glances. "And you came back here to work as an intern?" Anita asked. "Why?"

Jade swallowed as conflicting emotions fought for independence in her psyche. Guilt was one factor in her decision, but it wasn't the primary driver and, even if it was, she couldn't tell them that. She certainly couldn't tell them the actual reason.

"I wanted a change," she said. "I loved working for a fashion magazine, but even one as cutting-edge as Tres Chic can be a bit soulless after a while. I wanted to work somewhere more in line with my ethos and beliefs."

"And that's here?" Thomas asked.

"Yes. I think so. Beautiful You! has a powerful mission. It leads the world in sustainable fashion and ecologically sound products, whilst staying contemporary and stylish. It's not a simple thing to pull off and Rebecca does that time and time again with everything she produces."

"All right, girl, calm down," Thomas said with a chuckle. "We're not the ones hiring you. We don't need the whole spiel. You are getting paid, though?"

"Oh, yes. Of course." She tucked a strand of hair behind her ear. "I guess it's been a while since I was the new girl in the office. It's a bit daunting. But I'm glad to be here. You see, my mum died last year, and it made me realise how short life was. I made the decision that I should only focus on things that make me feel more alive, even if that meant I left my job in New York to start at the bottom here."

"That's cool, I guess," Lauren said. "And I'm sorry to hear about your mum. Were you close?"

Jade shrugged. "Once upon a time."

"Do you have any other family over here?" Anita asked.

She shook her head. "No. It's just me now."

A silence fell over the desks. Jade stared at the blank computer screen to her right, wondering if she should switch it on.

"Well, heads up," Anita whispered, gesturing over Jade's shoulder. "Rebecca has just arrived."

Jade twisted around in time to see the woman herself, Rebecca Burton-Webb, striding purposefully across the office. Her hair was tied back in a tight bun, but she still looked as elegant and striking as in every photo Jade had ever seen of her. She wore a beautiful cream blazer, accompanied by a simple knitted turtleneck in black and black bootcut jeans. What was immediately striking to Jade was how much shorter Rebecca was than she'd imagined. This titanic personality of a woman must only stand five-two in her stocking feet. Still, despite her diminutive size, she swept through the office like a force of nature - waving at people, greeting others with her perfect Hollywood smile as she passed by their desks - all the while talking to someone via the iPhone she had clamped to her ear.

"There she is," Thomas said. "Our glorious leader."

Jade didn't take her eyes off Rebecca. "It's not like that, is it? I thought she was a good boss. Fair."

"She is," Anita said. "Thomas' default setting is cynicism. You'll get used to it."

Thomas gasped in pretend shock as Rebecca disappeared into her glass-fronted office at the far side of the room. Jade turned back around to face her new colleagues.

"She is good to work for," Lauren said. "But since Kristen left, she's been all over the place."

"Kristen?" Jade asked.

"Her PA. She was Rebecca's right-hand woman. She did

everything for her. But she left two months ago to go work for 'she who must not be named'."

Jade frowned and looked around the group. "Who?"

Thomas narrowed his eyes. "The actress with the – *ahem* - scented candles. Rebecca views her as her main rival these days."

"Oh, I see."

"Yes, if you want to progress from your internship, I suggest you never mention her name within earshot of Ms Burton-Webb. Other than that, Rebecca can be a little hard work, but she's lovely. Just like me."

"Thanks," Jade said. "Good to know."

She glanced back over her shoulder. Through the glass, she could see Rebecca sitting behind her desk, squinting at a piece of paper in her hand. It was strange seeing her in the flesh, daunting even. But she would have to get over that feeling if she were to succeed. Rebecca might be one of the most influential women in the world, but she was a person just like everyone else. She had wants and dreams. She used the bathroom and farted. She could be hurt, and she could feel pain, and if pushed into a corner, she'd do what was needed to survive.

At least, that's what Jade was counting on.

3

"Yes, what is it?" Rebecca called out in reply to the knock on her door. It had already been a busy morning and she didn't need any more distractions. Glancing up from the piece of paper in her hand – the quarter two reports from their flagship stores in Europe - she saw Marsha through the glass partition wall, hovering outside the door to her office. There was another woman behind her she didn't recognise.

"Come in then," she mouthed, waving her through.

Marsha eased the door open. "Are you busy?"

Rebecca released a heavy sigh, resisting the urge to inform Marsha that, yes, of course she was busy. She was always bloody busy.

"What is it?" she asked.

"I've got Jade, the new intern. It's her first day. Would you like to say hello?"

Rebecca sat back in her seat, trying to recall any mention of new starters. It worried her she couldn't, and this brought with it further feelings of confusion and anger. It was too regular an occurrence these days, but she put it down to stress and lack of sleep.

"Rebecca?"

Marsha was waiting for an answer and with the young woman peering through the glass at her, she could hardly say no.

"Yes, of course. Please show her in."

Marsha stepped aside and the new girl stepped into the room. She looked quite old to be an intern, thirties if Rebecca was to guess, but she was good-looking, with shiny brown hair that fell over her face in a long wave.

"Good morning my dear..." Rebecca said, glaring at Marsha, who picked up the cue promptly.

"Jade Fisher," she said.

"Of course. Jade. Lovely to meet you. Please come in."

She remembered now. Or thought she did. Something about a magazine. If Kristen was still here, she'd have reminded her.

Bloody Kristen.

"Are you staying too?" she asked Marsha.

"No. I'll leave you to it," Marsha said, backing out of the room.

Rebecca waited until she'd left and the door was closed before turning to Jade with a winning smile. "Marsha is a fine woman and a brilliant HR manager, but she's very by the book. It doesn't always fit with my way of doing things."

Jade smiled back and Rebecca noted she had excellent teeth. Straight and white and perfectly proportioned.

"I suppose that's the nature of HR, though," Jade replied. "They have to be sticklers so the creative forces can flow unencumbered without cause for concern."

"That's an excellent way of looking at it. Please have a seat."

Rebecca walked out from behind her desk and headed over to where a small sofa and two chairs were set up around a small table on the other side of the room. She sat on the chair and indicated for Jade to take the couch, which she did.

"Thank you."

"Aren't you a little old to be an intern?" Rebecca asked once they were settled. "I'm sorry to be blunt, but there's little point in beating around the bush in this life. And it's a genuine question. I mean, you're still very young and vibrant, I'm sure. But most of the interns we've had are in their early twenties. And you aren't."

"It's fine," Jade said. "I've already been asked that question once this morning, so I get it. I don't know if you saw my application, but I was working as a Fashion Assistant at Tres Chic magazine in New York and felt I needed a change."

"Tres Chic?" Rebecca repeated. "Impressive. So, you know Angela?"

Jade nodded. "Angela. Yes. She's great."

"She's a hoot, isn't she? Did you ever go drinking with her? Bloody hell. I've never seen anyone be able to put away hard liquor like that woman."

"No, unfortunately not," Jade said. She looked uncomfortable suddenly. "I've been wanting to make a change for a while, and I love everything you do here. I've been watching the industry papers for any news about vacancies. And this intern job was the first one that came up and so I thought. Why not?"

"But the pay can't be what you were on at Tres Chic?"

"No. It's not. But I hope that you'll see something in me and this won't be my final role at Beautiful You! You see, I understand your vision so profoundly and I've wanted to work for you for so long I thought it was worth the jump. Plus, my mother died recently, and it's made me reassess a lot of things. What I want to do with my life. What I want to devote my career to. Your mission statement about sustainability and how you want to revolutionise the wellness industry is incredibly inspiring."

Rebecca raised her head. The new girl was laying it on a little thick, but she admired her drive and motivation. "That's wonderful," she said. "I like to know that everyone who works at Beautiful You! shares our vision. If not, it doesn't work, does it? I've always thought a career such as this has to be a vocation."

She smiled as she said it, but there were connotations around that word. *Vocation.* Meaning something you devoted your life to. Perhaps to the extent of everything else. It was true that Rebecca had certainly done that over the years, but as time went on, she wondered at what cost. She'd bled for her company. She'd lost friends, loved ones. She'd even pushed aside her once strong desire to have children in favour of building her brand. And, yes, on the surface she now had it all. She was often named one of the most powerful women in business, not to mention one of the wealthiest. But take away the company and what else did she have? The townhouse in Chelsea where she spent most of the year, the apartments in Paris and New York, the beachfront villa in the Maldives. These were just bricks and mortar. She often thought one of the traits that made her so successful was her inability to be entirely satisfied with her life, and it certainly kept her striving for more, but the older she got, the more she yearned for closeness

And that was the real rub, right there. Wasn't it?

For a weeks, now, she'd suspected Seb was up to his old ways. But was she surprised? People had warned her at the time that it was a bad idea to marry a man twenty years her junior, especially a man like Sebastian Turner. But she'd loved him. She still loved him. When they'd met, he was a young actor fresh out of drama school and ready to make his mark on the world. She'd loved his enthusiasm and passion for his work, so in tune with her own sensibilities. But the fact Seb hadn't made it as an A-lister lay heavy on her mind. At those times when she couldn't sleep - perhaps in between layovers or when the jet lag hit her especially hard – all she could focus on was that his failure as an actor was the only reason that he was still with her. Because just as much as Seb liked the ladies, he liked his elite lifestyle. He'd told her he'd stopped playing around and to keep herself sane she'd decided to believe him, but some days she could just smell it on him.

"What you've built here up to this point is wonderful," Jade was saying. "But your vision for the future inspires me even more."

"Interesting," Rebecca said. "What, in particular, inspires you?"

It was a valid question and one she would usually have longed to know the answer to, but the very notion of the future had already created a space in Rebecca's mind for a new mob of intrusive thoughts to muscle their way in.

The future? Best not to think about that, Becs! We know what the future holds, don't we? Because you're not getting any younger, and maybe it isn't just the jet lag making you forget what day it is. Maybe it's time to see someone and get a professional opinion like Seb keeps suggesting.

No.

Stop that.

She fixed her face into a kind smile as Jade talked about ethical branding and how she believed mental health, and women's health, in particular, were now an integral part of the conversation, which, of course, she meant as The Conversation. The big conversation. The new worldwide discourse. Clearly, this new girl was clever and savvy with it, but once more Rebecca found her attention drifting into the dark corridors of her mind. Because no matter how worthy their mission statement here at Beautiful You!, no matter how cutting-edge and innovative Jade thought the company was, Rebecca knew they were floundering. A global pandemic, followed by a new financial crisis, had hit everyone hard and they were feeling the full brunt. The quarter two report on her desk proved that without a doubt. They needed to do more. She needed to do more.

But how? And what?

The magazine launch had gone well but sales were nowhere near what they'd projected them to be and for only the second time in her life, Rebecca felt scared of what the next few years might bring. She refused to compromise her vision, but if they carried on this trajectory, something would have to give. Most of her time recently had been spent wondering what she could do to turn things around rather than on what she wanted to create next. Her mindset was focused on lack rather than abundance, and that never worked out well.

If Kristen was still here...

But there was no use in thinking about her. She'd gone to the dark side. For a while, after she'd resigned, Rebecca had considered reaching out to her in the hope offering her more money or a better office might lure her back. But each time she'd stopped herself. She still had some pride left and, being married to Seb for the last decade, there was only enough begging and pleading she could put herself through. Even Kristen wasn't worth more humiliation.

She raised her head to see the new girl had finished talking and was looking at her with an expectant expression on her face. The low glow from the pendant light above their heads highlighted her fine jawline and high cheekbones and, at that moment, she looked so familiar, as if the past had suddenly rushed in to meet Rebecca. Staring at Jade, she was lost in the abyss between two lifetimes. But the mind played tricks. She looked down at her hands, which were clasped in her lap, and when she raised her head again, the thoughts had diminished and she was back in the moment.

"I think you're going to fit in perfectly," Rebecca said, lowering her tone into a time-worn 'business' voice. The voice of Rebecca Burton-Webb, CEO and founder of Beautiful You! Third most powerful woman in business 2021. "Do you have any questions for me while we're here?"

"Well, actually..." Jade began, but then smiled and let out a nervous laugh. "No. I do have a few questions. But they can wait. It's my first day, so I think it's best if I settle in first and get the lay of the land as it were. Will we be able to talk again like this?"

Rebecca kept her smile in place. "Yes. I'm sure we can. But I'm not always here at head office, I'm afraid. I do jet around, unfortunately." Another image of Seb flashed across her mind, but it was gone before she could get a real grip on it. "You know how it is. People to see, things to do. No rest for the wicked."

She laughed and Jade did too, but she couldn't help but notice a glimmer of something in the young woman's expression. It was the way she narrowed her eyes ever so slightly, an instinctive movement. Like she hated her. But as soon as Rebecca noticed, it was gone.

"Well, thank you so much for meeting with me this morning," Jade said. "I really appreciate you taking the time out of your busy schedule."

"Not at all. We're a family here. And it's good to meet you. As I say, you sound perfect for the role, and I'm sure you'll be an absolute asset." She got to her feet and pointed her arm at the door. "Now, if you will excuse me, I do have a few calls to make."

"Yes. Of course. I'll see myself out." Jade sprang to her feet and headed for the door. As she got there, she paused and turned back to look at her. "And thank you, Rebecca, for this opportunity to work for you."

Rebecca returned her smile, but there was nothing more to be said. She waited as Jade exited the room before walking over to the door and making sure it was fully closed. Once done, she let out a long sigh that had so much more emotion in it than she'd expected. Tears formed in her eyes, but she blinked them away. No time for all that silliness. She had to ring the board and then work out what their next steps would be in terms of their stores in Brussels and Berlin. Turning to walk back to her desk, she caught sight of Nicole and Sariah, her Influencer Marketing team, through the glass wall of her office. They were standing near the photocopier, talking heatedly about something or other. They looked so young and vital. So full of energy and fire. Releasing another long breath, Rebecca moved her attention around the office, taking in her award-winning creative team, Louise and Hina in Finance, the Growth Marketing division and the new editorial team. Every one of them was at least thirty years younger than her. On a good day, that wouldn't have bothered her at all. She knew that experience was still the biggest lever to success. But what happened when your success was waning?

"What the hell are you going to do?" she muttered to herself, as her gaze shifted over to the far side of the office where Jade was returning to her desk.

She seemed like a nice enough girl and she knew a lot about the company and its ethos. That was reassuring. But if she was so clued up and experienced, what was she doing accepting a job as an intern? Didn't she know that most of her day would be spent going for coffee and answering the phone? And what about the way Rebecca had caught her looking at her just now? It was curious to her and slightly unnerving, but she was most likely being paranoid. Her mindset was off and she felt low, a clear sign it was best to step away from her thoughts for a while and get busy. That was how you got out of a slump; you went to work.

The same way she'd always done.

4

Thomas and the girls were great. Just what Jade needed after feeling so nervous about her first day at Beautiful You!

Anita had just been telling the group about a meal she had last week, which was 'totally amazing.' But now Thomas was staring at the poor girl as if he had her in his sights.

"What did you just say?" he asked.

Anita frowned at him. "What do you mean?"

"You said chorizo?" He pronounced the word the way she had done. The Castilian way, with the lisping ceceo sound for the 'Ch' and 'Z'. *Thoritho.*

"That's how you pronounce it," Anita said, wrinkling up her nose. "That's how they say it in Spain."

"Yeah, I know it is. But you're not Spanish as far as I know," he said. "I was just wondering where the line gets drawn between pronouncing things in the accent of the native speakers and it all being a bit - you know - dodgy?"

Lauren caught Jade's eye and rolled her own. "Come on, Thomas. Don't be silly. It's respecting their culture."

"Is it though? Or is it just Anita being a bit poncey?" It was his turn to catch Jade's gaze, but like with Lauren, she kept her face neutral. She was enjoying the banter; she didn't want to get involved. Not yet, anyway. Not until she'd got to grips with the social dynamics at play.

"I mean," Thomas went on. "If you went around to my gran's house, would you be asking her for 'mo' rice an' pea!'" He put on a thick Jamaican accent as he said it. Lauren snickered, but Anita huffed.

"No, of course not."

"Or if you were eating with an African tribe, would you pronounce dinner their way if it was all clicks and whoops?"

"No, Thomas, I wouldn't." Anita spoke through gritted teeth. "That's cultural appropriation. It's bad."

Thomas sat back and crossed his arms, grinning as if he knew he'd won. "Yeah. It's a minefield, isn't it? So, maybe just pronounce it CHoriZo then."

"Piss off," Anita told him. But she was laughing to herself.

Jade returned to her computer screen, to the series of PDF documents Marsha had sent over which comprised the company's HR policies. She was to read them all and put her e-signature on each. In the email, Marsha also mentioned she needed to see her 'Right To Work' information and two forms of ID for her personnel file. The request had provoked a swirl of fear in her belly, which Thomas's catty outburst had gone some way in distracting her from. But the fact remained, she had to provide documents she didn't have.

"How did it go with Rebecca?" Lauren asked, leaning around the side of her computer to address Jade.

She sat back, glad once more of the diversion. "Good, thanks. It's always weird meeting someone who you already know so much about, isn't it? But she didn't disappoint. She was great."

"She can be. She reminds me a bit of my mum." Lauren grimaced at herself. "Shit. Sorry, Jade. I didn't mean to bring up mums."

"Oh, god, it's fine," she told her. "She'd been ill for a long time. We were close once but I've not seen much of my family for the last six years."

"I thought you said there was only you left?" Thomas piped up.

"Yes. That's what I mean. Just me. And it's been like that for a long time."

Thomas frowned, but she was glad when he didn't pursue it.

"Must have been hard," Lauren said. "Being all alone in New York and not even a lifeline back here. That's really brave of you. I don't know if I could do it."

Jade shrugged. "It was good for me. I needed a fresh start at the time, and New York was the perfect city to achieve that." She returned her attention to her screen, but as she stared at the sombre document in front of her, she found it difficult to concentrate.

Everything she'd just told her new colleagues was true. In a way. But there was so much more to it than that. So much more that she couldn't tell them.

"Hey, guys! How is everyone?"

Jade looked up to see a young woman standing over their desk. She had white-blonde hair scraped back in a high ponytail and her pale blue eyes sparkled as she looked at Jade.

"You're the new intern, right? I'm Nicole. Influencer Marketing. Are these reprobates teaching you all their bad habits already?"

Jade smiled. "They're helping me settle in. I'm Jade, by the way." She stood up and reached her hand out over the desk.

Nicole smirked at the gesture but took her hand.

"Charmed," she said, affectedly, then frowned. "You're not like the usual interns we employ."

"A lot older, hey?" Jade replied, throwing up her eyebrows as Nicole released her hand.

"Well, yes. I suppose. Not that there's anything wrong with that..."

"Jade used to work at Tres Chic," Anita said, and the way she said it told Jade she didn't think much of Nicole. "She's just got back from living in New York. She wanted a change. A new start. Nothing wrong with that, is there?"

"Not at all," Nicole said and smiled. "Tres Chic, hey? That's big. I hope you don't get bored in this new role. Or do you have eyes on the big prize?"

"What's that?" Jade asked.

Nicole lowered her voice. "Rebecca's PA, of course. She's been without one since Kristen left and everyone can see she's struggling."

"Leave it out, Nic," Lauren said. "We all know Kristen pissing off hit her hard."

"She doesn't think she can replace her," Nicole added. "But I doubt that she'll get that luxury. The shareholders are keen for her to get back on top of things after the last few years, and she needs a PA. Kristen was her secret weapon." She straightened up and tilted her head to one side. "But it is great to meet you, Jane."

"Jade." She smiled back, not giving her the satisfaction. "And you."

"By the way," Nicole said, grabbing Thomas by the shoulders. "The reason I came over here. It's my birthday on Wednesday and we're going out for a few drinks after work. Nothing too extravagant. I wanted to go to Soho House but I appreciate not *everyone* is a member. So, I think we'll just go to

Long Bar. It'd be great if you could all make it. You too, of course, Jade."

Thomas leaned his head back to look up at her. "Unaccustomed as I am to drinking, you can count me in."

"Yes, us too," Lauren said. "Cheers Nic."

Jade strained to watch as Nicole sauntered back to her desk across the other side of the office. She swayed her hips as she walked like a true alpha female.

"So...that's Nicole," Thomas said.

Jade stuck out her bottom lip. "She seems nice."

"Does she?"

"Nothing I can't handle." Thomas winked at her and they returned to their work. Jade scan-read the first two policies and signed them as instructed and emailed them back to Marsha. The clock at the top of her screen told her it was 12:15 p.m. In her haste this morning, she'd skipped breakfast and, whilst she could sense her stomach rumbling, didn't want to be the first to leave. She decided to wait and see what happened. Twisting her chair around, she positioned herself so it looked like she was still reading her screen, but where she could also see into Rebecca's office.

It looked like Rebecca was talking to herself as she paraded in front of her desk, but more than likely she had her phone on hands-free and the speaker on. Despite her office having glass walls, which gave an impression of togetherness and transparency, Jade could tell when she was in there that the room was completely soundproof. There was something about the acoustics and the air quality that gave it away. But she had the boss in her sight.

She'd done it.

She was working at Beautiful You!

Working for Rebecca Burton-Webb.

Eyes on the prize, Nicole had said. It was certainly something along those lines, but Jade wouldn't call what she was after a prize.

Justice was closer to the truth.

You might even call it revenge.

5

The first day of a new job is always going to be somewhat of a rollercoaster ride. There are so many new people to meet and new names to learn. Not to mention new pieces of information to absorb. By 4 p.m. Jade was flagging and ready for home. Her contracted hours were nine to five but, from what Lauren had told her whilst out for a sandwich on their lunch hour, people often started later - and finished a hell of a lot later.

Marsha had also been over, pestering her again for her documents - which didn't help. For now, Jade had put her off, telling her they were at her friend's house, where she'd been staying for a few weeks after returning to the UK. Marsha had been rather unhappy about the situation but agreed that Jade could collect them at the weekend and bring them in the following Monday. That gave her a week to do what was required or to come up with a new excuse.

There was nothing like a deadline, was there?

It was 4:45 p.m., almost time to go home, when she heard a commotion over by the entrance. Looking up from her screen she saw Seb Turner enter the office. A quiver of nervous energy shot down into her groin as he strode past her desk and yanked open the door to Rebecca's office without knocking. Rebecca was sitting at her desk. She held her free hand up to him before pointing aggressively at the phone pressed against her ear. Seb said something that Jade couldn't hear before Rebecca gestured for him to shut the door. He spun around and looked both ways across the office before obliging her.

"Trouble in paradise," Thomas muttered.

"Don't be mean," Lauren scolded. "It can't be easy for her."

Jade rotated her chair back around. "What do you mean?"

"Come on, you know so much about Rebecca, you must have heard the rumours about her husband." She dipped her head and her already husky voice dropped to a croaky whisper. "Let's just say he's not the most monogamous of partners."

"Really?" Jade replied, acting shocked. She glanced from Lauren to Thomas and Anita. "Is that true?"

Thomas lifted his shoulders. "That's what people say. But from what I hear, she won't have it. She either turns a blind eye or won't admit it to herself. She thinks the sun shines out of his penis. But I don't blame her, to be honest."

Anita and Lauren both groaned at this and the three of them carried on chatting, but Jade phased them out as she leaned back to watch the exchange in Rebecca's office. Seb was leaning over the desk, pointing a sharp finger at Rebecca and going red in the face. She couldn't help feeling a little awkward watching the two of them.

"Does anyone want any water?" she asked, getting to her feet and picking up her aluminium water canister. She waved it in the air as the others glanced up at her. "I'm going to get a refill. Anyone?"

"I'm good thanks."

"Not for me."

Jade pushed her chair under her desk. "No worries. Back in

a second." She was thirsty, but filling up her water bottle wasn't the only reason she was walking across the office to the cooler furthest from her desk. Passing alongside the wall of Rebecca's office, she cast a furtive look into the room. Up close, she could see their lips moving but still couldn't pick out a sound. It looked heated, however, and Seb was doing most of the talking. At the corner of the office, she tilted her head to get a better look and saw that Rebecca was crying. Or at least, she was holding the curve of her forefinger against the bottom of her eye the way people often did when they were trying not to let tears ruin their make-up. But as Jade continued on her way, Rebecca stood and tossed her head back, fortitude and resilience tightening her expression.

She filled her bottle from the cooler without looking again and was heading back to her desk when the door of Rebecca's office swung open and Seb Turner almost walked into her on his way out.

"Shit! Watch where you're going," he snapped, swerving around and lifting his torso so as not to barge her.

"I'm so sorry, I didn't see you," Jade squeaked, jumping back. "I was just walking past."

"No. I'm sorry." He stopped and held a hand up, huffing out a breath. "It was my fault."

He shifted around, frowning as he faced her. "Have I seen you here before?" The frown twisted into a crooked half-smile and he raised an eyebrow. It was no doubt a well-honed look, one he might have even practised in the mirror. But it was also formidable.

"I'm the new girl," she said, holding her water bottle in front of her in two hands. "Today's my first day."

"I see. Great. I'm Seb, by the way, Seb Turner. Rebecca's husband." He held out his hand to her. "And you are?"

"Jade. Jade Fisher. Pleased to meet you." She shook his

31

hand; it all but enveloped her own, and the skin of his palm was soft and warm.

Seb narrowed his eyes some more at her. Conversely, to what she'd thought about Rebecca, he was taller than she'd imagined, and up close his rugged good looks were mesmerising. Despite his dark hair and stubble, his eyes were a striking shade of azure blue and, as he considered her, she felt her cheeks burn.

"Is she paying you enough?" he asked, nodding back at Rebecca's office.

"Oh, yes. All good. I'm here for the experience, too. I'm a big fan of your wife and everything she's done. She's a bit of a hero of mine."

"Is that so?" The smile turned into a smirk before dropping away. "Well, maybe you should see a doctor about that?" He stared at her with a penetrating look on his face.

Jade clung to the water bottle for dear life. "Oh... I..." She didn't know what to say, but she couldn't take her eyes off him.

He held her gaze for a second or two longer before erupting in a deep laugh. "Don't look so scared. I'm only messing with you," he said. "It's lovely to meet you, Jade Fisher. I'm sure you'll fit right in and become an integral member of the wonderful Beautiful You! family. Because that's what we all are here. One big happy family." There was bitterness in his voice when he said this last part, but then he laughed to cover it.

"Righto. Well, I'd better be going." He looked her up and down and shot her that same enthralling smile before nodding at the water canister. "And go easy on the poor fellow. You don't need to be that rough."

"What?" Jade looked down to see she had both hands wrapped around the metallic shaft of the bottle and was wringing it nervously. "Oh?"

She felt her cheeks flush some more before a wave of anger bubbled up inside of her, wiping out any nerves or trepidation she might have felt. At any other time, she'd have headed straight for Marsha's office after a comment like that, but today she just giggled and smiled and told him it was good to meet him. Something like that anyway. It was hard to focus with the extent of conflicting emotions swirling within her. She watched Seb strut out across the office before twisting the lid off the water bottle and taking a long drink. It was ice cold and she gulped down almost half the canister before hurrying back to her desk.

"What was that all about?" Lauren stage-whispered before she'd even sat down. "Did you and Seb have a nice chat?"

"He was just saying hello," Jade replied. "He seems nice."

"Watch yourself around him," Anita said sternly. "Most of the girls here know to give him a wide berth. I get bad vibes off him. And if Rebecca thought you were trying it on with her husband, I doubt you'd get past your first probation interview in all honesty. She's a fair woman, but she's as territorial as the best of us."

Jade nodded, putting on a serious face. "Thank you. Point taken. I'll make sure I keep my head down next time he's in."

Later that night, Jade sat at the kitchen table in the small flat she was renting in Chalk Farm. It was a decent enough place for the price and through her bedroom window, she could see the edge of Primrose Hill, where she'd played as a child. That was helpful. It kept her mind on the job at hand.

She eased open the lid of her laptop and swiped her finger on the mouse pad to wake the machine. As the screen flashed to life, she sat back and reached for the large glass of Wild Turkey she'd poured herself as a reward for making it through her first day. She'd got a taste for it over in the States and enjoyed the burn on her lips and down her throat as she took a sip. She had a good palette and picked up notes of peppermint and cinnamon, of vanilla and oak. But mostly it tasted of rebellion.

She squinted at the screen and smiled to herself as she flicked through the file of photos. Most of them she'd found on gossip pages or the websites of women's lifestyle magazines. Many were candid, taken by paparazzi, but there were some posed shots as well, even some on the red carpet at movie premieres. But, whatever the quality of the photo, the subject was the same in each of the ninety-three photos she'd so far collected. Sebastian Turner. Seb. Rebecca Burton-Webb's much younger husband.

Jade stopped on a particular shot of Seb leaving a nightclub a few years ago. Despite the hour he looked his usual devilishly handsome self and rather than acting annoyed at the press intrusion, he was staring down the camera lens and smiling that same crooked half-smile he'd floored her with this afternoon. She sipped at the whisky and let out a long sigh full of emotion

"Anita gets bad vibes off you, Seb," she whispered to the photo. "What do you think of that?" She took another sip of her drink and twisted her mouth to mirror that of the man on the screen. She raised her glass. "Sleep tight, Seb. And I'll see you soon."

6

It was 10 p.m. when Rebecca's car pulled up outside her house on Cheyne Walk. She thanked Michael, her driver, and told him not to bother getting out of the cab to open the door for her like he normally would. She'd manage on her own for once.

As he drove away, she stood on the pavement and inspected her large, three-storey townhouse. The garden was looking a little overgrown but other than that it was still a magnificent property and the fact she lived here still gave her a warm feeling inside. Running parallel to the river and boasting rows of stunning red-brick mansions, Cheyne Walk had been *the* place to live ever since the early 1900s. Bram Stoker had lived at number twenty-seven. In the late sixties, Mick Jagger and Marianne Faithfull resided at number forty-eight. It was the perfect address for someone like Rebecca.

As she walked up the steps to the front door, she noticed light filtering out through the lounge window. As she watched, it turned from green to stark blue to orange. No doubt it was Seb, watching the far-too-large flatscreen television they'd recently purchased. Or, rather, *she'd* purchased. Seb's finances were rather fluid presently. She had reminded him that working actors had to actually do some work to call themselves that, but it only led to an argument, so she hadn't brought it up since.

A welcome rush of warm air hit her in the face as she opened the door. She stepped inside, knowing not to call out to Seb if he was engrossed in some television series. He wouldn't answer, and it only made her feel bad when he didn't. She shut the door and slid the bolts home before walking the length of the hallway and through into the lounge where, as expected, Seb was lounging on the sofa with a glass of red wine resting on his stomach. On the television screen was some actor Rebecca didn't recognise. But that wasn't unusual. She didn't watch television these days. No time. No interest.

"Hello darling," she said.

Seb didn't look away from the screen. "Hey. What time is it?"

"Late." She placed her bag down on the chair and slipped out of her coat.

"And have you calmed down?" Seb asked. He said it like it was an off-the-cuff remark, but she sensed an undercurrent of bitterness in the question.

"Have you?"

"I'm always calm, darling. You know that." He finally turned to look at her. His blue eyes were full of concern. "I'm worried about you."

Rebecca placed her coat over the back of the chair and moved around the front. "Are you?" She sat and removed her shoes, rotating her ankle and wiggling her toes as she released them from the punishing leather. Taking off her shoes at the end of a long day had become an almost ritualistic act for Rebecca over the years, a signifier for her that work was over. Regardless of the tension knotting her shoulders and the ache in her heart, it felt good to relax. Albeit briefly.

Seb was still looking at her. "Of course I'm worried, Becs. You're working too hard."

Rebecca scoffed. "You're noticing that now." She sat back and let out a groan that she hadn't planned. "I have to work hard, Seb. People rely on me. The company relies on me. You know full well that the last two years have been difficult. We're not out of the woods yet."

Seb's full lips flattened into a thin smile. "I know."

"Do you? Because you're still spending our money like water."

"Jesus. This again?" He sat up and swung his feet down onto the polished hardwood floor, placing the half-empty glass of wine on the table next to the couch. "Come on, Rebecca. Out with it. Say what you really want to say."

"You still haven't answered my question." Her chest tightened as she spoke. She didn't want to be doing this. She didn't want to be thinking these thoughts.

Seb huffed like a sulky teen. "What question?"

"The one I asked you this afternoon before you stormed out. What was that hotel trip about last month when I was in Germany? Why didn't you tell me about it? You must have known I'd see it on the credit card statement. Do you just not care?" She startled and stepped back as Seb sprang off the couch like a wildcat. He was over to her in two strides. "I was playing golf. Okay? I was with Jonty and Mark. Ring them if you don't believe me." Those striking blue eyes, the same ones that had got him noticed straight out of drama school, were wide and fierce. She could smell alcohol on his breath. That wasn't his first glass of wine.

She held his gaze and breathed slowly down her nose, trying to retain an outward air of calm. "Where was it?"

"Up north somewhere. Derbyshire, I think. Mark arranged

it all." He raised his chin. "You know I did mention this to you before you left. I told you we were planning a golf trip."

A twinge of doubt fought with the toxins in the muscles of Rebecca's brow. "Did you?"

"Yes! You don't listen to me. Or you don't remember." He tilted his head to one side and his voice softened. "It's been happening a lot, hasn't it, you forgetting things? Do you not think you should go and see—?"

"Oh, for Heaven's sake, Seb! I remember that we've been through this countless times! My faculties are all intact, thank you very much. I'm just incredibly stressed right now. The least I expect is a little support from my husband. Is that too much to ask?"

Seb made a huffing sound and headed back to the sofa, shaking his head as he went. "There she goes again with the emotional blackmail. Typical."

Rebecca didn't respond. She was so angry she felt like she was vibrating. Angry and confused.

Why was he doing this?

Why was he saying these things?

She closed her eyes to compose herself, remaining where she was for a few more seconds before leaving the room and heading for the kitchen

The only lights on were the under-cabinet LEDs, and they cast the large Scandi-style kitchen in a welcoming glow as she entered. A bottle of claret stood on the edge of the central island with less than a glass left in the bottom. She picked a wine glass off the rack under the nearest unit and drained the bottle into it before taking a large drink. For the last five years, she hadn't drunk alcohol at home, but tonight she needed it. It wasn't just Seb that had upset her, there was far too much going on in her chaotic life right now for him to be the only reason, but he was all she could think about as she pulled a stool out from under the island and sat.

Her body was still tingling with a mixture of anger and misery and she made quick work of the wine. Seb had not told her about that golf trip. She was certain of that fact. But she'd been certain of a few other things recently and then proven wrong. Maybe she should book in with her doctor and get checked out. To put her mind at ease, if nothing else. Prove to everyone she wasn't totally losing it.

"Jesus, Rebecca."

She let out a bitter laugh as she poured the last droplet of wine onto her tongue and glanced down the hallway. The notion came to her to go back into the lounge and snuggle up with Seb on the couch. Sometimes it was easier to let actions do the talking. It would get her out of her head and away from these troubling thoughts if nothing else. But she remained where she was. The sad truth of the matter was she feared the possibility of rebuttal more than of being alone with her thoughts.

They'd been great together in the early days, she and Seb. He was funny and charming and so focused on her. He'd made her feel like the only woman in the world. The only person in his world. The age difference had worried her initially, but Seb had reassured her often that he loved her for who she was, and that her extra life experience was only a plus point for him. After six months of dating, she'd allowed herself to fall for him with every part of herself. And now here she was. Paranoid. Alone with everyone. Drinking mid-week. Letting things slide at work. She was famous in business for being meticulous. But how can someone who was so meticulous not see the drop coming? Everything was such a damn struggle these days. Everything.

Many people had shown up in Rebecca's life over the years,

but they never stayed long. She had plenty of acquaintances, and a phone full of contacts, but no one she could call a true friend. For a long time, it was the way she wanted it. So she told herself, anyway. Beautiful You! was her entire world. She lived it and breathed it and had no time for socialising outside of the industry parties and events she attended to help push the business forward. Friends were a drag. Friends drained your energy. And after everything that had happened, it was hard for her to allow people in.

Rebecca puffed out her cheeks as the memory grew legs. She hadn't thought about *her* past for so long. It was over thirty years ago, but thinking about what had happened still made the hairs on the back of her neck stand up. Occasionally, she'd see something, or someone would say something that made her think back to the old days, but even the happy memories were sullied and she quickly focused her attention elsewhere.

Tonight, however, Rebecca couldn't shake the thought of her. Because she needed a friend, someone she could talk to about Seb's less-than-husbandly ways, not to mention those blasted shareholders that were constantly pecking at her head. The two of them had been so close once. Like sisters.

Rebecca got up from the island and carried the empty wine glass over to the sink. Onwards and upwards. That was her motto now. She was Rebecca Burton-Webb, for Christ's sake. She was strong, savvy, a leader of industry.

She washed her hands and headed down the hallway. A good night's sleep and she'd feel better in the morning. She was probably just tired and emotional. It happened. As she passed by the door to the lounge, a small voice inside of her told her to go to Seb, to share with him her thoughts and fears. But she shooed the idea away. She couldn't voice her worries about their relationship to him at the best of times, and definitely not after he'd drunk almost a bottle of wine. As for the other thing playing on her mind this evening, that would never be talked about with anyone. Ever. Everyone had secrets, but this one she would carry to her grave. She had to. There was no way she could tell Seb what they'd done, what she'd done. It was too horrible to even contemplate sharing.

It could never come out.

If it ever did, she'd lose everything.

7

Despite not getting to sleep until well past midnight, Jade woke up at five and forced herself to go for a run. Dressed in her black Lycra leggings and running top, and with her headphones blasting Lady Gaga's debut album, she ran from her flat on Belmont Street, up Primrose Hill and back along Adelaide Road, passing Chalk Farm tube station. Back at her flat, sweaty and panting, she checked her distance on the running app and was pleased to discover she'd covered almost five kilometres in under thirty-two minutes. Not bad going, considering she'd let her routine slip recently. She viewed this as a good omen. It meant she was on the right path. Things were going to work out for her.

Once showered, she selected a suitable outfit - burgundy checked jacquard pants from Joseph and a black georgette blouse from Karen Millen – and ate a slice of toast whilst getting dressed and applying some make-up. Leaving the flat, she headed back towards Chalk Farm tube station, where she jumped on the Northern Line to Tottenham Court Road and then caught the Central Line to Marble Arch. From there, it was only a two-minute walk to her new office. In fact, from door to door, it had taken her just twenty-five minutes. Not bad going for London and, as she entered the front entrance of the Beautiful You! building, she felt a prickle of something approaching regret. She would have been happy working here, she thought, as she called the lift and rode it up to the third floor. It could have been the new start she'd been searching for after splitting with Jacob.

But, no. She rolled her shoulders back as the lift came to a stop and by the time she'd stepped onto the third-floor landing, had quashed the ridiculous notion. She was here for one reason only. She had to remember that.

"Here she is! Her second day and she's already taking the piss," Thomas called out as Jade entered the office and headed for her desk. As she got closer, he made a show of looking at his watch. "What time do you call this, babe?"

"Piss off," she told him. "It's only a quarter past nine. I'm early compared to everyone else. And I was told it was a relaxed start here."

"It is. For regular employees."

"Oh? And what am I?"

Thomas pulled a face. "The help? The tea lady?" He laughed at his own joke. "Sorry, hun, I'm just messing with you. How are you?"

She took off her jacket and hung it over the back of her chair. "I'm actually feeling very motivated today."

"Oh, God. We'll soon knock that out of you." He grinned. "But I do think you're a good fit for this place. For us lot, especially."

"Yeah," Jade said. "I agree."

Over the next half hour, the office filled up with people and Jade applied herself to her new role: doing the rounds, asking her colleagues if they needed any stationery fetching, and whether they had any errands she could handle for them. It was a little awkward at first, but she felt it was good to show willingness. Now that Marsha's desire for documents had been dampened until Monday, she didn't feel the need to avoid her so much and after lunch, Jade accompanied her up to the fourth floor, where Marsha introduced her to sales and finance teams, as well as the legal team who she was due to do some work for this afternoon.

Despite the roles on fourth being more corporate than those down on third, the people up here were all as young and good-looking as their more creative counterparts, and all incredibly warm and welcoming towards Jade. It was nice. At Tres Chic, the atmosphere was more impersonal, and the ethos focused on getting your head down and working hard. Here, people stopped and chatted with each other in between their desks. They shared ideas and designs and seemed happy to pitch in where they were needed. This was no accident, however - many of the articles Jade had read about Rebecca Burton-Webb, dealt with her vision for her brand, and how she was keener than ever on creating a culture of inclusion and diversity at Beautiful You! She'd crafted a culture where all her employees felt part of the greater whole and where hierarchy and glass ceilings were a thing of the past. It was admirable and, with each article Jade had read, she'd found it harder and harder to marry the Rebecca she knew in her head with the one on the page. Now that she'd met the woman in person, she was even more confused. She was firm and stoic and somewhat scary up close but seemed to emanate genuine warmth and kindness. It gave Jade cause for concern. Which was why she was trying to keep her feelings out of it and focus only on facts. On what she knew to be true.

"Jade. Hey again."

Back at her desk a few hours later, she looked up to see Sonya from legal standing over her.

"Hi, Sonya." She smiled to conceal any annoyance that might have shown on her face. She'd only just sat down after walking over to Mayfair and back to post off a box of samples to Italy that was missed off a recent shipment. The veins in her legs were still throbbing. "Did you need me for something?"

"I was wondering if you could do me a favour." She waved a large manila envelope at her. "I've got some papers I need Rebecca to sign but I've got to leave for a meeting in Birmingham and she's not back yet. I don't want to leave them on her desk and have them get lost. Can you go in when she's back and put them in her hand for me?"

Jade took the envelope. "Yes. No problem."

"You're a bloody lifesaver," Sonya exclaimed. "She's due in sometime this afternoon, but I'm not sure when."

"That's fine."

"Wonderful. I owe you one. Right. I must dash. See you all later."

She hurried away and Jade placed the envelope down next to her keyboard.

"Don't forget," Anita said, lowering her chin and regarding her through her fringe. "Sonya's a bit like Rebecca. A sweetheart, until you piss her off."

"What happens then?"

"She turns into a winged harpy and rips your throat out," Thomas joked.

"I think I'm safe," Jade said, winking at him. "I don't forget things. Not important things, anyway."

The rest of the afternoon was spent compiling a draft guest list for an upcoming promo event, which just involved Jade cutting and pasting email addresses from past guest lists and putting them in a new Excel document. It was the sort of thing she could do with her eyes closed, but it passed the time and was straightforward enough that she could join in the banter with her new colleagues. Thomas had a date that evening and was entertaining them all with stories of his failed but illustrious love life.

"Well, what would you do if you looked down at someone and it looked like their bloody eye was hanging out?" he went on, acting shocked as the three girls giggled behind their hands.

"What was it?" Lauren asked through stifled laughter.

"It turned out he had a severe dog hair allergy. He didn't realise as somehow he'd never been close enough to a dog before. But usually, I let my little Boo sleep on the pillow next to me. I ended up having to take this guy to A and E. He had this massive fluid bubble built up in the membrane of his eyeball. Bloody disgusting."

"Jesus," Jade said. "Did you see him again?"

"Oh yeah. The following week. He was cute. Apart from the eye stuff, you know. But at his place that time."

Jade shook her head and was about to ask him for more when she saw Rebecca march through the main entrance and make a beeline for her office. She straightened her spine, feeling nervous. It reminded her of that feeling she got right before she had to do a presentation or speak in front of a room. It was because she wanted to get this right.

Lauren was starting a story of her own, but before she got too engrossed in it, Jade got to her feet and picked up the manila envelope.

"Are you going in straight away?" Anita asked, nodding at the envelope with a frown. "Bit keen, aren't you? She'll prefer to get settled first."

"I want to get it over with," she said. "It's best she has it."

She walked off before Anita or any of them could reply. Keeping her pace slow, she timed her walk so she arrived at the

Rebecca's office once Rebecca was inside and had hung her coat up. Taking a deep breath Jade knocked on the door.

"Come in!"

Jade eased down the handle and pushed the door open, peering around the side. Rebecca was standing with her back to her, in front of the large printer unit that stood on a plinth at the far side of the room. She was huffing and cursing under her breath, tapping at the printer's touchscreen control panel with one hand whilst scrolling through her phone with the thumb of her other.

Jade let the door close behind her but remained standing in front of it. She folded her arms across the large envelope clasped to her chest. A second went by. And another. Should she say something? She opened her mouth, ready to mention the envelope Sonya had asked her to pass on. But she closed it again as, at that moment, Rebecca shot a sharp glance over her shoulder.

"I don't suppose you know anything about Bluetooth bloody printers, do you?" she asked, before returning her attention to the control panel.

"Umm. Not so much. But I can have a look at it for you." Jade joined Rebecca in front of the machine. "Oh, Sonya asked me to give you this." She handed her the envelope and Rebecca snatched it from her, holding up her iPhone in response.

"I need this printed today," she said.

"Okay. Let me see."

Rebecca sniffed and shoved the phone at her. "Here it is, a contract from one of our new suppliers. The bloody machines just aren't talking to each other."

A ripple of electricity shot down Jade's back as she took the phone from her boss. "Thanks. I can't promise anything, but I'll —" She stopped as Rebecca's desk phone chimed to life, the high-pitched tone filling the room.

"Excuse me," Rebecca said, marching over to answer it. "I need to take this."

Jade turned back to the printer as Rebecca picked up the receiver. "Hello, Rebecca Burton-Webb, speaking..."

Jade tensed as she stared down at the screen of Rebecca's private phone. It made her dizzy. She assumed there to be so many famous people's information on here, not to mention all of Rebecca's email correspondence. In the wrong hands, it could be a weapon. In the right hands too. She held it close to her face, trying to read the tiny text on the screen. The contract appeared to be from a supplier based in Nairobi. She glanced over at Rebecca, who was deep in conversation, waving her arm around as she talked. She seemed angry, telling whoever it was she needed to set up a meeting 'as soon as yesterday.'

Rebecca pinched at the screen to enlarge the document, but it contained so much legal jargon it was impossible to understand. She noticed the phrases 'bio-diversity' and 'sustainable methods' and 'ethical practices', however, which made her think it was probably above board. But why wouldn't it be? Rebecca was a savvy businesswoman. She wouldn't be so powerful in the industry if she hadn't learnt from her mistakes.

If only everyone had that opportunity.

Jade's I.T. knowledge was average, at best. But average knowledge could make you appear like a boffin to the right people. People like Rebecca who had grown up without the internet and who always had other people to solve her technical issues for her. Jade switched off the Bluetooth option on Rebecca's phone and did the same on the printer. Next, she switched the printer off at the mains and clasped the buttons down on the side of the phone to instigate a hard reboot.

As she waited for both devices to reload, she shifted her attention back to her hearing. Rebecca was responding with heavy tutting noises to whatever she was being told, but she didn't sound angry as much as despondent. Despite Rebecca's reputation for being so calm and collected, Jade detected an air of desperation. She was tense. Possibly missing her old PA more than ever. But that was a good thing. She could use that.

"I don't have her number or, of course, I would do," Rebecca barked down the phone. "Lara Bamford is a tricky person to get hold of."

A shiver ran across Jade's shoulders, making them twitch. It was hearing the name that did it. Lara Bamford, the first female CEO of one of the biggest hedge funds in North America. She was indeed a hard woman to get hold of. But not impossible. She smiled to herself as Rebecca's phone screen illuminated.

"Fine. Let me know if you hear anything. And if you speak to her PA, then I trust you'll pass on my details. I need this, Julian. Do you understand? Yes... Fine..."

She slammed the phone down without saying goodbye. "Merde," she said in a perfect French accent.

A surge of adrenaline shot through Jade's body. She cleared her throat as she turned. "Is everything all right?"

Rebecca didn't look up. "Yes, fine." She laughed. "I mean, no. Not really. But nothing for you to concern yourself with."

"Did I hear you mention Lara Bamford?" Jade asked, pushing through her nerves. "CEO of The Castle Group, yes?"

"That was a private conversation," Rebecca said, raising her head. She looked at Jade and frowned.

"Oh, yes, of course," Jade yelped and coughed. "I didn't mean to listen in... I was just... I couldn't help but pick up on the name, that's all. You see, I've been reading about her, and she was in the front of my mind, I guess. She's quite a woman."

"Yes. And one hard to get a handle on. Unfortunately, I need to speak with her rather urgently and the amount of gatekeepers she has is ridiculous. I know if I could just get in front of her for five minutes—" She stopped herself and huffed.

"Apologies, you don't need to hear any of this. I'm just a little... perturbed right now, that's all."

Jade pushed her shoulders back. "Did you know she was attending the BVCA Gala this week?"

Rebecca had ripped open the envelope Sonya had Jade deliver and was peering inside, but on hearing this, her head snapped up. "What?"

"Lara Bamford. She's over in London to attend the venture capitalist's yearly dinner event this Thursday."

Rebecca's eyes widened. "How do you know this?"

"It's not common knowledge, but I have Google updates set up for people in the industry, and those I feel are worth following. Lara is a bit of an inspiration. First female CEO at Castle, managing the biggest portfolio in the western world but focused on retail sustainability and off-setting carbon emissions. And all before turning forty."

Rebecca almost smiled. "You know your stuff. But how...?"

"As I say, I have Google updates set up. Last week I got a notification from a business site about her visit. I think they must have posted it out of turn though because they deleted it almost straight away. But I'm pretty certain she's going to be there. Might be worth seeing if you can get a ticket?" She shrugged.

"Yes. It might be." Rebecca said, nodding at her. "Brilliant. I know the organiser. Well, done...erm..." She grimaced and waved her hand in the air.

"Jade," Jade offered.

"Of course! Jade. Thank you, darling. You're a lifesaver."

She smiled. "You're the second person to have said that to me this afternoon."

"Hmm. Yes. Where did you say you came from again?"

"Tres Chic."

Rebecca wagged a finger in the air. "That's right." She

pulled a concerned face and shot her a look up and down. "And being an intern isn't beneath you?"

Jade shrugged again. "I'm a hard worker and I don't mind getting my hands dirty. Metaphorically speaking, at least. I'd say an internship at Beautiful You! beats most fashion assistant jobs elsewhere."

Rebecca flashed her eyes at her. "Good answer."

"Losing my mother made me reassess my life," Jade continued, the words sending a ripple of nervous energy running through her body. "I know it's a cliché, but I'd rather be at the bottom of a ladder I want to climb... You know?"

"I do. And I'm sorry for your loss."

The words hit Jade hard, but she kept her smile in place. "Thank you."

"Did you study?" Rebecca asked her.

"Yes. At Saint Martins. Fashion Design with Marketing." She didn't take her eyes off Rebecca.

"Isn't that something?" she exclaimed and tilted her head back as if to better take Jade in. "You know that's the exact course I took?"

"Oh, I know," Jade told her. "You visited and gave a talk when I was in my second year. It was... inspirational. I've followed you ever since. It was why, when I saw the intern position come up here, it felt like fate was guiding me. I was already considering moving back to the UK and now this... I know it sounds silly."

"No. Not at all. It doesn't sound silly to me."

"Right, well, I'd better get back to work and leave you in peace," Jade said. "Oh, but I think I sorted this." She lifted the phone and tapped print and a moment later the machine next to her whirred into life. "Here you go," she said, stepping over to Rebecca's desk and handing back her phone.

"Brilliant!" she cried. "Thank you, Jade."

"No problem." She lowered her chin and smiled. "Thank you. For hiring me. For giving me this opportunity to learn from the absolute best."

Without another word, she spun on her heels and headed for the door. She could sense Rebecca watching her as she eased it open and slunk out into the low afternoon hum of the main office. As she walked back to her desk, she couldn't stop the smile from spreading across her face. That couldn't have gone better if she'd rehearsed it. An excellent result, considering it was only her second day here. For the first time in a long time, she felt pleased with herself. Hell, she might even get a decent night's sleep tonight. Wouldn't that be something?

8

The next day was Wednesday and Jade's morning was spent in Finance, helping Hina with some archiving that was long overdue. Once Jade was given her instructions - she was to marry up invoices and receipts and seal them in huge box-like envelopes for storage - she switched to autopilot, completing the task like she'd been shown, but with little thought given to it. Which was useful, as her mind was racing with a host of other things.

She'd fallen asleep relatively early last night, but it wasn't the type of rest anyone could describe as 'a decent night's sleep.' Weird, confusing images and ideas had plagued her consciousness, and she'd woken up in a cold sweat. She'd remembered at the time what she'd been dreaming about and it had bothered her a great deal, but she was damned if she could recall it now.

By the time she'd finished in Finance, it was gone twelve. For the previous two days, Jade had followed her colleagues' lead and not taken lunch until well into the afternoon. But this morning she'd felt too discombobulated to eat breakfast and was feeling weak with hunger.

"I'm going out to get a sandwich," she told Lauren and Thomas once back down on third. "Does anyone want anything?"

The two of them both looked up from their screens, staring at her as if she was speaking an alien language. "Sorry?" Lauren muttered.

"Lunch. Do you want anything brought back?"

"Oh, no thanks."

"I'll pop out for something in a bit," Thomas told her. "Anita's got a meeting in Soho, but I doubt she'll want anything. She doesn't eat lunch if she knows she's going out. She'd rather save the calories for the wine. Are you still coming?"

"Tonight? What's going on?"

Thomas opened his mouth in mock horror. "Nicole's birthday drinks. Don't let her know you forgot about her!"

Shit.

She had forgotten. And now she'd made plans. Still, it was nothing she couldn't rearrange. Drinks later sounded good. Plus, she hoped there'd be valuable things to learn from her new colleagues, once the alcohol had loosened their tongues and they'd let their guards down.

"I'll be there," she said. "I'm looking forward to it. Have you bought Nicole anything? Is there a card going around?"

Lauren snorted. "No. We don't do that sort of thing. It's rather cheesy, don't you think? Get her a glass of fizz later. That's all she'll care about."

"Gotcha." She grabbed her bag and jacket off the back of her chair. "I won't be long."

She headed for the lift, and as the doors slid closed she pulled her phone out of her bag and fired off a quick text, explaining that she couldn't make it this evening after all. Under the circumstances, it was understandable. Drinks with her colleagues were important. For many reasons.

54

She rode the lift down to the ground floor and, once outside the building, stopped to breathe in the cool early autumn air. Despite what she'd been telling people, it had been an incredibly hard decision to move back to London. New York had become her home and if it wasn't for the nagging and guilt trips she'd endured for the last year, she'd still be there. She might even have patched things up with Jacob. Stranger things had happened. Yet, today, with the crisp air tingling her skin and the sights and sounds of London filling her awareness, a not-unpleasant wave of nostalgia washed over her. This was her hometown, after all.

On Jade's first day at Beautiful You! Marsha had mentioned a smart, modern deli down the next street that most people from the office went to for lunch. It certainly sounded her thing, and she could smell the freshly cooked in-house sourdough as she got to the corner. Yet something compelled her to walk past, and she headed instead for Marble Arch tube station.

She swiped her Oyster Card on the barrier and caught the next tube over to Piccadilly Circus. She could have walked it in around twenty minutes and been there and back within the hour, but although her contract stated she had a full hour allocated for lunch, most people got takeout and ate it at their desks whilst working. In the short while she'd been at Beautiful You! she'd gained a lot of goodwill and impressed many people. She didn't want to spoil that. Not yet, anyway.

Having been here thousands of times before, she didn't give the bright lights of Piccadilly a moment's glance as she crossed the road and walked down Glasshouse Street. Keeping her head down and quickening her step, she walked to the end of the street, where she took a right onto Brewer Street, heading into Soho.

Here she perked up, eyes darting around, taking in all the eating establishments, many of which weren't here the last time she visited over three years ago. And there it was, a hundred metres in front of her on the left. Gorkem Cafe. Winding around the sea of ambling tourists and steadfast office workers, she made her way and stood outside to read the menu. She wasn't a massive fan of Turkish food. But she'd read good things about this place.

A blanket of glorious smells enveloped her as she opened the door and stepped inside. The café was only the size of a single unit but was buzzing with life. All but one of its eight tables were occupied, each filled with plates of exciting-looking delicacies. But as she glanced around the room, taking in each diner, her heart sank. He wasn't here.

She moved over to the counter and squinted up at the chalkboard above. Most of the words on it she didn't recognise, but she enjoyed trying new food.

"Hello, dear. What can I get you?" a kind-faced woman asked from behind the counter.

"Hmm. Not sure," Jade replied. She turned and pointed to a stew-like dish on a nearby table that she'd spotted on her way over here. "That looks good. Can I have one of those, please?"

"That is Iskender kebab. Is thin meat in tomato sauce with bread."

"That sounds great. Thank you," she said, before noting the clock over the woman's shoulder. "Could I get that to go? Please?"

"No problem." The woman looked to her left, shouting through to the kitchen in Turkish before turning back to Jade. "That's six-ninety-five, please dear. Do you want a drink? It is included."

"Great. I'll have a bottle of water," she replied, scrambling in her bag and pulling out her credit card. She swiped it against the machine and waited until 'Approved' flashed up on the screen before replacing it and smiling at the woman. "Will the food be long?"

"Is ready right now," came the reply, as a large man with dark skin and black swept-back hair bustled into view carrying two metal takeout cartons. The woman took them from the man without acknowledging him and placed them in a brown paper bag with paper handles. "Enjoy," she said. "You can choose a bottle of water from the fridge near the entrance."

"Excellent. Thank you." Jade grabbed the handle and stepped away from the counter.

Giving the room one more look in case she'd missed him the first time, she shuffled over to the tall glass-fronted fridge in the corner. An old man was sitting in front of it with his chair pulled out so she could only open it a few inches and had to snake her hand awkwardly around the side of the door to grab a bottle of Evian. Because heaven forbid, she might have to engage with a stranger and ask him to move. She might have called New York home for the last six years, but she was still an awkward Brit, with all the weird social conventions and odd niceties that came with it.

With the mineral water in her clutches, she closed the fridge door. Coming all this way was a bloody stupid idea. London was an enormous city. Even if he was eating here today, why would he be here in this five-minute window?

She shook her head.

Idiot.

She moved over to the door but stopped before she got there as she saw someone on the other side. They had their head turned and were shouting at someone further down the street, but she recognised the voice immediately. As they turned and opened the door to the cafe, a yelp of excitement bubbled up in her chest. Idiot, was she?

She stepped forward as he entered the café.

"Hey. It's you," he said, eyes twinkling as he looked her up and down. "The new girl, right?"

"Yes. That's right," she said, tilting her head to one side. "Hi, Seb. Fancy seeing you here."

9

"What are you doing at Gorkem's?" Seb asked, his arresting blue eyes gazing into hers. "I mean, it's an amazing place, but it's a bit of a trek from Beautiful You!"

He held Jade's gaze, eyes crinkling up at the corners as a flutter of nervous energy worked its way into her pelvis.

"I read a feature on it," she replied. "It sounded great, and I fancied something new." What she didn't say was that the feature in question was an old interview with Seb Turner himself. One of those silly Q & A one-pagers in a gossip magazine. The sort of piece that asked identical questions each week to different celebrities. Favourite place in the world? Favourite quote? What would you do if you had one hour left on earth? That sort of thing.

'Marrakesh', 'To create is to live twice' and 'Have sex' were Seb's responses to those particular questions, but there was also a question about his favourite place to eat and he'd mentioned Gorkem Café in Soho. He went on to say that he ate lunch here at least twice a week and, hyperbole or not, she thought she'd risk it. It seemed to have paid off.

"Well, it's good to see you again," Seb said. "I'm about to get lunch. Do you want to join me?"

"Oh. I can't," she said, lifting her takeout bag to show him. "I should get back to the office."

"Come on, it'll be nice to have some company." His lips tilted into that crooked half-smile. "We didn't have time for a proper chat yesterday."

Jade looked down for a moment and then back up, regarding him through her eyelashes. "I'd love to. But I can't. It's only my third day and I don't want people to think I'm flaky."

"How could they? And don't worry about Rebecca. If she has a problem with you having a relaxing lunch with an interesting companion, then you tell her to come to me."

Jade grimaced. "Do you think it'd be okay?"

"Of course. Besides, I don't think Rebecca is in today. Meetings, of some description. If anyone else has a problem, you really can tell them to piss off."

Jade giggled. "Thanks."

"We're in luck. There's a table free. This way." He placed his hand on the small of her back and guided her across the café to a table near the back. As they got closer, the woman behind the counter saw Seb and smiled.

"Mr Turner!" she cried. "Good to see you, my darling. Everything okay?"

"It is now, Pinar. I'm ravenous."

"You want your usual?"

"Of course! We'll sit here if that's cool." He gestured to Jade. "Can you bring out a spare plate for my friend, too, please? She's going to keep me company."

Pinar gave Jade a knowing smile. "No problem. I am over in a minute."

Seb stepped back and gestured for Jade to sit, waiting for her to get settled before sitting opposite. She'd read he was a real

60

charmer, but she hadn't countered on him being so attentive. It was nice. It made a change.

They stared at each other for a moment as a fresh wave of nervous energy tickled at Jade's sensibilities. But it wasn't unpleasant. Seb hardly knew her, and whilst she'd spent the last month researching every aspect of his life, she'd only met him for the first time yesterday. It should have felt more awkward than it did. But there was something about Seb's relaxed, confident manner that calmed a fire inside of her. She could see why women liked him so much, but being married to someone like Seb must cause Rebecca grief. She almost felt sorry for her.

"So, Jade, tell me about yourself. What do you like to do? What are your dreams?"

"Erm... Wow... My dreams," she stammered. "I've not thought about those for a long time. I suppose I want to do something important in the world."

"Yawn. Boring," he said. "And far too vague. What does that even mean?"

She looked at him and frowned, but he grinned back.

"Okay then," she said. "I suppose my big dream is saving the planet whilst making a lot of money at the same time."

"Now we're getting there. And you don't think those two things are mutually exclusive?"

"Not at all. Rebecca is a prime example of someone who's doing just that."

Seb sneered, and his demeanour dropped. "Yeah, maybe. Let's not talk about Rebecca, okay?"

"Sorry. I shouldn't have..."

"It's fine. I'm just a little tired of being known as Rebecca's husband, you know. I mean fucking hell. I've got a career too."

"I know. You're brilliant. I'm a big fan."

That was enough for his mood to rise again. He sat back and looked at her out of the corner of his eye as if trying to work out if she was being serious. "Really? You've seen some of my work."

"Absolutely. I've seen most of it. Rebel Soldiers is one of my favourite action films."

Seb made a sound like the air being let out of a car tire. "Now I know you're taking the piss."

"I'm not. I know people think it's a bit cheesy. But your character has real depth. That last scene where you're talking about your dead friend. It's incredibly powerful."

This was pushing it. She'd had to force herself to sit through the entirety of the film last week and it had to be one of the most self-obsessed and ridiculous things she'd ever seen.

"What do you think of my monologue in the waterfall scene?" Seb asked.

"Oh, that? Amazing." She was struggling for more superlatives when Pilar appeared by the side of the table, carrying a tray.

"Here we go," she said, placing three dishes down in front of Seb. "Your usual, Mr Turner."

"Thank you. It looks delicious. As always."

Pilar placed a fresh plate down in front of Jade, along with cutlery for them both, wrapped in white paper napkins. "Enjoy," she said but didn't move away. She stood at the end of the table with her hands on her hips, smiling at Seb like a proud mother. "When are we going to see you on our television again?" she asked.

"Ask my agent," he replied. "But soon. Hopefully." He looked at the food and for a split-second, Jade detected a hint of shame flash across his face. But then he was back to his charismatic self, squeezing Pilar's arm in thanks and telling her she was looking younger than ever.

"You've got to try the hummus here," he told Jade as Pilar wandered off beaming. "Yes, I know - hummus, how very dull and obvious - but this stuff is something else. I don't know what they put in it. I mean, I've asked them, but they won't tell me. Not even after I gave them that."

He pointed to a framed photo hanging above the counter. Jade hadn't noticed it earlier. It was a signed headshot of a much younger version of Seb Turner. She turned back to watch as he tucked into his dinner. It seemed odd that he would brag about something so trivial and lame as having a photo on the wall. But maybe that told her something else about who he was. It was no secret his career was on the wane, and whilst she didn't know many actors personally, she suspected the received wisdom was true, that they all had incredibly fragile egos and lived for compliments and reassurance. She was pleased with herself for bringing up Rebel Soldiers. She'd been shooting from the hip, but it was a savvy move on her part.

"Are you not eating?" Seb asked, pointing to the takeout bag sitting on the table beside her.

"Yes. I will. I was just...forget it." She pulled the paper bag towards her and peered inside. A bright red oil had seeped out onto the top tray, but it smelled great. "I can't remember what I ordered," she said, not meaning to play the ditsy girl but doing so anyway.

"It's all fabulous." Seb swallowed the food in his mouth and sat back to take her in.

Jesus.

That stare. It was unnerving.

His eyebrows twitched. "You used to live in New York, is that right?"

"How do you know that?"

"I can't remember. I heard someone talking about you. It might have been Rebecca, I don't recall. Don't look so scared. I've not been stalking you or anything."

She let out an involuntary yelp, shooting her hand over her mouth to catch it.

If you only knew!

"I've got shares in Beautiful You!" Seb went on. "So, I like to keep abreast of who works there. Especially the interesting ones. Such as yourself."

The subtext in his words was as subtle as his performance in Rebel Soldiers.

"Interesting," she repeated, composing herself enough to catch the look he gave her. He was flirting now, no mistake, but rather than her finding it encouraging, she was full of insecurities. Despite this being the exact response that she'd hoped for, she couldn't stop her leg from juddering under the table. She'd rarely been around men with such flagrant sexual appetites and the actuality of being here cast a heavy shadow of doubt over her.

Seb waved a piece of flat bread at her, catching her attention. "I was considering moving to LA," he said. "It's the place to be if you want to make movies. But then I met Rebecca..." He trailed off as if that explained everything. And maybe for him, it did.

"These days that doesn't matter so much, does it?" she asked. "I thought most actors self-filmed their auditions now, or did them over Zoom?"

Shit.

Even before she'd finished speaking, she knew it was the wrong thing to say.

"Do they?" Seb sniffed. "Maybe I should let my agent know that." He stabbed his fork into a lamb kofte and stuffed the whole thing in his mouth.

Bugger.

She needed to pull this back. The sexual tension had made

her anxious, but there was a happy medium. She was here for a reason, after all. The plan. Stick to the plan.

She smiled at him as he chewed, desperately thinking of something to say. Before anything came to her, she felt her handbag vibrating next to her. Saved by the bell.

"Ooh, I'm ringing."

Seb shrugged. "Go for it."

Pleased at the distraction, she pulled out her phone, ready to divert the call. But when she saw the name on the screen, her heart did a somersault. She got to her feet, tilting the phone screen away from Seb.

"Sorry," she said. "I have to take this. It's important."

10

"What are you calling me for?" Jade hissed into the receiver. "I'm at work. We agreed you wouldn't call me at work. It's dangerous."

The line buzzed, as the person on the other end was sighing heavily into the microphone. "And hello to you too! You just sent me the briefest of texts informing me you aren't coming tonight. But that's not fair Jade. One of the reasons why you came back to the UK was to help me. We also agreed on that."

"Listen to me!" Jade snapped. "You don't know what sort of fucked up roller coaster ride these last few days have been. Do you know who I'm having lunch with right now? Seb Turner." She paused to allow the words to sink in. When there was no answer, she continued. "Yes. I thought that would shut you up. I'm doing it. Okay. I'm getting there. Like we *agreed*."

"Seb, really? That is good going. What's he like?"

Jade bit her lip. "Like we expected him to be," she said. "An arrogant prick with a massive ego and a wandering eye."

"But you're getting him onside? Do you think he likes you?" Her tone was still sharp but had mellowed somewhat.

"Erm. Of course. Who wouldn't?" She laughed to lighten

the mood, but no laughter came back. "Don't worry. I've got this."

The phone buzzed again. Another deep sigh. "Why can't you come over tonight?"

"It's someone's birthday. A girl called Nicole. Everyone's going out for drinks. I said I would before I realised what day it was. But I think it'd be valuable. Plus, Nicole is the only person I've met so far who's been a bit off with me. I need to get her onside, too." She turned around. Through the window, she saw Seb talking to Pilar, gesticulating at the food, bringing his fingers up to his mouth and kissing the tips with dramatic gusto. He must have sensed her watching him because he looked straight at her. As their eyes met, he smiled and mouthed 'Are you okay?'

She nodded, feeling her cheeks flush at the same time.

"Someone in the office might have some dirt we can use," she said, turning around. "I'm hoping once people have had a few drinks, the gossip will flow. But I am sorry about bailing on you tonight. I know how hard it is for you."

"Do you? Do you really?"

"Yes! I do!"

The line went silent, to the extent that Jade lifted the phone from her ear momentarily to check they were still connected. "Are you still there?"

"Sorry. I've got to go," came the curt reply. "Good luck tonight. Be cool, you know, be safe. Let me know how it goes."

She hung up before Jade could reply, leaving her standing in the street in a cloud of contradictory emotions. Did she not realise this was hard on her just as much? Until three months ago, she was living in New York working on her career. She might not have been 'living her best life', as they say, especially not after it being apparent she and Jacob weren't getting back together, but she was content. She hadn't asked for any of this.

"Bloody hell." She swiftly dabbed at her eyes as she felt tears forming. "Pull yourself together." She tossed her hair over her shoulders and stuck out her chest. Back into the role. There'd be plenty of time for tears and contemplation once this was all over. For now, she had to stay focused.

"Everything all right?"

She was startled as Seb appeared beside her.

"Yes. Fine. Thanks." He had her handbag slung over his shoulder and was holding her jacket and the takeout bag. "Here, let me put this on for you. It's freezing out here."

He handed her the takeout, and they did an awkward dance as Seb helped her into her jacket and she flipped the paper bag from hand to hand to slide her arms into the sleeves.

"Thank you," she said. "That's very chivalrous of you." She meant it. She couldn't remember Jacob ever helping her with her jacket. He'd probably have actively scoffed at the very idea of it.

"I've got to make a move, I'm afraid," Seb said. "But thank you for joining me. Albeit fleetingly."

"I'm so sorry," she said, holding up the phone still in her hand. She shrugged. "It was my bank. There was some suspicious activity on my account. But it's all sorted."

"Good. You can't be too careful." He slipped her handbag off his shoulder and handed it over.

"You said it." She opened the bag and went to place her phone inside. "Shit! Is that the time? I need to get back to the office."

She swung the bag over her shoulder and glanced down the street. It was ten to one. It would take her at least twenty-five minutes to get back to her desk. People were going to notice. Marsha would notice. Would she tell Rebecca? Would that be the end of it? Her heart was beating fast and loud in her chest as she glanced up at Seb.

"Don't worry," he said. "My car will be here in a minute. I'll drop you off. You'll be at your desk by one. Guaranteed." He grinned. It was like he'd read her thoughts.

"Are you sure?" she asked.

"Of course. Here he is now." He raised his hand in the air, looking over her shoulder. She stepped back as a black SUV pulled up alongside them.

"Here we are." Seb leaned across her and opened the door. "We'll have you back in no time."

She climbed in the back of the car, nodding and smiling at the driver, a bald man with a round face.

"This is Jez," Seb told her, climbing in the car beside her and sitting down heavily on the leather bench seat. "Jez, this is Jade. She's just started working at Beautiful You! I said we'd give her a lift to the office if that's cool?"

"You're the boss," Jez called out, pulling away down the street. He met Jade's gaze in the rear-view mirror. "Pleased to meet you, Jade. What are you doing hanging about with this rascal?"

She gasped at the question, but Seb leaned into her. "Jez is an old mate of mine," he said. "And a damn good actor. But since he gave up drinking, I thought it'd be cool for him to be my driver. It means we can hang out together."

"Yeah, lucky me," Jez said with a chuckle.

"That's cool," Jade told them. "And sweet, really."

"That's me," Seb said, leaning in even closer. "Cool *and* a total sweetie."

He didn't move back to his side of the seat and, up close, she could smell him. He smelled good.

"Thank you for this," she said, turning enough so that she could see his face. "I think you are a sweetie."

He tilted his head back and laughed. "You're only saying that because you don't know me well enough yet."

"Yet?"

He shrugged and closed his eyes with a smile. And there he was. The arrogant prick with the massive ego. Whether or not he was showing off in front of Jez, she was glad to see him through this lens. It was for the best.

"You can drop me off on the corner if it's easier," she told them, as they drove up Park Street towards Oxford Street.

"No need," Jez replied. "The one-way system takes us past the building. It's no bother."

"Thank you," she lied, as a fresh wave of nervous energy washed over her.

Jez swung the car onto Oxford Street and slowed to a stop opposite the Beautiful You! building.

"It was good to see you again," Seb said. "But I still don't feel like we've got to know each other at all. Maybe we could have a drink sometime?"

"Umm. I don't..." Jade glanced at Jez's eyes in the mirror as her breath caught in her throat. She lowered her head along with her voice as she turned back to Seb. "I mean, you're married to my boss. Isn't that...bad?"

"I'm only talking about a drink, Jade." It felt to her like he was staring into her soul. "I like to get to know all the new employees. Men and women. Rebecca's fine with it."

She didn't believe that for a second but found herself smiling and nodding. "Okay, great," she said, reaching around for the door handle.

"No. Please. Allow me." Before she could protest, he'd opened his door and jumped out into the flow of traffic.

She caught Jez's gaze again and smiled nervously as Seb walked around the back of the car and opened the door for her.

"Out you get, M'Lady," he said, holding his hand out and bowing theatrically.

"Thank you... M'Lord!" She giggled as she took his hand and he helped her out.

They stood on the roadside and looked at each other for too long before Jade remembered where she was. "Right. I need to get back. Thanks again."

She hurried across the road before he could respond, winding through the oncoming traffic. Once on the other side, she turned back to wave, but the car had already pulled away. Lowering her arm, she looked around to make sure no one had seen her. The streams of people on the street walked past as if she was invisible. That was London for you, and she was glad of it. But as she glanced up at the glass building in front of her, she froze. Someone was standing in the window up on the third floor. From this distance and with the low autumnal sun in her eyes, she couldn't make out who it was, but something about their stance bothered her. They'd been watching her; she was certain of it. They'd seen her getting out of Seb Turner's car. That wasn't good. It wasn't good at all.

11

Nicole's birthday drinks party was already in full swing as Jade and Anita arrived at the Sanderson Hotel that evening. It was the first time Jade had been to the hotel's Long Bar, and the design impressed her. She viewed, with delight, the host of greenery that hung down over the bar and the concealed lighting under the counter. As they moved further into the venue, however, the pictures of menacing eyeballs adorning the backs of each of the bar stools were slightly off-putting. It felt as if the room itself was watching her.

She'd had enough of being watched for one day.

"Here they are. We thought you weren't coming," Thomas cried as they approached the table where he and Lauren were sitting along with Sally and Mia, who she'd only met in passing but were part of the Influencer Marketing team along with Nicole. Jade and Anita had intended on getting a taxi along with Thomas and Lauren as soon as work was over, but Anita had forgotten a change of shoes. Ever the people pleaser, Jade had agreed to accompany her to Zara where she'd purchased a cute pair of beige and black sling-backs.

"Come here, let's have a look at them." Thomas stood, sloshing his full glass of fizz over the table. Side-stepping around the seated guests, he stepped out into the open space to get a better look at Anita's new shoes.

"They were a total steal," she said, lifting her foot and tilting it around so he could get the full effect. "Nice, huh?"

"Love them!" Thomas told her, placing his hand on Jade's shoulder. "Now let's get you bitches some drinks. What are you having? We've got a shitload of Prosecco on the go but some people are on the cocktails already."

"Prosecco is fine," Jade said.

"Coming up." He lurched over to the bar, where rows of elegant tulip glasses were pre-filled with sparkling wine. Grabbing two glasses, he walked back over and handed the drinks to Jade and Anita. "Here we go. Rebecca's paying for the first two hours apparently, so get a move on. You two are playing catch-up."

"God, is everyone already pissed?" Anita asked.

Thomas gulped back a mouthful of his drink. "Getting there."

"I might try to pace myself, actually," Jade said, eliciting a vicious side-eye from Thomas.

"I knew there was something strange about you," he said and even though it was clear he was joking, the words sent a shiver down Jade's spine.

No. She wasn't strange. She fitted in. She was part of the team. That was how it was supposed to be.

"I mean... I'll have a few drinks."

"Good girl." He stepped forward and lowered his voice, but only into a stage whisper, speaking out of the corner of his mouth. "Nicole is already completely wasted."

Anita laughed. "Typical. She always is."

"Where is the birthday girl?" Jade asked. She was hoping

she wouldn't have to deal too much with Nicole this evening, but it would be both polite and pertinent to say 'hello' and wish her 'happy birthday.'"

Thomas looked around and shrugged. "She was here. She might be outside vaping."

"I'm sure we'll see her soon enough...unfortunately," Anita said, nudging Jade playfully.

"You're bad, you know that? I'm the new girl. I'm going to get black-balled before I have a chance to find my feet hanging around with you."

"Come off it," Anita said. "Everyone loves you. Can't you tell? I was watching you yesterday when you were in with Rebecca. Whatever you were saying must have impressed her."

"How do you know?"

"Because she was standing still for once, and looked like she was actually listening to you."

Jade frowned. "Doesn't she normally?"

"No. She used to be a part of the action. We'd have weekly meetings where she encouraged everyone to throw ideas on the table - anything, no matter how crazy or outlandish - but lately... since the pandemic, she's been distracted and stressed out. I've been working for her for over ten years and I've never seen her look so tired and unhappy."

"That's a shame," Jade said, surprising herself that she meant it. "What do you think the reason is?"

"Probably a few things. The worldwide malaise, business not going as well as it should be, the magazine failing. Sorry, I know you're going to be working on it, but the truth is, it was a stupid venture. I said so at the time. It's almost impossible to launch a new hard-copy magazine these days. Yes, the big hitters are still getting numbers in print. But they've got history. And whilst Beautiful You! is still a relevant brand, it's not the golden goose it once was. Those days are over." She gulped back a mouthful of Prosecco. "Rebecca has done amazing things in the industry, but she's sixty-five this year and still trying to compete with people a lot younger than her. She's not got her finger on the pulse like she used to. She's getting old and fatigued with the industry and deep down, I think she knows that. And the fact her husband is a total shit can't help."

Jade swallowed. The way Anita said this last part made her uneasy. It felt like she was accusing her of something.

Was it her in the window?

Was this her way of warning her off?

"Is he as bad as people say?" she stammered.

Anita sniffed. "Who knows? He's a man, so..."

"Yes. Sure."

Jade had been sipping at her drink while Anita talked and now found she'd drunk the entire glass. There was nothing like a bit of social anxiety to help you overcome your proposed abstinence. She waved the empty glass at Anita.

"I'm going to get another. Do you want one?"

Anita grinned. "Nice. I knew you were one of us. Don't listen to Thomas. And yes, absolutely."

"I'm going to use the bathroom first," she said. "Do you know where they are?"

Anita scrunched up her face. "I think they're over on the other side of the bar. I've not been here for ages."

"I'll find them."

Jade made her way across the room, waving to a few people she recognised from the office as she went. There was still no sign of Nicole, but she hoped now that she'd shown her face she could slink away without reprisal. Drinking on an empty stomach, she was already feeling the effects of that first glass of Prosecco. Hopefully tonight she'd get a proper night's sleep. The hallowed eight hours. It had been a long time since that had happened.

Winding through the throng of people, she came out at the far side of the bar and saw the bathrooms in front of her. Quickening her step, because now she really needed to pee quite urgently, she half-ran, half-skipped across the remaining floor space and pushed open the heavy wooden door. The room beyond was stark and modern, with low sink units on one side of the room and a row of stalls on the other. Not stopping to admire the décor too closely, she headed for the nearest stall and locked the door behind her. She was glad of the music, piped in from the main bar at a decent volume as she sat on the polished wooden seat and relieved herself. After she'd finished, she immediately felt less panicky than she had done. Probably it helped that she was away from the crowds, but another glass of Prosecco would also help. One more glass, then she'd make her excuses and go. Maybe two more.

Leaving the stall, she headed for the sink unit opposite and twisted on the classy bronze tap. Leaving the water to warm up, she administered a globule of Jo Malone pomegranate handwash from the cream dispenser into her palm. As she washed her hands, she raised her head to look at her reflection in the round individual mirror above the basin. She looked worn out. That was her first impression. The stark overhead lights in these bathrooms didn't help, but there was only so much excuse one could give in terms of unflattering lighting. If her mother was here, she'd tell her she needed a good night's sleep and a decent meal inside of her. Jade smiled at the memory, but as more thoughts of her dear mum formed in her mind, they brought with them another bout of anxiety and panic.

A toilet flushed behind her and she returned her attention to her hands, lathering up the soap before rinsing it away.

"Did you have a nice lunch date?"

She shot her head up to see Nicole's reflection in the mirror. She was standing in the open toilet stall with her arms folded.

"Nicole!" Jade gasped, turning around to face her. "Happy birthday! Are you having a good time?"

"Yes. I'm having a whale of a time," she replied. "But I asked you a question."

Jade sucked in a deep breath. *Lunch date.* At least now she knew who was in the window this afternoon. She wiped her wet hands on the top of her corduroy skirt. "What do you mean?"

"You know what I mean," Nicole said, uncrossing her arms and stepping towards her. "I saw you getting out of Seb Turner's car. What were you doing?"

"Nothing," Jade replied.

Nicole was so close she could smell the wine on her breath. Without the bright red killer heels, the two of them would probably be the same height. As it was, Nicole towered over her. Her white-blonde hair had been curled for the occasion and hung down over her shoulders.

"Are you fucking Seb?"

"What? No!" Jade said, laughing despite herself. "I bumped into him in a café in Soho. He recognised me from the office and offered to give me a ride, that's all."

"He offered to give you a ride? Did he now?"

Jade frowned. "Come on, Nicole. Don't talk that way. That's Rebecca's husband." The indignation in her voice was real. She forced herself to hold eye contact as Nicole jutted her face closer to hers.

"I'm watching you," she whispered. "There's something not right about you."

"You're watching me?" Jade straightened herself up to her full height. "What the hell does that mean?"

"I saw the way Seb was talking to you the other day in the office. It was like you were old friends."

"I swear that was the first time I've met him," Jade said, holding her arms out. "Honestly, Nicole, you've got it wrong.

Yes, Seb is kind of handsome, if you like that sort of thing. But he's not my type. At all. And even if he was, I wouldn't do that to Rebecca. I have too much respect for her. Not to mention that I value my job too much."

"Yes, that's another thing," Nicole said, pointing a long bony finger in her face. "Why does someone leave their job as a fashion assistant at one of the best magazines in New York to work as a lowly intern?"

The way she said the word *intern*, she might as well have said *child killer*.

Jade rolled her eyes, about to respond in kind, but stopped herself. She squeezed her fist together to calm herself.

"Listen, Nicole," she said, putting as much warmth in her voice as she could muster. "Can we start again? Please? I've told everyone the reason why I've taken a step down. Losing my mum made me reassess my life. And I've wanted to work at Beautiful You! forever. I'm happy doing a bit of the grunt work for a while if it gets me in the door. I like it. It's fun."

"Is it?"

"Sort of." She smiled. "Nothing is going on between me and Seb, and I've got no ulterior motives. I promise you."

Nicole huffed out a heavy breath but appeared to be calming. "Well, I think you're crazy."

"Maybe I am." She lowered her chin. "Shall we get out there and get some drinks?"

Nicole watched her for a moment as if she was trying to get a read on her. "Fine," she lifted her arms and pulled her ponytail tight. "You don't want to be bothering with Seb Turner, anyway. The man's a waste of space."

Jade tilted her head to one side. "Is he? I thought he and Rebecca were a good team?"

"Maybe for the press," Nicole said, nudging past her and running her hands arbitrarily under the water tap. "But he's a total bastard. The way he talks to her sometimes... I wouldn't stand for it. Not from some failed actor with a drinking problem who can't keep his penis in his pants." She twisted off the tap and flicked her hands to dispel some of the water before reaching for a paper towel off the pile at the back of the sink. "But she loves him. And that's the tragedy of her life. She can't see what he's really like." She dried her hands before scrunching up the paper towel and tossing it in the bin.

"That's so sad," Jade said.

"Yes. It is. But we all have our crosses to bear, don't we, sweetie?" She gave Jade a hard stare before moving over to the door and yanking it open. "Right then, more drinks. A Cosmo, I think. See you in there." She disappeared, allowing the door to swing shut behind her.

Jade waited for a moment to put some space between them. She'd rather not have to encounter Nicole at the bar. She checked herself in the mirror, applied two new streaks of rouge vermillion lipstick and headed for the door.

We all have our crosses to bear.

Wasn't that the truth?

She opened the bathroom door and headed back to the party. Another drink beckoned. She'd damn well earned one.

12

J ade rubbed at her temples as the computer screen flashed
to life, casting her bare arms in a bluish glow. They looked
paler than they ever had done and emphasised her need for
a holiday. Somewhere hot and peaceful. Maybe she'd treat
herself once this was all over. She certainly needed a holiday.
She was already worn out, living on her wits every single day.
Yet, whatever the outcome, it would all be over soon enough.

She had to keep that in mind.

It was Thursday morning, the day after Nicole's birthday
party and, despite it being almost half past nine, she was the first
person in the office. After three (or was it four?) more glasses of
Prosecco, she'd managed to steal herself away from the Long Bar
without being seen and was safely home and in bed before she
turned into a pumpkin. Despite – or more likely because of - the
alcohol, she'd fallen asleep relatively easily but had woken up at
4.50 a.m. wide awake and with the painful knowledge she
wouldn't get back to sleep. Now, four hours later, all she had
was a throbbing head, bad skin and a tonne of unhelpful
thoughts for her troubles. But she'd spoken to Nicole, at least,

and quashed any theories she might have held about her and Seb. Or so she hoped.

Behind her, muffled voices grew louder as the main door opened. Looking up, she saw Mia and Sally entering the office. They waved, on their way over to their desks and Mia made a gruesome face which Jade took as an expression of hangover solidarity. She waved back before returning to her screen and logging into the Beautiful You! intranet portal. She checked her emails and replied to invites from different departments, offering her job shadowing opportunities. It was part of the course as an intern, but she could do without it. She opened up a new internet browser window and read the day's news. It was all bad news. It always was. Ten minutes went by, then twenty and thirty. She didn't look up as she heard more people arriving. The clock on her computer told her it was almost 10:15 a.m. They were late now in anyone's book, but from their voices, they didn't sound concerned. In fact, they were laughing and jeering, and as she glanced over; it surprised her to see Rebecca herself in the group.

"Well, it sounds like you had an excellent evening," she said, shaking her head at whatever the others – Nicole, Lauren and Anita – had been telling her. "And I'm glad you had a good birthday, Nic."

Jade sat back and let out a sharp sigh. It shouldn't have been surprising Rebecca was like this, given everything she'd heard. But in her experience, there was often a sizeable gap between the legend and the truth.

As the group of four got up to the first bank of desks, Rebecca split off from them, striding around the perimeter of the space towards her office. Her long white coat gave her the look of an ice queen, Jade thought. Or maybe that was just her projecting. She sat upright as Nicole walked by and gave her a sharp look. Jade opened her mouth to say something but, when Nicole followed up with a wry smile, she shut it again.

It was fine. They were fine.

"Morning," Lauren said, slumping in her seat. "What time did you get home last night?" She sounded like she'd smoked a whole carton of Marlborough Lights.

Jade glanced at Lauren and then at Anita, who was eyeing her suspiciously. "You never said goodbye!" she hissed, but she was joking.

"I know. I'm a lightweight," Jade told them. "I was asleep by midnight, but I've still got a bit of a bad head. How are you guys?"

"I feel like shit," Anita said.

"I want to curl up into a ball and die," Lauren added.

"Oops." Jade laughed, and they did too. "Rebecca sounded like she didn't mind her entire workforce turning up hungover."

"She's cool when she wants to be," Lauren said. "I think she likes to live vicariously through the pretty young things. Probably why most people here are under thirty. No offence."

Jade frowned. "How did you know I wasn't?"

"Well, you aren't, are you?" Lauren glanced at Anita. "I just assumed... sorry."

"It's cool. Yes. I'm probably one of the oldest people in the office. Maybe that's the reason why everyone has a hard time accepting I'd take this role." She'd meant the statement to sound light-hearted, sarcastic even, but her words hung heavy over their desks and when neither of her colleagues responded, Jade lowered her head behind her screen.

"Hey there, bitches. How's everyone feeling today?"

Jade relaxed her shoulders as Thomas joined them. He held his arms out and stuck out his bottom lip. "Oh, dear. Are we all feeling a tad delicate this morning?"

"Piss off," Anita muttered. "Go sell your positivity somewhere else."

"Charming! Well, I feel great. I've just been to the gym. Sweated it all out."

"Must have been a lot of sweat," Lauren said.

Thomas gasped theatrically as he pulled his chair out. "How dare you? I only had one or two glasses of fizz last night."

"Yeah, right," Jade said. "One or two glasses per half-hour."

"Someone's found their feet already," he said, glaring at her as he sat. "You look okay. See, girls, it is possible to go out and not feel like something from Middle-earth the next day."

Lauren and Anita both hissed at him, but shut up quickly. "Heads up," Anita whispered, and as Jade followed her gaze, she saw Rebecca striding towards them.

She stopped and smiled. "Are we all good?"

"Wonderful," Thomas said. "I, for one, am feeling on top of the world."

Rebecca beamed. "I can always count on you, Thomas." Her expression turned serious, and Jade's heart fell into her stomach as she turned to address her. "Jade, do you have five minutes? In my office?"

"Erm. Yes. Of course." She got to her feet as Rebecca twisted around and headed back the way she'd come.

"Do you think you're going to get fired?" Thomas whispered as she glanced down at the three of them.

"Shut up, dickhead," Lauren hissed. Then, to Jade. "Don't worry, babe. She's probably got some menial tasks for you to do and doesn't want to embarrass you in front of everyone."

"Awesome. Lucky me," she said, forcing her smile.

She hurried after Rebecca, catching up with her as she entered her office and catching the door before it swung shut.

"There you are," she said, not looking around.

"Is everything okay?" Jade asked, following Rebecca over to

83

the large walnut desk. "I know Marsha is still chasing me for my documents, but I'll be able to—"

She stopped as Rebecca waved the idea away with a swipe of her hand. "I'm not concerned about all that," she said, gesturing at one of the two cream leather chairs in front of the desk. "Please, take a seat."

Jade did as instructed, whilst Rebecca sat in the much larger black leather chair on the other side. Once settled, she leaned across the desk and clasped her hands together. She hadn't taken her coat off. Was that a bad sign? It seemed like a bad sign.

"You're a hard person to get a read on, Jade. Are you aware of that?"

Holding her resolve, Jade crossed one leg over the other. "Oh?"

"On one hand, you've got this wealth of experience and understanding of the industry. Yet at the same time, you're more than happy to take a step down and get stuck in with basic admin tasks. I've had reports back from all sides telling me how helpful and motivated you've been."

Jade twisted her mouth to one side with a shrug. "I'm enjoying being here. Enjoying the variety."

"Hmm. I see that. But that's also rather curious for me. I'd have thought someone in your position would be much more cynical and – please excuse the pun – *jaded* by the industry, and would have turned her nose up at some of the humble tasks ascribed to them. But I don't see that in you."

Jade cleared her throat and sat forward in her seat. "I suppose I was yearning for a change in direction - and I see this as the perfect route. My mum worked hard to provide for me and my sister and did her best to remain positive, handling situations with a lightness of touch. I think she instilled the same in me. I like to be busy. I like to work hard. I'm not saying I want to do menial tasks forever. But I meant it when I said that working at Beautiful You! is a dream come true for me."

Rebecca smiled. "That was what I was hoping to hear." She unclasped her hands and leant back, shuffling her shoulders as they made contact with the back of the chair. "I take it you've heard about Kristen, my PA, who left rather abruptly last month."

"Yes. I mean, only that someone called Kristen used to work here. And she was your PA..." She trailed off, grimacing internally at her response.

"I had the notion, initially, that I'd soldier on without her," Rebecca said, flicking her eyebrows. "But the shareholders don't like that idea and to be honest, the last four weeks have been difficult. Kristen was someone I could always rely on. Right up until I couldn't. She worked hard and wasn't just an excellent gatekeeper but was more than capable of coming up with her own solutions and ideas. Whatever she did, it was in support of my vision for the brand."

Jade smiled. "She sounds like a brilliant assistant."

"She was." Rebecca gazed at a spot over Jade's shoulder for a second and her eyes glazed over. "But great PAs aren't born, they're created." Her eyes sparkled back to life as she returned her attention to Jade. "The reason we're having this conversation, Jade, is that I see great potential in you. You're smart and zippy and there's fierce energy in you that's almost tangible. I like it. I think we could work well together. What do you think?"

"Sorry, Rebecca," Jade said. "What are you saying?"

"I'm saying, Jade, that I'm prepared to upset a few people and take a chance on you. As you know, I don't do things by the book and regardless of the fact you've started here as an intern only a few days ago, I trust my guts more than my head. I was incredibly impressed with the information you provided on

Lara Bamford's attendance at the BVCA gala. If that's the level of commitment and creative thinking I can expect from you, then – if you're interested - I'd like you to take over as my PA."

Jade swallowed. But her throat had gone so dry it was hard to. "Are you serious?"

"I wouldn't joke about something like this, Jade. It would be on a trial basis at first, and I'll have to discuss it with Marsha and Hina regarding the matter of your salary. But what do you think?"

"I think...Yes!" Jade said, working hard to maintain a level of decorum. "Thank you, Rebecca. You won't regret this decision."

"Très bon!" Rebecca said. "I'll be honest with you; I've been winding myself into the ground recently and I'm going to need you to hit the ground running. I'll speak with Marsha tomorrow and we'll sort out the details, so please keep this to yourself until then. For now, I'm going to forward you a few emails I'd like you to deal with and I'll grant you viewing permissions for my calendar when I get a chance."

"Great. No problem."

Rebecca got to her feet and brushed down the front of her coat. "Now I must go. I wanted to do this face-to-face and I'm glad I did, but I'm due for a manicure in thirty minutes. The gala is tomorrow night, after all, and I need to look my best for Lana."

"I don't doubt that you will," Jade said, also standing. "She'll be putty in your hands."

"You see. That's another thing," Rebecca said, lowering her voice conspiratorially. "I do appreciate a little cheerleading now and again, but it has to feel sincere. And you've got that in spades, I'd say. You seem to instinctively know what I need to hear, and I like that. But on the flip side, I don't need a yes-woman. Understood? Challenge me. Tell me if you think I'm making a mistake. I need that just as much."

"I will."

"Good." Rebecca held her arm out and guided Jade to the door. "I'm excited. I think this is the start of a wonderful working relationship."

"Me too," Jade replied, stepping to one side to allow Rebecca to open the door. "And thank you. I won't let you down."

She left Rebecca's office, not daring to look back as she returned to her desk in case Rebecca saw anything in her face which might give her doubt.

Shit.

Shit! Shit! Shit!

She'd done it! And faster than she'd ever hoped. Thomas and the others looked at her with quizzical expressions as she sat.

"She just wanted to thank me for my hard work," she told them, hiding behind her screen so they couldn't see the bizarre mix of excitement and trepidation she was feeling, expressed on her face.

You won't regret this decision.

How the hell she'd said that without bursting into flames, she wasn't sure. But maybe she was better at playing this role than she'd given herself credit for. Still, despite the fact the plan was going well, it was no time to get complacent. Now things got serious.

13

Jade bowed her head, trying to remain calm. There was a knot in the polished hardwood floor in front of her that looked a bit like a clown's face. It grinned up at her, but she couldn't work out whether it was a good or bad omen. She puffed out a long breath and raised her head as, beside her, Marsha clapped her hands together and addressed the room.

"Everyone! Can I have your attention, please?" She waved at Sally across the room. "Can you finish that call and put the phones on hold? Thank you!"

It was 11 a.m. the next day, and Jade spent the last twenty-four hours unable to think of anything but this moment. A surge of nerves turned her stomach, as every pair of eyes in the office homed in on her. In her peripheral vision, she saw Thomas lean around the side of his screen and regard her with a questioning expression. She ignored him, focusing on a light switch on the wall across the room.

"Okay all," Marsha said once the room was quiet. "We have a thrilling announcement to make. You've all met Jade here by now and I'm sure you're aware of how well she's fitted in at Beautiful You! and has already made herself rather indispensable." She turned and smiled at Jade. It wasn't an entirely genuine smile, but she'd take it. "Well... Rebecca thinks so too because she's asked Jade to take on the role of her new personal assistant!"

Jade stiffened as stifled gasps and whispers rippled around the space. It was to be expected and she held her nerve, smiling proudly as Marsha continued.

"Rebecca has seen great things in Jade, which I'm certain we all have. So, can you all please welcome her as a permanent and vital member of the Beautiful You! family."

"That's awesome news!" Thomas yelled out. "You go, girl!"

"I hope you haven't got any plans for the next three years!" Lauren added.

People laughed, but as Jade scanned the room, she saw Nicole over in the far corner with a face like a crumpled cigarette packet.

"Thank you, everyone," she said. "I know it's a bit of a shock. It is to me as well. But I already feel I'm very much a part of the team after you made me feel so welcome. The culture and atmosphere you've all created here is fantastic and I hope together we can only improve on the creativity and influence that makes Beautiful You! such a wonderful and important place to work." She could tell she was waffling, so she shut up. Nicole was still giving her the death stare, but she tried not to look at her as a smattering of applause covered her walk back to her old desk.

"Wow!" Anita said, looking her up and down. "You don't waste any time, do you?"

"I guess I don't." She'd vowed to stay humble, to not piss anyone off any more than she had to. But she had many reasons to be pleased with herself.

"But well done," Anita said. "I'm glad you'll be staying on for good. And Christ knows Rebecca needs an assistant!"

"Yeah, congratulations, Jade," Lauren said. "You'll be a great PA. But I meant what I said, *you ain't gonna get noooo rest, lady!*" She said this last part in a gruff American accent. It made Jade laugh and lightened her mood.

"I get it," she said. "But I'm ready. There's nothing she can throw at me I can't handle."

She hoped that was true, but as she logged onto her computer and clicked open her emails, her elation faded. A new message from Marsha was waiting for her at the top of the page. She must have gone straight back to her desk and sent it. Jade puffed out her cheeks and clicked it open, scan-reading the brief message that was to remind her she still needed to bring in her documents. The fact Marsha was now requesting them via email meant she was creating an e-trail and wasn't going to let it drop. Jade gritted her teeth and typed out a reply, telling her no problem, and that she was still visiting her friend at the weekend and would pick up her passport and papers then. This was a lie. There was no friend and the last thing she wanted to do was show anyone associated with Beautiful You! her passport. Her hope was, now she was being thrown headfirst into the PA role, she could put Marsha off for another few weeks. Her only other concern was her bank flagging payment when the name on her account didn't match the one on the payroll. But that shouldn't be a problem until next month and by then she'd be long gone. One way or another.

"Does anyone want a coffee?" she asked, seeing it was almost twelve. "My shout."

Thomas raised his head. "Ooh, hark at her. Big spender, now she's got her promotion."

"Leave her alone," Lauren scolded. "And thanks, Jade. I'll have a soya latte, please."

"Coming up."

She took the other's orders – the same for Anita and a flat

white with an extra shot for Thomas – and grabbed her coat and bag before heading for the lift. The doors opened as she pressed the call button and she stepped inside, feeling more blessed and in tune with the universe than this small happenstance should have allowed. She moved to the back of the metal box, smiling to herself as she pressed the button for the ground floor and turning to face the doors as they slid shut. The situation was moving fast, but that was down to hard work and plenty of research.

"Hang on." The doors had almost closed when a thin, willowy hand snaked through the gap in the doors. As they reopened, Nicole stepped inside the lift, giving Jade a sinister smile. "Well, well, well…" she muttered, as the doors closed and the lift vibrated into life.

"Excuse me?"

"Nothing, babe. I'm happy for you. You're obviously the right person for the job. There can't be anything else in it."

Jade raised her chin. The voice in her head was on repeat, telling her not to get drawn into anything with Nicole. But she couldn't help herself.

"What else could it be?"

"I don't know. Yet. But I stand by my initial estimation. There's something not right about you."

"Is that so?" She stepped aside so she could face her. "Listen, Nicole, I can only assume you had your eyes on the role yourself. I mean, you practically admitted it when I first met you. And I am sorry you were overlooked but Rebecca saw something of value in me and whilst I might not deserve the position in terms of time served and all that crap, I'll be a damn good PA. I've got the personality and experience to—"

"Jesus, babe! Please tell me you didn't say all that cliched shit to Rebecca. Is that why she offered you the job?"

"No. She offered me the job because I'm motivated, keen

and I can think on my feet. And because I don't sit back and wait for people to give me things. One thing I've learned in this life, Nicole, if you want something, then it's down to you alone to go out and get it." She spat the words out and then gulped back a mouthful of air, unsure why she felt the need to defend her promotion so forcefully.

The lift came to a stop and Jade rolled her neck around her shoulders as they waited in silence to be let out into the lobby.

"Yes, well. I'm watching you," Nicole said, pushing her chest out. The lift pinged and she strode out across the white marble space before the doors fully opened. Jade held back a second, giving Nicole time to reach the exit before stepping out herself.

She was shaking, and worried for a second that she might throw up. She glanced over at the girl on reception, but she was looking the other way. When she looked back at Nicole, she was already exiting the building.

"Screw you," she whispered after her. "You watch me all you want, *babe*. You won't get anywhere."

She was walking across the lobby when she felt her phone vibrate in her jacket pocket. Pulling it out, she saw she had a new message, but from a number that she didn't recognise. As she opened it, she saw it was from Rebecca, informing her that this was her personal number and that she wasn't to share it with anyone. It went on to explain that she'd text her again from her business line, so she had that number as well. Jade could share this number with those she deemed worthy.

She was about to reply when another message popped up. From Rebecca again, this time asking Jade to meet her tomorrow morning at eleven at her house in Chelsea. She ended the message with a link to the address and the lipstick kiss emoji, which Jade thought was slightly weird. Her first reaction was to reply and remind Rebecca that tomorrow was, in fact, Saturday but she stopped herself. Of course Rebecca knew tomorrow was Saturday, but she didn't stop working just because it was the weekend and nor did she expect her PA to. Working for someone like Rebecca Burton-Webb wasn't just a full-time job, it was a lifestyle. You lived and breathed the role or you fell by the wayside.

Jade texted back, telling Rebecca she'd guard her number with her life and that she looked forward to seeing her in the morning. Despite her nerves feeling taut and brittle and knowing she was unlikely to catch up with her sleep anytime soon, she found herself smiling as she pocketed the phone and headed for the exit.

This was it.

Tomorrow morning, she would have access to Rebecca's house and, in turn, her secrets. If what she was looking for existed, then it had to be in that Chelsea townhouse. She took a deep breath and headed out the door.

14

Nicole gnawed on the inside of her top lip as she watched the skinny boy behind the counter shove a handful of olives onto her sandwich. "Do you want any sauces?" he asked in a voice that seemed far too deep for his build.

"What is there?" she asked, before screwing up her face. "In fact, no. A bit of salt and black pepper, if you have it."

The boy grunted and reached for a large plastic salt cellar. At least he didn't have to change his blasted gloves again for this part. Nicole sneered as he applied the seasoning before wrapping up her sandwich and sliding it along the counter to the girl on the till like he was Tom Cruise in Cocktail.

For Heaven's sake.

What the hell was she doing here? It was probably a reflection of her state of mind that she'd entered the first eating establishment she'd come across. Normally for her lunch – if she ate lunch at all – she'd go to the Mediterranean deli in Soho for a fresh salad, or Pret at a push. The last time she was in a Subway she was at university. Maybe that had something to do it with it, too. The subconscious mind was a strange thing.

"Do you want any crisps with that?" the cashier girl asked.

"No thank you."

"Drink?"

"Just the sandwich." The girl rang up the price and Nicole waved her card at the machine until she heard the beep. "Thank you."

She grabbed the girthy sub roll from off the tray and hurried away, making to leave the establishment. But where could she go? If she had purchased a salad, she'd have taken it back to the office to consume or, in summer, walk over to Soho gardens to enjoy it in the sunshine. She couldn't do that with this huge doughy creation. Even if it was only a six incher, even if she'd only got veggies and no sauce, she would feel too self-conscious eating it in front of people.

With a sigh of acceptance, she took a seat in the window, unwrapped the sandwich and took a bite. It had the strange sensation of being overly dry and too wet at the same time. But it tasted pleasant enough. She hadn't eaten breakfast and the salt fed her hangover even if the limp cucumber and tangy green peppers did not.

She swallowed what was in her mouth and shifted her gaze through the large window in front of her onto the street outside. It was a cold autumnal day and many of the people passing by were huddled into their coats and scarves, faces grim with determination to get to wherever they were going. The sky was a light grey colour and even the shop fronts, usually so bright and colourful at this end of town, appeared drab and insipid. As if she was looking at them through the sepia filter on her phone. It felt to Nicole in that moment like the entire world reflected her inner experience. Today negativity ruled and try as she might she couldn't focus her energy on feeling good about her life.

That bloody new girl.

She took another bite of her sandwich, a bigger bite this time, not caring now how she looked as she gnawed it down. For seven years she'd been working at Beautiful You! and had given every bit of herself to Rebecca and that company. She'd sacrificed relationships, turned down exciting opportunities, lost friends. All so she could focus her attention on being the best Influence Marketer she could be. And she'd been successful too. The numbers didn't lie. You could read any report from that time to see her appointment had seen a marked uptick in the brand's standing, especially with the desirable twenty-to-thirty-year-old bracket. She'd helped elevate Beautiful You! from a luxury heritage brand into a brand that was also innovative and vital.

But did she get any thanks?

Did she hell.

Jennifer, her old friend from back home in Birkenhead, used to tell her she was too eager, and that she pushed people away by trying too hard. But Jennifer was just jealous and after enduring her negativity for as long as she could, Nicole cut all ties with her. She hadn't been back to Birkenhead or Liverpool for years now. After successfully losing her accent, she felt no affiliation with her hometown. London was her home now. Beautiful You! was her world.

Which just made what had happened so much more painful.

The PA job should have been hers. She'd intimated to Rebecca on more than one occasion that she'd love to be considered for the role if it – God forbid - ever became available. And it wasn't like she hadn't proved she had what it took. There'd been that week a few years ago when Kristen was laid up with a twisted ankle and Nicole had stepped into the breach. She'd spent two whole days folding cardboard flyers around tiny essential oil samples for Rebecca. She hadn't expected a medal, but she had expected Rebecca to remember her commitment. When Kristen upped and left, she'd been distraught like everyone else, wondering what her abrupt departure might do to the already visibly strained Rebecca, but she couldn't help but feel a touch of exhilaration. Surely this was her time to shine. To step up to the plate. To show the world what she could do. Her stuffy, old-fashioned parents might not understand – or care – what an Influence Marketer did, but they'd know what a PA was. They'd understand that her being the CEO and founder's assistant was a major step forward for her. They might even start talking about her with pride to their friends like they did her brother Robert. Just because he was a managing director and he'd given them two grandchildren.

A sliver of lettuce fell out of her sandwich, and she scooped it up and snaffled it down. As she did, her focus shifted from the street outside the window to her reflection in the glass. There she was, hunched over her meal as if she hadn't eaten in weeks. The restaurant's stark lighting cast deep shadows on her face. What a fright.

She dropped the sandwich onto the wax paper wrapping and sat back. Her career had been everything to her these last seven years. But maybe it was time to accept that no one at Beautiful You! actually cared about her. Or indeed anyone. When she'd first started at the company, it felt like a real team, a family, even. People were supportive and friendly; the atmosphere was one of joy and creativity. It felt as if they were all dedicated to the same goal.

But not anymore. Now it was all about the bottom line and doing whatever they could to stay relevant in such volatile and uncertain times. Rebecca was floundering. Anyone could see that. But that was why she needed someone beside her who knew what they were doing, who cared about the brand, who had given everything of themselves to it.

Jade Fisher was not that person. She was attractive and held herself well and knew what to say and how to say it. But she was playing a game.

Why could no one else see it but her?

But no matter. She'd keep an eye on her like she'd warned her she would. No one was that good. She'd mess up eventually and when she did, Nicole would be there to pick up the pieces.

The woman looking back at her from the window grinned. She looked rather demonic and a bit like a female version of The Joker. But there was also determination in her expression. She might be down, but she wasn't out. She wasn't going to let someone like Jade Fisher steal what was rightfully hers. That woman was hiding something, and Nicole was going to damn well find out what it was.

15

Jade was due to arrive at Rebecca's house at eleven, but the clock above the rear-view mirror in her Uber car told her it was only 10:33 a.m. as it pulled up outside the white Victorian townhouse on Chelsea's Cheyne Walk. But it was good to be early, she told herself. It showed willingness. Plus, she'd planned on being early. It was important.

After thanking the driver, she climbed out and took a moment to ground herself and gazed up at the impressive building, much like she had done on her first day at Beautiful You! With a view of the Thames through the leafy trees opposite, it was certainly in a wonderful location and she wondered if Rebecca appreciated her lot. It would be wrong to call her success luck. Jade knew how hard she'd worked over the last thirty-plus years. But she also knew what else Rebecca had done to get where she was.

Was it worth it, Jade wondered?

Putting on a bright smile, she walked up the stone steps to the front door of the house where an intercom system was attached to the wall with a small camera lens pointing at her.

She pressed the button and stepped back, rocking on her heels as she waited for a response.

The speaker clicked and she heard what sounded like a groan. Then a man's voice. Seb.

"Hello?"

"Hi, it's Jade." She positioned herself in front of the camera and smiled. "Rebecca asked me to come over to help her with some things. Is she in?"

She looked away, feeling awkward suddenly.

"One minute," Seb said and the speaker clicked off.

Jade took the time to straighten herself, picking a piece of lint off the shoulder of her woollen coat and flicking her hair back over her shoulders. She'd washed and curled it this morning and she was glad she had done. She'd intended to impress on her first assignment working for Rebecca and she knew on the surface she'd achieved that aim. Even if she said so herself. She looked the perfect mix of attractive but professional with a hint of wholesomeness thrown in for good measure thanks to the cream turtleneck and nude make-up. The exact look one strived for in the fashion, beauty, and well-being industry.

Nevertheless, she still felt a shudder of anxiety as the door opened to reveal Seb Turner and that crooked half-smile of his. He was wearing a pair of light grey sweatpants that left nothing to the imagination and a white t-shirt that, although slubby, gripped him in all the right places. She swallowed, willing herself to keep her eyes fixed on his face rather than them doing another tour of his impressive physique like they so wanted to do.

"Morning Jade," he said, rubbing at his head and leaving his hair tousled. "Rebecca's out having her hair done."

"Oh? Is she? I am sorry." She smiled. She already knew that

because she had access to Rebecca's calendar. "I thought it would be good to get here early."

"Not to worry. Come in. It's freezing out there this morning." He stepped back but held the door for her as she entered so she had to shuffle past him to get into the hallway beyond. As she did, she got another whiff of his scent. He smelled even better than he had done in the car the other day. He was wearing the same cologne but today it was filtered through his natural muskiness that tingled her scent receptors, and more besides.

"Wow, what an amazing space," she said, looking around. She meant it, too. The hallway walls were painted a rich blue and the floor was tiled with the most beautiful Victorian tiles she'd ever seen. "But I knew Rebecca's place would be amazing."

"I live here too, you know," Seb said, closing the door behind her. "I did have a say in the décor."

"Oh, God!" she gasped, spinning around to look at him. "I don't doubt it. I'm sorry, it's just that... You know..."

"Yes. Rebecca is the visionary. I'm just the dumb himbo she keeps around to help her feel young."

Jade swallowed, unsure of what to say to this. But then Seb laughed and even though she didn't think he was entirely joking, she laughed as well.

"Do you want a tour?" he asked. "Or some coffee? I've just put a pot on. It's good stuff."

She smiled and dropped her shoulders, hoping the act would communicate to her nervous system that all was well, and it could stop it with all the adrenaline.

"Coffee would be great," she said.

"No problem. Come through to the kitchen." He walked past her and she followed him down the wide hallway to the room at the far end

The kitchen was as beautifully decorated as she'd imagined it would be, with a huge black granite-topped island in the centre of the room, and units on either side in contrasting shades of walnut. A double Belfast sink looked out over a lush garden full of exotic trees and tall plants. It was charming, sensuous and sophisticated. Just like Rebecca.

"I was only joking just now," Seb said, grabbing an upturned clay mug off a shelf and flipping it around. He placed it down on the worktop in front of him. "About Rebecca just keeping me around to feel young. Don't tell her I said that."

Jade chuckled. "Your secret's safe with me."

She watched as he reached for the jug of filter coffee from out of the American diner-style machine and poured some out for her. He was muttering to himself as he did, but she couldn't make out the content of his words. However, it was interesting he'd say that about Rebecca. It seemed to confirm a few ideas she'd already had about their relationship.

"Here you go." He handed her a steaming cup of coffee. "Milk? Cream? Sugar?"

"Some milk, please."

"No worries." He walked over to the biggest domestic refrigerator unit Jade had ever seen and opened one of the two doors before looking over his shoulder with a grin. "Now the question is, what kind of milk? Soya? Oat? Almond? Good old cow's milk?"

"Oat, if you have it."

He came back with a carton and filled her mug up with a waiter-like flourish, ending the pour with a flirtatious wink. "Enjoy."

She took a sip and kept the mug to her lips, hoping the heat from the liquid would cover the blushes already warming her cheeks. The coffee was strong and bitter, but she didn't mind that.

"Rebecca tells me you're her new assistant," Seb said, leaning back against the worktop. "Congratulations. I think. I hope you know what you're in for."

"You're not the first person to say that."

"I think it's good," he said. "You're clearly very bright and, God knows, Rebecca needs the support right now. It'll be nice to get to know you better." He lowered his head to meet her gaze as he said this last part and it was all she could do to not let out a nervous laugh.

She forced herself to maintain eye contact. "I agree. I expect we'll be seeing a lot more of each other."

The tension in the air was palpable. Neither of them spoke for what seemed like minutes but was probably seconds.

Seb broke the silence. "Where did you say you were from, originally?"

"I grew up in Chalk Farm."

"Right. Cool. Very hip. Was it fun growing up there?"

"I don't know. My childhood wasn't great, I'll be honest. My dad died when I was eighteen months old and my mum found it hard to cope without him. She never really got over it. She died last year."

"Oh, shit, I'm sorry."

"No. It's fine. It was a long time ago. But that's life, I suppose. Or, rather, it's death. You can't fight these things. It is what it is."

Seb stuck out his bottom lip and nodded as if her hackneyed words were the most profound thing he'd ever heard. "I've lost both of my parents, too. It's hard, isn't it? But I suppose as you say, it's inevitable. The circle of life."

She wasn't the only one utilising the cliches this morning, it seemed. Jade tightened her jaw as the Elton John song played in her head. But this was good. They were connecting.

She was about to ask him about his childhood when she

103

noticed the clock on the cooker behind him. It was almost eleven. Rebecca would be home any minute.

"I don't suppose I could use the bathroom, could I?" she asked, placing the coffee mug down on a raffia coaster on the kitchen island. "Before Rebecca gets back. I don't want to be nipping away once we get started."

"Of course. There's a toilet down the hall but use the main bathroom upstairs. It's much nicer. Go on up the stairs and it's directly in front of you on the landing. Do you want to me show you?"

"It's fine. I'll manage." She was already heading for the door. "I'll be back in a tick."

With her breath held tight in her chest and a fresh surge of adrenaline making its presence known, she walked down the hallway and hurried up the wide staircase to the first floor. The landing was done out in blush pink wallpaper, which had a swirling design in rose gold that was picked out by the light as she moved. It was stylish and timeless and reminded Jade of an iconic Biba design she'd seen. Another stairwell on the far side of the landing lead up to the third floor, which was most likely where Rebecca and Seb's bedroom was situated. She imagined a grand suite, taking up the whole of the top floor and with an equally luxurious bathroom attached. That was what she'd have done with the house if she owned it.

Maybe one day.

As well as the stairwell, five doors lead off from the wide landing, two on either side facing each other and one in front of her, which she took to be the bathroom. But she wasn't interested in the bathroom.

With her heart pounding in her chest, she approached the first door on the right and grabbed hold of the brass door handle, turning it slowly and easing the door open in case it made a noise and alerted Seb she was on the prowl. The room beyond looked to be a spare room and was sparsely decorated in neutral white and beige. A large king-size bed stood against the nearside wall and the only other pieces of furniture were a vintage wardrobe that stood on the far wall and an elegant old bureau facing the bed. But no bookcases, no shelves, no filing cabinets. Not what she was after.

She backed out of the room and hurried over to the next door along, mindful of her footsteps but also the time. There had to be something here. On opening the door, she was met with a large room done out in dark wood and leather with shelves floor to ceiling along one wall. There were books and files and stacks of papers and magazines covering every available surface. She stepped inside, trying to remain calm as her awareness dealt with the plethora of stimuli and possibilities the room contained. Was this what she'd been looking for? An immense walnut desk topped with maroon leather stood in the middle of the space and a laptop sat closed on top. It was quite a masculine space, she thought, doing a full three-sixty turn and scanning the shelves for anything relevant.

She walked over to a large lean-to bookcase next to the window and squinted at the rows of box files stored there. They had words such as 'Accounts' and 'Receipts' and 'Correspondence' scrawled on the sides of them, but the dates on them were all too recent.

Yet Jade knew Rebecca was meticulous about her finances. In almost every interview and feature Rebecca had ever done, the journalist had pointed out the dichotomy between Rebecca's contemporary, blue-sky creativity and her old-fashioned business sense. And it was this that was integral to the plan. Everything relied on the fact that Rebecca's systematic nature meant she'd kept a record of the shadowy transaction she'd made thirty years ago. If she had, then it was in this house somewhere.

But if the document in question was in this room, it was nowhere immediately obvious and she couldn't start rifling through box files and papers on the off chance of finding it. Not today, at least.

Exiting the room, she flitted across the landing, finding two more guest bedrooms behind the remaining doors.

Damn it.

But she'd expected as much. And now there was only one more room to try. The master bedroom up on the top floor. Before she could talk her way out of it, she scurried over to the stairwell and, gripping the handrail, hauled herself up, taking the steps two at a time. At the top of the stairwell, she stopped, astonished at the room in which she found herself. It was more of a self-contained flat than a bedroom, done out predominantly in cream, walnut and black. Over to her right was a large lounge area, complete with an enormous marble fireplace and the sort of luxurious couches one could get lost in. Next to the lounge, glass bi-fold doors opened out onto a white-rendered terrace where a table was still set up for breakfast, surrounded by a jungle of green plants.

On the other side of the room was the bedroom space, comprising an immense bed covered with an ornate satin throw that looked to be vintage and was probably worth more than Jade's entire apartment. A series of built-in wardrobes and shelving and drawer units took up the entire back wall, beautifully constructed in dark walnut and with concealed plinth lighting that showed off the impressive furniture as a piece of artwork in itself.

As if on autopilot, she walked over to the nearest wardrobe and placed her hand in the smooth recess on the door, the perfect size and shape for a female hand. Her heart felt as if it was going to burst out of her chest as she slid it open and was presented with rows and rows of dresses, coats, jumpers and jackets. She could have easily spent the rest of the day and most of the night pulling out pieces to admire, but that wasn't why she was here. Dropping to her knees, she swiped away a few of the long dresses and almost toppled over as she saw not one but three identical safes at the bottom of the wardrobe. Each stood a metre tall and was made of black painted steel with a touch-sensitive keypad in the middle of the door.

"Well, there we go," she whispered.

This confirmed it. What sort of person had not one but three safes in their house? What was Rebecca keeping in there that she didn't want anyone to see? Jade suspected she knew the answer to that question, but without access to the safes, she had no proof. And without proof...well, they'd had that discussion and had decided that categoric proof was needed before any further action was taken. That was why she was here, risking her freedom and perhaps even her life.

She was startled as she heard a noise. It sounded like a person coughing and as she listened more closely she heard footsteps.

Shit.

Shit. Shit. Shit.

She stood and slid the wardrobe closed as stealthily as she could before hurrying over to the stairwell on her tiptoes. As she got there, she sensed a presence on the landing below and stepped back as Rebecca appeared at the foot of the stairwell. Jade glanced around, frantic, assessing what to do. Should she hide in the wardrobe? Under the bed? Could she exit via the terrace and scale over the wall onto next doors terrace?

She stood, frozen on the spot, not daring to breathe.

"Jade, are you up there?"

A shrill yelp escaped her. She gritted her teeth, but it was no use. "S-Sorry," she whimpered, stepping back as Rebecca climbed the stairs and entered her bedroom. She was wearing dark glasses and had an emerald headscarf wrapped around her freshly coiffured bob.

She looked Jade up and down. "What the bloody hell are you doing in my bedroom?"

"I was looking for the bathroom," Jade replied, concentrating on keeping her voice steady. "I think I took a wrong turn somehow. I wasn't thinking..." It sounded lame. There was no way anyone would believe that explanation.

Rebecca lowered her head and regarded her over the top of her glasses. She didn't look happy, but she didn't look ready to call the police either.

"A wrong turn, was it?" she said. "That's a new one."

Jade tried to swallow the air bubble stuck in her throat, but it didn't want to shift. She scratched at her neck before remembering that was a surefire sign of guilt. "I'm sorry," she said, shoving her hands behind her back, opening herself up physically. "I suppose I was a little curious about seeing your amazing house as well. I know that's bad of me. But I haven't touched anything. I wouldn't. I absolutely adore what you've done with the place and I found myself up here before I knew what I was doing. I'm so very sorry. But it's beautiful. Really beautiful. Not that I expected your house to be anything other than that."

It was a bold move, perhaps, owning up to her mistake. But she knew Rebecca liked boldness in people and, really, what else could she say without making matters worse? She didn't dare move as Rebecca removed her glasses, making a noise that could have been a laugh or a sigh.

"Thank you," she said. "It needs a lick of paint here and there, but I like it."

"It's wonderful," Jade said, side-stepping towards the stairs. She had one hand on the handrail when Rebecca scoffed.

"Where are you going?"

Jade stopped. "I was going downstairs."

"The hell you are," Rebecca said. She took off her coat and flung it on the bed. "You're here now. We may as well get started."

"Oh?"

"That's why you're here," Rebecca said. "I need you to help me pick out an outfit for tonight. I was going to buy something new but I've decided to go classic instead. I think Lana will appreciate that more. Don't you?"

"Yes," Jade stammered. "I think you're right."

"Come along then," Rebecca said, striding over to the wardrobe Jade had just been looking inside. "We've got a would-be investor to impress, my dear."

16

I n truth, Rebecca had been rather perturbed to find her newly appointed PA alone in her bedroom. But there was little point in reprimanding the girl too severely. She'd been caught out and the look on her face said she was suitably embarrassed and chastised by the experience. Besides, Rebecca couldn't blame her for being a little nosey. If she was to be believed, then Jade was a big fan of hers. It was understandable she'd want to see the inner workings of her life. So, she'd allow her this transgression. But that was it. No more mistakes. Or she'd be out on her ear before she even got started.

Rebecca let out a bitter laugh.

Who are you kidding?

She needed an assistant now more than ever and Jade was the right person for the job. Yes, she hadn't known her for long. And, yes, both Marsha and Seb had voiced their concerns that she was promoting her too soon. But she had a good feeling about this one. Jade was clever and confident and had genuine passion burning behind her eyes that she couldn't help but be drawn to. It would be a cold day in hell when Rebecca Burton-Webb didn't trust her instincts.

But her sense of which clothes looked good on her these days?

That was another matter.

"This one is beautiful," Jade said, holding up a fitted black dress. She walked over to Rebecca and held it up in front of her so she could see the effect in the free-standing mirror they'd set up. The bottom half of the dress was covered in sequins and the top was an intricate lattice-work of lace and appliqued black roses. Rebecca would have said it was a McQueen but she couldn't recall. She didn't remember where or when she'd bought it either. There were so many dresses. So many years gone by.

"Too over the top." She dismissed it with a wave of her hand and Jade laid it on the pile of discarded outfits on the bed. They'd been doing this for the past hour and the pile was already plentiful.

Rebecca drew back a long breath and sighed it out. Nothing looked good on her. Nothing was suitable when you were old and frumpy and indecisive. She had hoped getting her hair done might have given her a new lease on life, but she felt worn out. Rebecca Burton-Webb, CEO and founder of Beautiful You! was still a force of nature and as integral to the company as ever. At work, she operated from instinct and experience. She trusted herself. But at home, as Rebecca the person - Rebecca the wife - she couldn't have felt more out of touch with her professional persona. The fact she was being so indecisive was a worry in of itself. She was never like this. She was bold and savvy, with a fire in her belly and passion in her heart. The sword of Damocles that hung over her company didn't help, of course. Nor did it help she'd become so forgetful. Apart from the odd glass of wine when she really needed one, she'd stopped drinking alcohol. Yet her days were spent in a cloud of confusion and worry, as if constantly hungover.

Beautiful You! had gone through hard times before, especially at the start, so she knew that stress could leave one feeling this way. Yet, she'd been younger back then and so full of ideals that nothing could faze her. Even when the absolute worst had happened, she'd rode it out and picked herself up. Not just that, but she'd been able to learn from her mistakes and come back even stronger. These days she felt battered and broken by experience rather than forged by it. Seb didn't help, but he wasn't the only worry in her life. On days like this, she wished she still had someone close to her she could lean on. A friend. A confidante. A business partner.

She tsked loudly and screwed up her eyes. Why the hell was she putting herself through this? It had been years since she'd allowed memories of her past to exist as anything other than a momentary glimmer in her psyche. Thinking about what had happened always upset her and never helped. Normally, if a memory from that time popped up unexpectedly, she'd shift her attention onto her work until the dark thoughts faded into the recesses of her mind.

"Is everything all right?"

Rebecca opened her eyes to see Jade looking at her with a concerned expression on her face.

"What?"

"You looked like you were in pain," Jade said. "Are you okay?"

"Yes. Of course." Rebecca consciously relaxed her torso and smiled. "I'm just thinking about Lana Bamford. I've never liked this part of the job, that's all, discussing finances and asking for money. I'll be honest with you, dear. A lot is riding on tonight."

"I understand," Jade said. "But I'm certain you'll suitably impress her, and she'll be more than eager to get involved in Beautiful You! as you take us into the next phase of its development." She smiled and, for a brief moment, Rebecca had the urge to hug her. Jade's words were what she needed to hear, but it was more than that. She provided a warm, calming, and even familiar presence.

"Thank you," Rebecca said. "I'm a little tired this morning and not feeling myself. I'll be okay later."

"Of course you will! You're Rebecca Burton-Webb. You're a firebrand. Lana Bamford will be enchanted by you, just like everyone else is. This time tomorrow, I'm certain we'll have her on-side and she'll be eager to be involved."

Rebecca couldn't help but smile.

Enchanted.

She liked that. Yes. She'd picked Kristen's successor well. There were still some things she could get right. She wasn't going to seed just yet. Smiling, she took Jade in, marvelling at her bright, eager eyes and that smile, so full of enthusiasm and compassion. Just like...

Gosh.

Rebecca gasped as she finally realised who her new assistant reminded her of. She screwed her face up once again. Why the hell was her past haunting her with such force today?

"Rebecca, are you sure you're okay?" Jade stepped towards her. "You've gone very pale."

"Have I?" She held her hand to her chest. "I haven't had much to eat this morning."

"Ah. I see." But the concern on her face didn't fade.

"You know, you remind me of someone." Rebecca said it before she realised what she was doing. A frisson of fear ran down her back, but she ignored it.

"Oh. Really?"

"Yes. Someone from my past. Someone I've not thought about for a long time." She waved her hand in front of her. "Ignore me. I'm being silly and nostalgic. I don't know what's wrong with me today. I've got a lot on my mind."

She gestured for Jade to select another outfit, but she didn't budge.

"Was she nice – this person?"

"Yes. She was. She was my best friend."

"What happened to her?"

Rebecca sighed and it felt like her entire upper body had deflated. What had happened to her? That was the big question. They'd been so close, once. Why did she have to go and do what she did? They could have worked through it.

Things would have been so different.

Rebecca gave Jade what she hoped was a reassuring smile. "Nothing happened. We just drifted apart, that's all. I had my work, she had hers. Forget I ever said anything. But needless to say, she was very beautiful. Like you."

The comment had the desired effect. Jade giggled and looked away; her interest suitably deflected by the compliment. "I don't know about that," she muttered.

"Nonsense," Rebecca said, pointing into the wardrobe. "Now let's have a look at that navy blue number there. I seem to remember liking myself in that one."

17

J ade eyed the clock on Rebecca's kitchen wall with
concern. She'd planned on heading home before going out
this evening, but that was unlikely now. Her fault. She'd
been stupid to presume the task of finding an outfit for her
boss would only take a few hours. It was late afternoon before
Rebecca was satisfied with her outfit - the black McQueen
number, with lace and appliqué that Jade had suggested four
hours earlier – and then she'd insisted Jade wait with her whilst
a young girl from Harrods, who did home visits for people like
Rebecca, did her make-up.

The time was now a few minutes after five and Jade was
sitting at Rebecca's kitchen island, sipping a glass of iced
sparkling water whilst Rebecca told tales of past galas and
dinners she'd attended. The stories were amusing and
interesting in parts, but Jade sensed her boss was being careful
to only share so much. She brushed over names and times and
there was an ambiguity to each tale that wasn't the result of a
fading memory.

A wave of heavy emotion had overcome Jade earlier - and
she still wasn't entirely sure whether it was excitement or panic

- when Rebecca had stared at her in that whimsical way and mentioned 'her'. Jade even wondered for a split-second if the game was up, but had pushed her for more regardless, desperate to hear Rebecca talk more about her past. At one point, she was certain she was going to divulge something significant, perhaps even speak 'her' name. But it had all come to nothing and that was probably for the best.

"I didn't realise you were still here."

Jade looked over to see Seb standing in the kitchen doorway. His hair was now gelled back and the slubby outfit was gone in favour of pressed black trousers and a light blue shirt that emphasised his biceps.

"We've been upstairs getting ready for the gala," Rebecca said. "It takes me a long time these days."

"Come off it," Seb said, going to her and placing his hands around her waist, holding her at arm's length. "You look amazing. Like a model."

Rebecca scoffed. "Don't overdo it, Seb."

"Hey, you've still got it. You're still beautiful. Isn't she, Jade?" He looked over at her, a twinkle in his eye as he did.

"Absolutely," she said. "It's a stunning dress and you look stunning in it." She frowned at Seb. "Aren't you going to the gala too?

"No. These sorts of events aren't Seb's thing." Rebecca said, in a voice full of subtext. She pushed him away and glanced up at the clock. "Merde! My car will be here any minute. Whereabouts are you again, Jade?"

"Chalk Farm," she said. "But I'm visiting some friends tonight, over in Angel."

"Ah shame, the gala is up in Mayfair. I could have taken a detour to Chalk Farm but Angel is a little far..." She grimaced. "I'm sorry I've kept you so long. But I do appreciate you very much. You can get a cab, yes? And of course, you must remember to keep all your receipts from now on. Hina collects expense forms around the twentieth of each month."

"No worries," Seb said. "Jez can drop her off on our way over to Tower Hill."

Rebecca shot him a sharp look. "What?"

"I'm going to my club. I did tell you this." Seb shook his head at Jade. "She doesn't listen to me. Either that or you really are losing it." He said this last part to Rebecca. There was humour in his voice, but Rebecca's expression told a different story. But it wasn't anger as much as alarm behind her eyes.

"When did you tell me?"

"Yesterday. And this morning. Honestly, Rebecca." He looked at Jade again. "Can you try to get through to her? She needs to get checked out. It's only because I'm worried about you, darling."

Jade flapped her mouth, eyes darting between her boss and Seb. She wondered if this was what children felt like when their parents were arguing. But she'd never known that feeling. She mumbled a few words of placation before a rhythmic knocking on the door saved her.

"That's Jez," Seb said. He leaned down and kissed Rebecca on the forehead. "Jade? Are you ready?"

"Oh. Erm." She stiffened, feeling like a deer in headlights. "I don't know... Should I...?"

"Go with him," Rebecca told her. "It'll save you having to hail a cab."

"Are you sure?"

"Yes. And I mean it. Thank you for today."

Seb was already walking down the hall to the front door. "Come on, let's go."

Jade nodded at Rebecca and then hurried after him as he opened the door and headed down to the roadside where the same black SUV from before was parked up with its engine idling.

"Where to, ma'am?" Seb asked, opening the door for her and bowing his head.

"If you can drop me by Angel tube station, that's great," she said, climbing in the back of the car and acknowledging Jez. "Hello again."

"We meet again."

"Rebecca has made Jade her PA," Seb told him, climbing in beside her and shutting the door. "So, you'll probably be seeing a lot more of her. That's if she goes the distance." He smirked to himself as Jez pulled the car away from the curb and drove along the side of the Thames before taking a left down Royal Hospital Road.

"Did you say you were going to a club?" Jade asked, once the silence in the back of the car - and the knowing glances between Seb and Jez - became too much for her.

"It's not the sort of club you're thinking of."

She nodded and looked out the window. She knew exactly what sort of club he meant, but he apparently had her down as some sort of party girl. As Jez took a left, taking them around the back of Parliament Square, she smiled to herself. In different circumstances she'd have been insulted that Seb thought of her in this way, but as things stood it was probably a good thing. In her experience, people underestimated you at their peril.

As she looked back, she caught him watching her. His blue eyes were intense, even in the half-light of dusk, and at once she felt intimidated and alive. "It's called The Baccarat Club," he said. "It's an exclusive, member's only club for those in the media."

"Ah, I see," Jade said, playing along. "Is it hard to get into?"

Seb snickered under his breath. "It was, once upon a time.

But now they seem to let anyone in. Even the likes of me!" He leaned in and lowered his voice. "Do you want to join me?"

Jade felt her chest flush. "Oh. No. I mean... I'd love to. Normally. But I have to be somewhere this evening. My friends are expecting me. Thank you, though. I appreciate the offer."

Seb didn't take his eyes off her. "Shame. I think we'd have fun. In fact, I know we would." He smiled and his eyes crinkled up at the corners. "Another time, perhaps."

"Would Rebecca not mind?" She felt nervous asking this, but she needed to know. What was it Sofia had said to her?

If you can't be bold and fearless, become someone who can.

Seb cleared his throat and glanced at his driver via the rearview mirror. "I don't think we'd need to tell Rebecca," he said. "You've got to appreciate, Jade, Rebecca and I are very different people. She's a strong, powerful woman with a lot of responsibilities and an empire to run. Whereas me, I'm more of a laid-back soul. Don't get me wrong, Rebecca is great, but I have needs and desires. I like to have fun and she...doesn't."

In the rear-view mirror, she saw Jez raise an eyebrow.

"I'm not sure it's a good idea," Jade told him. "I mean, you're a great guy and easy to talk to, and I do enjoy your company. But Rebecca is my boss. I wouldn't want to do anything that jeopardised my—"

"Hey, hey, hey," Seb cut in, holding his hands up. "Let's not get ahead of ourselves here, Jade. All I did was ask if you wanted to join me for a drink?"

Now her cheeks were burning for a different reason. "Right! Yes! Sure!" She gritted her teeth and looked down into her lap.

Bloody idiot!

Not so much bold and fearless as clumsy and foolish.

Play it cool, will you?

The car fell silent as they drove down Farringdon Road and Jade was relieved when they passed by Sadler's Wells Theatre a few minutes later. It meant they were nearly at her destination and she could remove herself from this embarrassing and potentially perilous situation. Why the hell had she said all that? The implication was there. She didn't need to bloody well spell it out and scare him off.

"You can drop me here if that's better," she called out to Jez as he pulled up at the lights for City Road. "I can walk from here."

"Are you sure?" he replied. "There's not much in it."

"No. It's better here," she replied, clicking off her seatbelt. "It's only a five-minute walk."

"As you wish." He yanked the steering wheel around and eased the car over to the side of the road.

"Thank you," she told him, glancing at Seb, too. "I appreciate it. And I'm sorry. For putting you out of your way. And everything."

Feeling like the biggest fool ever, and trying to ignore the niggling sense that she'd just blown things, she reached over for the door handle.

"Wait. Allow me." Seb released his seatbelt and was out of the car before she could respond. She rubbed at the back of her neck as he walked around the back of the car and opened the door for her. "Here we are." He held out his hand and after staring at it for a moment, she took it.

He helped her out of the car and they stood on the roadside, staring at each other. It was awkward and strange and she had a powerful urge to walk away. To never stop walking. To walk back to New York if she had to.

Seb's mouth tilted into that now familiar half-smile and he leaned down so his lips were next to her ear.

"I want you," he whispered. His breath tickled her neck and she shuddered. She opened her mouth to respond, but no words came to her. Then Seb stepped back and regarded her with a knowing look before grasping her gently by the shoulder and giving it a squeeze. "I'll see you soon." He climbed back into the car and shut the door. As they pulled away, Jade held her hand up and waved, unsure of what else to do.

Bloody hell.

This was it.

It was happening.

So why was she plagued by a chorus of doubting voices in her head?

She shivered again and folded her arms around herself. It was a chilly night, but it wasn't only the elements she was shielding herself from. Yes, this was what she wanted. It was part of the plan. But her situation had become very scary all of a sudden. She was a fashion assistant, not a spy or a secret agent. Standing on the side of the road as Seb's car disappeared from view, she worried she wasn't a strong enough person to do what was required of her. Even if she found Seb attractive - and had once joked it would be a decent perk of the job - he'd unsettled her just now. It was like she'd stepped out of the playground and into the real world and was now regretting it with every fibre of her being. This type of work needed someone with steely nerves and unwavering strength of mind. She'd thought that was her, but maybe she was wrong.

She puffed out a breath. Not for the first time, she wondered if it was too late to back out. She wanted answers and, more than that, she wanted what was rightfully hers. But at what cost?

Her phone buzzed in her pocket and as she pulled it out, she saw it was already ten past six. There was a message asking her where she was. Without responding, she shoved the phone back in her pocket and set off walking.

18

S ofia must have been watching out for her because she opened the door before Jade had a chance to knock. She looked tired and strung out. But that made two of them.

"You're late," she snapped, wandering back into the house and leaving the door open for her.

Jade closed it and followed her into the kitchen. "I'm sorry. I couldn't get away," she said. "She had me picking dresses out for her all day long. You should see how many she owns. There are three enormous wardrobes jammed full of clothes. I don't know where Seb keeps his stuff, in one of the spare rooms I imagine. Poor bastard."

It was odd talking about him like this after what had happened between them only a few minutes earlier, but she'd always been good at compartmentalising different parts of her life. She'd been Rebecca's PA, then she was with Seb, and now she was here. Different things happened here. She was a different person.

Sofia picked up the kettle and walked it over to the sink. "Do you want a drink?" she asked.

"Do we have anything stronger?"

"It's pretty early for that, isn't it?"

Jade pulled a chair out from under the kitchen table and sat down. "Depends how you look at it."

"Fine. I could do with a drink as well, to be honest." Sofia opened the tall pantry cupboard on the far side of the room and, stepping to one side, waved her hand over the middle shelf to present two bottles of red wine and a half-empty bottle of Gordon's gin. "What are you in the mood for?"

"Gin," she answered, without pause.

"Good answer." Sofia placed it on the table in front of her. "I think I've got some small cans of tonic under the stairs. Hang on."

Jade sat back in her seat and surveyed the room. The kitchen looked like it always did. Even the kettle and toaster were the same ones they'd had since she was about thirteen. Which said something about their quality, perhaps. She might have even considered them a fitting metaphor for something or other if she wasn't so exhausted.

"Here we are." Sofia returned with two glasses and two small mixer cans of tonic water. She placed them down beside the bottle of gin and sat in the chair next to Jade. "There's no ice, sorry."

"Ah, no."

"Piss off. I've not had time to think about making bloody ice." The rage coming off her seemed excessive, but also understandable. "You're not the only one who's stressed, you know."

"Yes. I do know."

"Do you?"

They sneered almost in unison. Sofia grabbed the bottle of gin and twisted off the top, pouring a generous serving into each glass.

"So, then?" she said. "Tell me. What's been going on? You were at her house. Did you find anything?"

Jade didn't shift her gaze from the glass in front of her. "Not really. I managed to get upstairs alone for a few minutes and had a look around. She's got a big office with loads of files, but I'd need hours to look through everything."

Sofia opened the mixer cans and shoved one at her. Jade picked it up and poured the whole thing into her glass as she continued.

"But in her bedroom, in one of her wardrobes, there are three safes. Maybe one of them is full of expensive jewellery and heirlooms, but not three. So, what else is up there?"

Sofia nodded as she sat back down. "Can you get the access codes?"

"I don't know." She picked up her glass. "This whole situation is a lot harder and scarier than I thought it would be."

"Is it?" Sofia's voice was cold and brittle. "We knew it wouldn't be a walk in the park, J."

Jade gulped her drink. It was lukewarm and far too strong, but it was alcohol and right now, she needed the buzz. "Perhaps I didn't take everything on board properly," she replied. "I was focusing on the exciting aspects rather than the gritty reality of what I have to do. Now I'm there in the middle of it all... I don't know... I can't help but feel uncomfortable and a bit weird about it."

"Fucking hell!" Sofia spat. "Don't tell me you've got Stockholm Syndrome already! We knew Rebecca was charming and interesting – on the surface. I told you to be careful about being sucked into her world. I know what you're like."

"It's not just Rebecca," Jade told her. "It's everything. Seb, my new colleagues, this horrible woman at work who seems to hate me. It's a lot to deal with, you know. A real lot."

"Oh, I am sorry," Sofia said, looking away. "How awful for you."

A stony silence descended over the table. The two of them drank their glasses of gin, looking everywhere but at each other. Jade could sense the spikey energy coming off of Sofia. She placed her glass down.

"How is she?"

Sofia looked at her as if she'd just asked whether the sun was hot.

"That bad?"

"Go up and see her if you want. She's awake."

"Yeah. I will. Maybe after I finish this." She grabbed her glass, about to finish the remaining gin when Sofia reached out and touched her hand.

"If you want to say hello, I'd do it now. I'm hoping she'll be asleep soon. We had an awful night last night. She's tired. We both are."

We *all* are, Jade thought. But she didn't say it.

"Okay, I'll go up." She scraped her chair back. "It's not like my ice is going to melt while I'm gone, is it?"

"I told you to piss off." But there was a little more warmth in Sofia's voice now. "Do you want me to come as well?"

"No, it's fine." She walked out into the hallway and, looking up the stairs, noticed the landing light was off. With night having arrived in the last hour, the beige-carpeted steps appeared to ascend into a black void. There was *definitely* a metaphor *there*. Or was it a simile? Sofia was the journalist, not her.

Holding the handrail, she made the walk she'd made a thousand times before. The steps creaked and groaned under her feet as she took each one, going steady, stepping into the person she needed to be to deal with what she would find at the top.

As she reached the landing, she flicked on the switch, illuminating the wide corridor in front of her. Passing the bathroom and the doors to the other bedrooms without a second glance, she walked down to the door at the end. It was hanging slightly open and a low light shone through the gap. She couldn't hear anything, but that didn't mean she was asleep. They had put a television in the room for her to watch, but it was rarely used. She eased open the door some more and poked her head around the side.

"Hey," she whispered.

The woman lying in bed looked over at her and smiled. "Hello, love."

Jade stepped into the room, fighting to keep her face on the pleasant side of neutral, rather than it display the sadness and shame in her heart.

"How are you today?" Jade asked, moving closer. Her stomach churned as she saw how thin the woman looked. The skin on her face and arms was practically translucent. She wasn't even that old. This wasn't fair.

"What day is it?" she asked. "Is it Monday? It is, isn't it? I need to get up. I've been so lazy lately."

"It's fine, you stay put. You're okay where you are."

"Easy for you to say." She looked Jade up and down and frowned. "Sylvia? Is that you?"

"No, it's me, remember? It's Justine."

"Justine? But she's..." She lowered her head and her eyes went dull. It was as if she was an android powering down, her circuit boards burning up. Another metaphor, perhaps, but it didn't boost Jade's mood at all. If anything, it only heightened the guilt blossoming inside of her. Because essentially that was what was happening here. Her circuit boards, her neural pathways, were burning up.

Jade perched on the edge of the bed and reached out for the

woman's hand. It was bony and cold, but after a second or two she returned the grip.

"Justine." It was as if a light had gone on briefly. She raised her head and smiled. "I've not seen you in a while. You look well."

It was all she could do not to break down. She smiled through the pain, grinning with all she had in the hope the muscles twitching up her cheeks kept the tears in her eyes.

"I know," she said. "But I'm here now."

"It's good to see you."

"Yeah. It's good to see you too, Mum."

19

Sofia was sitting where she'd left her at the kitchen table when Jade returned. It looked like she was on her second glass of gin. Maybe her third. She didn't look up as Jade joined her.

"She's asleep," she said.

Sofia nodded, but still didn't look at her. "Let's hope she sleeps through the night. I was up from three this morning with her. She was screaming and shouting, hitting me. It was horrible."

Jade picked up her glass and sipped at the remnants. "I'm sorry, Sof. I know how hard it is for you."

Finally, she lifted her head to glare at her. "I know you do. And I know what you're doing is just as hard in a way. But we can't falter now, Justine. We have to follow this through to the end."

She coughed. "I know it sounds daft. But, for now, can you call me Jade?" She grimaced at her own pomposity. Because that's what it sounded like coming out of her mouth. But she had good reason. When Sofia flicked up an eyebrow, she went on. "It's hard trying to remain in character the whole time and I think it'd help me feel more confident when I'm there, playing this role, if I only thought of myself as Jade Fisher. You know, like method actors do."

Sofia laughed, but it was devoid of joy or humour. "Fine. Jade it is. *Jade.*"

"Thanks. I know it sounds silly, but every little bit helps right now."

Sofia rubbed at her chin. "She's getting worse, you know. I mean, she has good days, but they're becoming fewer and far between."

"She knew who I was, just now," Jade said. "Eventually."

"But you don't see what she's like. It's me who's cooped up in the house looking after her twenty-four hours a day." She leaned over the table towards her. "I know we agreed you were more Rebecca's 'type' and had more experience in the industry, and I stand by that decision. You should be the one to—"

"Risk my neck?"

Sofia gave her a dark look. "Come off it, it's not that bad."

"Isn't it? I don't know, Sofia. I've got a lot of doubts about whether I can pull this off. It's nerve-wracking."

"At least you're still out and about in the real world. I had a good job. I was a brilliant journalist. I had publications fighting for me to write for them. But I gave that up to care for mum whilst you were in New York. Because I love you and I knew it was important to you. But this is more important. We must do this, J."

Jade spun the now empty glass on the table in front of her. "Do you think these experimental drugs will help?"

"From everything I've read, yes. But they're still unregulated and the MHRA is well and truly on the fence. It's not looking like they'll be available in the UK for years. We need the money. Not only for the treatment but to cover the last three years when we've been eating into all our savings. It's only going to go so far. Plus, we also need to make that bitch pay for what she did. Where is she tonight?"

"At a gala dinner, trying to impress a potential investor. She's completely stressed out, as well. I don't think the company is doing so well behind the scenes."

"Fucking good." She banged her fist on the table. "Jesus. Look at your face. Do you give a shit? I was half joking before about Stockholm Syndrome. Do you actually feel sorry for her?"

"No. Of course I don't."

"Don't forget what she did to mum. Don't forget what she did to this family."

"I know." Jade swallowed, not sure if she should voice the thoughts in her head. She sucked in a deep breath and went for it. "Are we certain, though, that it happened that way? I mean, mum's not exactly the most reliable of sources these days." Jade was already wincing as she spoke, and when Sofia slammed her fist down on the table for a second time, she jumped.

"Are you serious? You were here that day. You heard what she said. I know she's getting worse, but she has moments of clarity and she sounded pretty damn lucid to me."

Jade thought back to that time, two years earlier. She was back in the UK visiting her family and they'd taken their mum for a walk around Primrose Hill. She was fitter then, still able to walk and feed herself even if the early onset dementia had ravished a lot of her personality and memory. But Sofia was right. She had sounded coherent, even like her old self. What she'd told them was vague and there were holes in the story which she wasn't able to fill no matter how hard her daughters pressed her. But her words rang true.

Until that day, neither Justine nor Sofia had ever heard their mother mention Rebecca Burton-Webb. They knew their mum had studied at Imperial College Business School and had worked as a financial analyst in the city when she was younger, but she'd never mentioned Rebecca or Beautiful You! Their primary memory of their mum was as a loving single mother, who baked and played games with them, and took them on long walks at the weekend. There were moments when she'd get a sad look on her face and hurry off into the kitchen on her own, but it had been a happy childhood. Neither of the girls remembered their father, so they didn't miss him and there was enough life insurance money they could live in a decent house in a good part of town. Indeed, they'd wanted for nothing.

But on that fateful day two years ago, whilst sitting on a park bench looking out over central London, their mother had informed them that it wasn't their father's life insurance money that had granted them the life they'd had. It was the big payout she'd received from Rebecca Burton-Webb.

At first, they'd put the claim down to their mother's condition. But in the subsequent weeks, after Jade had returned to New York, Rebecca was mentioned regularly. Their mum would go off on rambling asides, muttering to herself how it was 'All her fault...' Sofia had sat with her for hours, trying to get the full story out of her, until deciding she'd do what she did best and investigate the claims herself.

It wasn't easy. Beautiful You! was formed in an era before the internet existed for most people and the little information she found online regarding the early history of the company only added to the established narrative - that Rebecca Burton-Webb was the sole founder of the company and had started it after leaving university and becoming frustrated with the toxic excesses of the eighties. But, ever the hardy journalist, Sofia kept digging, visiting the British Library every day for two weeks whilst her mum was being cared for by Sylvia, a kind woman whom they'd hired from an agency before it became financially unfeasible. Sofia read everything she could find on Rebecca and Beautiful You!, poring over old articles and interviews. She'd almost given up when she finally found what she'd been searching for - an old document in the Companies House archives. Back then, the company listed was called The Ethical Beauty Company, rather than Beautiful You! but Rebecca Burton-Webb was listed as one of the directors alongside Margaret Taylor. Their mother.

And there it was.

Another deep search using the term 'Ethical Beauty Company' threw up an old student newspaper based out of Saint Martins. In issue fourteen, there was an interview with Rebecca Burton-Webb on the eve of her third store opening on the Kings Road. By this stage Rebecca was already well on her way to becoming an influential figure in the beauty world, and the company was turning over a million a year in revenue, but perhaps because it was a student magazine, she seemed much more candid and open than in any other interview she did around this period. The feature was only a half-page long, but in it, Rebecca mentioned Beautiful You! had initially been called the less catchy Ethical Beauty Company and that she'd started it with her best friend, Mags, before creative differences had them parting ways just after they'd opened their second store.

"'It's all her fault' that's what mum said," Sofia reiterated, jabbing her finger at Jade.

"But that doesn't mean Rebecca screwed her over," she said. "It might have been an amicable buyout?"

"Do you really believe she'd have sold everything if she was thinking straight? They had two stores by then, and the brand was skyrocketing. No way. Rebecca screwed her over." Sofia lowered her voice. "Did you know mum suffered from post-natal depression after you were born?"

Jade flinched. "No. You never said."

"I was only two and a half myself. I've only just found out. She was already struggling and then dad died. Do you think she was in any fit state to make a business deal? I found some old medical notes in a file under her bed. She was taking all sorts of pills. Rebecca would have known she was mentally unwell and played on it, leaning on her to sell her part of the company. And sure, it was probably a decent amount of money at the time. But the last time I looked Beautiful You! was valued at five-hundred-and-thirty-eight million dollars. We're owed some of that, Jade. Rebecca owes us. She took advantage of a sick woman and took our legacy away from us."

"We don't know any of this for certain," Jade tried, but her statement was met with an icy glare and she shut up.

"I know for certain!" Sofia hissed. "And you know too, deep down. You're just getting cold feet because we're getting closer to the truth. But you need to hold your nerve, Sis. There has to be a record of that payout. Solicitors and brokers would have been involved. If not, there'll be bank statements at least. In fact, it's even better if no lawmen were involved. It'll mean she'll pay to keep it quiet. If we can line the dates up with mum's illness, we've got a real case, I think. We can put it to Rebecca that if she doesn't give us what we want – let's say ten million – then we'll go to the press and tell them how she fucked over a sick woman. I know it's grubby and you're the one getting your hands dirty. But this is how we help mum. How we get justice for her. For our family." She was speaking fast, without pause and not for the first time since she'd arrived back in England. Jade worried that her older sister had dug herself in too deep.

She sat back and watched her as she continued talking, telling her how important it was she stayed close to Rebecca, and get into those safes somehow. Sofia was the stronger and more intelligent of the two of them. As well as the most forthright. But when she got like this, eyes blazing with ferocity, speaking so rapidly and incessantly that spittle foamed at the corner of her mouth, she gave Jade cause for concern. Sofia was no crazy conspiracy nut or YouTube warrior, but it was safe to say she'd willingly jumped down the rabbit hole where Rebecca and their mum were concerned.

"What if I speak to Rebecca?" Jade asked. "What if I explain to her who I am and we're upfront about it? She might be pleased to see us. If we tell her about mum and her illness, she could help with her treatment?"

"We've talked about this," Sofia snapped. "But it's gone beyond that, Justine. Jade. Whatever. And it's too risky. What if she says no? What if she says she bought mum out fair and square and tells us to piss off? We'll never get close enough again to find out what we need."

Jade puffed out her cheeks and stared into the bottom of her glass. It was hard to know what to think. Everything seemed so complicated.

"She still might tell us to piss off," she said. "Even if I find proof, it's only our word against hers. And mum can't testify."

"A fair point," Sofia said. "And if that's all we had to go on, then I might feel the same as you. But I've found something else. Something huge."

Jade sat up. "What?"

"I didn't want to tell you just yet, as it's not one hundred percent confirmed. But I've got a contact - a source - who was around at the time. He remembers talk around Fleet Street about there being some sort of scandal involving Beautiful You! and the use of non-ethical products and horrific sweatshop conditions." She flashed her eyes at her sister, noticing Jade was now all ears. "I thought that might pique your interest."

"Whoa. If that's true, I've never heard about it."

"No one has. It never came out for whatever reason. My source is looking into it for me. I wasn't going to say anything until I knew more. But do you see? Rebecca isn't the wonderful moral woman she purports to be. Or at least, she wasn't always.

I'd say there are a few skeletons in that wardrobe along with those safes. She must have covered it up somehow. If you can get evidence of this too, we'll be golden. Once we have that as leverage, she'll have to give us what's rightfully ours. We deserve this, J. Mum deserves it. You can't back out now."

Jade nodded. She couldn't argue with her reasoning. Plus, she was in the role now. Like it or not, she had to see it out. For her mum. For her and Sofia as well. Family.

"Fine," she said. "I'll get what we need. One way or another. We'll take that bitch down."

Sofia reached for the gin bottle. "Good girl."

20

After waving her sister off in an Uber, Sofia wandered back into the kitchen and slumped down at the table. She had hoped Justine would stay the night – it would be good to have company, plus she wanted her to see first-hand what mum could be like – but she understood she wanted to get back to her own flat. There was every possibility Rebecca would call or text her first thing in the morning, and she wanted to get 'back into character' in case she did.

Sofia found it rather ridiculous she'd insisted on being called Jade, but she was the one putting herself out there, stepping into the lion's den. We all do what we have to to survive. If staying in character helped her little sister get what they needed, it was fine by her. She just hoped the renewed motivation she had when she'd left, remained with her long enough for them to succeed. It was clear she was having second thoughts about the plan.

There was enough gin left in the bottle for one more drink. She sloshed it out into her glass and took a large gulp of the neat spirit. It tasted foul, but part of her liked that it did. Not everything in life was sweet and enjoyable, and it was good to be reminded of that fact. Most of the time, life was as bitter and hard to swallow as this gin. She picked up the two glasses and walked them over to the sink, placing them in the basin before leaving the kitchen and heading upstairs.

From the stillness in the air, she could tell her mum was sleeping even before she poked her head around the door. As usual, she was laying with her head and upper body propped up on her three pillows. She had such a serene look on her face, with even the hint of a wry smile teasing her lips, that it was hard to believe she wasn't the kind, witty, intelligent woman she'd always been. Sofia walked over to the side of the bed and brushed a strand of grey hair over her ear. She'd been meaning to get a home dye kit for her but had yet to get around to it. But she would. Just as soon as all this was over and she could think about other things again. Right now, her brain capacity was full of theories and ideas. But despite her sister's doubts, she knew they were doing the right thing. It was dangerous and illegal and morally dubious, but no worse than what Rebecca had done. Sometimes you had to fight fire with fire.

Stepping to one side so she could open the top drawer of the bedside table, she picked out the blister pack of sleeping pills sitting on top of a box of tissues. She pressed two out into her hand and pushed them, one by one, through a gap in her mother's lips. She groaned and tried to move her head, but Sofia persisted. Picking up a glass of water from off the table, she leaned her mum's head forward and helped her drink.

"That's it, Mum," she whispered. "This will help. Swallow it down."

Water spiralled down the side of her mum's face onto the bedspread, but some went in and she swallowed what was in her mouth. That would do it. The doctor had prescribed the pills for Sofia a few months ago. She'd gone to see him in the hope he'd give her something for her low moods, but when she'd mentioned she was having difficulty sleeping, he'd suggested she try these first. The way she saw it, having her mum sleep through the night was a better solution than taking them herself.

"Night, Mum." She lowered her head back onto the pillow. "We're going to make this right. I promise."

She watched her for a moment longer before leaving the room and switching off the light. Hopefully, now, she'd sleep until morning, but Sofia left the door open ajar and the landing light on in case she woke up and became distressed.

It was still relatively early, but Sofia was tired and there was nothing else for her to stay up for. After brushing her teeth and washing off her make-up, she retired to her bedroom at the top of the stairs. Taking her jumper off over her head as she entered, she flung it on top of the clothes already piled up on her chair in the corner.

For God's sake, Sofia!

What a bloody mess.

She hoped Jade hadn't looked in here when she was upstairs. Seeing the room now through someone else's eyes, she realised just how much of a tip she'd allowed it to become. It was embarrassing, is what it was. She was thirty-four years old, living like a chaotic teenager.

Once this room was Sofia's favourite place in the world. It was her haven, a place to hide from the pressures and strains of being a teenage girl living in London. It had been hard leaving it behind. Of course, she could have stayed at home whilst attending Goldsmiths to study for her media and communications degree, but she'd wanted to get the full university experience. Her mum had pushed her to move out, also, saying it would be good for her. Little did either of them know that just over ten short years later, Sofia would be back here to care for her. In all that time, her mum had kept the room exactly as it had been and that pleased her. The antique mahogany writing desk still stood along one wall and the matching vanity unit was next to the window. But, now, whereas the room had once been an inspiring and creative space, it was untidy and disorganised and resembled the grotto of a serial killer. Newspaper and magazine articles about Beautiful You! and Rebecca Burton-Webb covered the walls - and the vanity unit, and its integral stool where she'd spent hours experimenting with her hair and make-up, existed only as storage for piles of papers and files. Screwed-up documents and cotton wool balls blackened by mascara littered the floor.

Stepping over the debris, she headed for her desk where her laptop sat eternally opened and plugged in. The internal battery had given up the ghost a long time ago.

Swiping at the tracking pad to awaken the screen, she found her email account already open in the browser window. She clicked to refresh the page, but there was nothing new since the last time she'd looked. She sat on the edge of the bed and let out a long, deliberate groan, which alleviated some of the tension across her shoulders and upper back.

"What a fucking life," she muttered to herself.

But it was all still to play for. She had to remember that. Justine was smart and much stronger than she had made out. She could do this. Soon things could look very different for the Taylor women.

Sofia narrowed her eyes at the computer screen. The top email was from Dustin, the freelance investigative journalist she'd known for years and the contact she'd mentioned to her sister. The one looking into the alleged Beautiful You! scandal. She prayed he came back with something big, something they could use that would finally solidify what she suspected. It felt like she had all the pieces of the puzzle spinning around in her head, but couldn't work out where they all fitted together. Rebecca Burton-Webb was evil, she knew that much. She'd taken from them. She'd fucked her mum over when she'd needed her the most. That was unforgivable.

Looking around the room, she noticed her pair of old navy yoga pants hanging over the arm of the chair in the corner. They were so sheer she didn't even feel comfortable wearing them in front of her mum, but they were also the comfiest item of clothing she owned. She slid off the bed and went to grab them when the laptop let out a familiar chirp. The sound of an email arriving.

Even now, after being part of the information superhighway since she was eleven years old and having her own email address since she was thirteen, she still got a dopamine rush whenever a new missive arrived. More than likely, it was spam or from a company she'd bought something from six months ago offering her a discount or asking her to fill out a survey. Yet there was always the possibility it was something else. A nugget of salacious gossip, a lead on a story...or the exact email she'd been hoping for!

As she leaned over to read the screen, she saw it was from Dustin.

Flinging the yoga pants over her shoulder, she hunched over the laptop and clicked the email open.

Dustin was a busy man and his message reflected that. It was brief and to the point. Just two lines of text.

Hi, Sofia. Me again. I think we were right about the BY! stuff. I've found something that seems big. Call me when you can and we'll meet. Could be what you're after. D

140

Sofia chewed on the inside of her cheek as she composed her reply and hit send. This was it. It had to be. They had her. Rebecca Burton-Webb was going to regret ever screwing over Margaret Taylor and her daughters.

21

The hallway light was on, but Rebecca could see no other lights on in the house as she walked up the stone steps to her front door. It was almost midnight and - whilst the gala dinner had been a success, and she'd secured a verbal agreement of investment from Lana Bamford – the fact the hallway light was still on told her Seb was still out. And this knowledge alone made all her hard work tonight fade into insignificance.

But what was she expecting? He always stayed out late on the weekend. On weekdays too increasingly. Rebecca lived and breathed for her company and what it stood for. She knew the road to mental well-being and contentment in life was to swap your expectations for appreciation. But Seb was her husband. When they'd talked earlier, he'd told her he'd be home before her. Surely, she was allowed to expect some things from him. Like basic respect.

Unlocking the front door, she went inside. The heating was on, which was something, but the air felt still and the house far too quiet. She walked through to the kitchen and over to the fridge, yanking the door open. Her eyes landed on a half-empty bottle of Catena Chardonnay and she reached for it instinctively, the rising frustration and despair diminishing any notion about being properly hydrated before going to sleep.

She poured the entire contents of the bottle into a glass and carried this through into the lounge, sipping at the ice-cold wine as she went. It had taken her a while to get in front of Lana tonight and she was already two Martinis down when they'd finally spoken. After that, she'd spent the rest of the night quaffing Champagne. She didn't know how many glasses she'd had, but it was a lot.

She placed the glass down on the small table beside her favourite armchair and sat. It felt as if the large, plump cushions were enveloping her. As she sat back and she imagined herself sinking into the chair and disappearing. She didn't think that would be too bad a thing to happen right now. If Seb came home and found her gone, it would teach the bastard. Although he'd be happy about it.

She slapped the arms of the chairs. "Fucking hell!" she cried out. "What are you doing? What the hell are you doing?"

Even this exclamation of rage sounded pathetic. She wiped at her eyes with the base of her thumb, opening them wide so as not to smudge her mascara. It was waterproof and expensive, but everything had a limit. She suspected if the waterworks opened tonight, they'd soon become floodgates. The tears might never stop.

She sniffed back and shook her head.

Stop this. Pull yourself together.

She wasn't sure why she felt so despondent. On the surface, it felt like Seb's lack of presence had done it, but demons lurked under the surface of her consciousness. Each had the potential to destroy her if she let her guard down.

For the first time in years, she found herself thinking about Flick. How she wished he was still around. He was a good man.

He'd loved her just as much as she loved him. If things had turned out differently and they'd got married instead, she was certain he'd have been home waiting for her, eager to hear how her important night had gone. Seb hadn't even texted. He never did. It was always radio silence whilst he was out at one of his clubs and vague and defensive explanations the next day if she asked him how his night had been.

"Oh, Flick," she whispered into the empty room. "I wish you were here."

It wasn't useful to dwell on the past. She knew that more than anyone. The past was gone. Who he was, who she was, those people didn't exist except in her memory. And she knew all too well that memories could be deceiving. They could trip you up. As if to highlight this, a new image flashed across her mind. She and Mags. Dancing at The Wag Club in the early days.

Bloody hell.

Her brain was taunting her this evening. Until today, she hadn't thought about Mags at all. Obviously, there was a good reason behind that. Yet they had been so close once. Inseparable in those early days. Maggie Taylor was Rebecca's last real friend. Tonight, she yearned for the closeness they'd shared.

No! Stop this!

Stop this now!

She reached for her glass and gulped down a large mouthful of Chardonnay. It tasted good, but more so, she hoped it would dilute and dispel the dark memories bubbling up in her awareness. Like Flick, Mags was part of her past. And that past didn't belong to her anymore.

Wiping at her face, she stretched her jaw to focus herself back into the present. What happened had to happen, she told herself. Terrible things had transpired, but she'd acted accordingly. She'd done what she needed to do to survive.

Because she was Rebecca Burton-Webb. She was creative and strong and she took no shit from anyone. Giving these ludicrous thoughts so much attention was pointless and destructive. She took another big gulp of wine. The truth of it was, she had a hell of a lot to be thankful for. She was married to a young, handsome man, who she loved. She was successful and well-liked in the industry and the world at large. Not only that, tonight she'd secured important backing that would appease the shareholders. Things were on the up. She should have been walking on air right now.

So why was she so damn miserable?

The glass of wine was poised at her lips, ready to be finished off, when she heard someone at the front door. Placing the glass on the table, she flattened her hair and sucked her stomach in as a blast of cool air entered the house. Rebecca remained still, listening as her husband eased the front door closed and hung up his jacket. He was trying to be quiet, but doing a lousy job of it.

Rebecca felt a rush of anxiety or was it adrenaline, as he stepped into the front room.

"Becca," he said. "I thought you'd still be out."

"Did you?" She pursed her lips and frowned in a show of confusion. "Because I'm pretty sure I told you I'd be home before midnight. And you told me you'd be home a long time before then."

Seb rolled his eyes. "I said nothing of the sort, darling. You remember I told you I was seeing Michael and Lance, yes?" He stared at her, swaying on the spot.

He hadn't told her that. She was sure of it. She released her stomach muscles.

"Where have you been?"

"I just told you! With Michael and Lance."

Rebecca nodded. Her jaw ached with the resolve she was

holding onto. Perhaps Michael and Lance had started wearing women's perfume, but she very much doubted it. She could smell it on him, even from this distance. Black Orchid by Tom Ford. It was one of her favourites. Or it had been.

"How was the gala?" he asked. "Did you to get an audience with what's-her-name?"

"Yes. I spoke to Lana Bamford. It went very well. She's keen to be involved."

"That's great. Well done you."

"Thank you."

"Are we okay?" Seb asked, waving his hands in the air between them.

"I don't know," she replied. "Are we?" She could feel tears forming and opened her eyes as wide as they'd go. It probably made her look psychotic, but she'd rather have that than look weak.

Seb dropped his shoulders and walked over to the couch, sitting on the side nearest the armchair. He smiled at her, his eyes big and doleful.

"I'm sorry for the confusion, darling. But I told you what I was doing. You said I should have fun." His voice was soft and he was speaking slowly. Like a therapist might. It was comforting, bordering on patronising. "You've been forgetting a lot of things lately though, Becs. Haven't you?"

She looked up at the photo on the mantelpiece. A picture of the two of them on their wedding day. It seemed like a long time ago now.

"You didn't tell me, Seb."

"I did, darling."

She turned to him as he leaned forward, a concerned expression creasing his beautiful features.

In her drunken haze, she didn't know what to think. It felt as

146

if she was suffocating. Who was she? What was she doing here with this man who didn't love her?

Flick.

Mags.

Why did it all have to go so sour?

"Don't get mad," Seb said. "But maybe it's time that we put some...systems in place. Just in case."

"In case of what?" she snapped. "What are you talking about, Sebastian?"

"You know what I'm talking about." His voice remained low and gentle. "We've talked about this. Many times. We need to put something in place for when – for if – the worst happens."

Rebecca chewed on the inside of her bottom lip. She knew what he was getting at. He wanted her to grant him the power of attorney, to give him control over her money. Even at the start, when she'd genuinely believed love was the driver in their relationship, she'd been cagey about giving him access to her wealth. It was why she'd had the pre-nuptial agreement drawn up, which was probably why they were still together. As it stood, the only way he got access to her fortune was if she died. The bastard was waiting down the clock, knowing he had at least forty years of fun left once she'd gone. Maybe more if the stress and anxiety didn't finish her off sooner.

The thought brought more tears to her eyes and this time she couldn't stop them. Until now, she hadn't ever voiced these thoughts to herself in actual words. The notion had always been in there, lurking in the depths of her psyche. She'd felt its dark presence in her soul many times. But whether it was the drink, the smell of Tom Ford, or just Seb's clumsy way of broaching the matter, tonight the demons reared up, screaming at her to take heed.

"You're not getting your hands on my money, Seb." She

glared at him as the words came out of her mouth. They sounded like they were being spoken by someone else.

Seb sat back sharply as if she'd struck him. "Excuse me?"

"You heard what I said." She held his gaze. Her fists were gripped so tight in her lap they'd gone numb. Stick to your guns, she told herself. She loved Seb, but she couldn't trust him. Tonight was a case in point. He was self-centred and arrogant. He didn't care about anyone but himself.

"How dare you? I'm thinking of you and your legacy. That's all I care about. Fucking hell, I couldn't give a shit about your money." He got to his feet, looming over her as he went on. "This is typical of you, Rebecca. Anyone who tries to help you, or gets close to you, you push away. You're losing it. Do you know that? The company is going to the dogs and it's all because of you. You need to book an appointment with the doctor. Tell them what's going on. You're becoming toxic and you're a fucking mess!"

Rebecca sprang to her feet with a litheness that surprised her. Before she knew what was happening, she'd slapped her husband around the face with as much power as her small frame allowed.

"What the fuck?" Seb spat, his hand going to his cheek. "You need help, Rebecca. I'm serious—"

"Stop it! Stop it!" She lashed out, eyes screwed up and hands slapping at his face and chest. The room was spinning like a merry-go-round and she couldn't feel her body. Whether she was crazy, or just paranoid and drunk, she'd had enough. All the success she'd enjoyed, all the glass ceilings she'd broken through, meant nothing to her. All she wanted was for this prick to love her.

"No! You stop!" The room ceased spinning as Seb grabbed hold of her hand. His usual, dreamy blue eyes burned with fury as he gripped her wrist. Rebecca struggled and whimpered, but he held on, raising his other hand above his head. He was going to hit her. He was actually going to hit her.

A strange serenity washed over her at the realisation. Did she want him to? Did she deserve it? Or was it just that thing, where once your worst fears were realised, there was some relief in the knowledge you couldn't fall any further?

Seb lowered his hand and pushed her away. "You're pathetic, do you know that?" He shook his head and walked out of the room.

"Where are you going?" Rebecca called after him, but he didn't answer. She slumped back down on the chair as tears poured from her eyes and her chest convulsed with emotion.

It wasn't fair. Her life wasn't supposed to turn out this way. She'd had a dream and it had been realised ten times over. She should be happy and content and readying herself to take her foot off the pedal in her later years, to enjoy the life she'd created for herself. Instead, she was more frazzled and nervous than she'd ever been.

But maybe this was her penance.

Maybe this was why the past had been on her mind lately. Because, whatever happened, whatever she did, what happened thirty years ago hung over her head like a black cloud.

She closed her eyes, sensing sleep was close by. That was something, at least. For a few blessed hours, she'd have relief from the turmoil swirling in her head.

22

J ade had been sitting behind her new desk for just a few minutes when she saw Marsha approaching her across the office.

Shit.

She squinted down at her computer screen. She hadn't even logged in yet, but she frowned at the flashing cursor and gave the mouse button a few clicks to look busy. It was no use, sitting here alone outside Rebecca's office she was in open water.

"Jade. How are you getting on with those documents?"

"Sorry? What?" It was a juvenile response, but Marsha had caught her off guard and she had nothing. It was only a few minutes after nine, for Heaven's sake.

"Have you got them or not?" Marsha asked. She folded her arms and rocked her weight onto her back foot. "I'm assuming that's a no?"

"I'm so sorry," Jade replied. "I was meant to visit my friend as I told you. But she was ill, COVID I think, so I couldn't go around. I will get them for you, though. I promise." She bared her teeth, making a troubled expression. "Is it going to be a big problem for you?"

She glanced past Marsha and saw Thomas arriving at his desk. He noticed her at the same time and scowled as if to ask what was going on. She shrugged in response. It was a shame she'd had to change desks - she could do with some of his catty asides to Marsha right now.

Marsha let out a long breath, full of subtext. "It's not a *big* problem for me. But I do need to see the original documents. And soon. We'd be in a lot of bother if The Home Office found out you were working here illegally."

"I know. I'm sorry. But don't fret, I'm completely legit. Just a bit forgetful." Jade put on her best smile. "I promise I'll get you the documents."

Marsha nodded. "Good. I'll see you later."

She wandered off and Jade turned back to her screen, typing her password into the relevant box and hitting the return key with gusto. It was her first day proper as Rebecca Burton-Webb's assistant and, despite her bolstered desire for justice after speaking with Sofia, she was excited to see what the new role would entail. As her screen loaded, she saw seven emails waiting for her, all of them from Rebecca and sent over the weekend. She sat back in her seat, about to click on the first of them when her phone vibrated on the desk in front of her. As she leaned over to see who was calling, her chest tightened and, in one fluid movement, she scooped it up and tapped the screen to answer.

"That's twice now you've called me at work," she hissed as she moved the phone to her ear. "What did we agree about keeping a distance and allowing me to stay in character?"

It sounded like Sofia was chuckling to herself. "I know what we agreed, but this is important."

Jade sat back in her chair, scoping the office in case anyone was looking. Her eyes met with Nicole's almost straight away. She'd been watching her. Jade smiled and nodded, but Nicole didn't flinch. Her expression was one of mistrust and loathing.

"I can't talk here. I'm out in the open," Jade whispered. "Give me a second." With the phone held out in front of her, she strode around the perimeter of the room and through the door that led to the staff bathrooms. Hurrying along the corridor, she headed for the women's bathroom, at the far end. Once inside, she moved along the row of stalls, pushing at the doors to check they were unoccupied before entering the stall furthest from the door.

"Okay, Sof. I'm in the loo. I can talk now." She locked the stall door and placed the seat down before sitting and pressing the phone to her ear. "What's going on?"

"Do you remember I mentioned I had a source who thought there'd been some kind of Beautiful You! scandal?"

"Yes. And?"

"Well, he's got back to me. He's got information that he reckons could change everything."

Jade leaned forward, cupping her hand over her mouth at the sound of footsteps outside the bathroom. "What information?" she whispered.

"He wouldn't tell me over email or on the phone," Sofia replied. "He is a bit cloak and dagger like that. He likes the drama. But he wants to meet tomorrow night. Can you come with me?"

Jade paused, listening as the footsteps carried on down the corridor and faded away. "I don't know. I might have to work. Where are you meeting him?"

"A bar in Hackney, near where he lives. Please J. I want you to hear what he has to say first-hand. You might have questions I don't think of. It'll be good for us. A united front and all that. We are in this together, after all."

"Fine." How could she say no to that? "What about mum? Who's going to look after her?"

Sofia sighed. "I've got some strong sleeping tablets from the doctor. I'll give her a couple with her dinner and she'll be asleep all night. At least until I get back."

"Jesus, Sof. Is that safe?"

"I don't need you getting on your high horse about this, J." She huffed out a bitter laugh.

"Okay, okay, don't get angry," Jade told her. "But still... She's so thin these days."

"She'll be fine. I've given her these pills before. All they do is help her sleep. Trust me, she'll be fine. I'll only be gone a few hours. Please come. I need you."

Jade tongued her back molar as she thought about it. It had been made clear to her on more than one occasion that being Rebecca's PA was a full-time job. As in, she was on call every minute of every day. But there had to be caveats to that. And if Rebecca needed her to run an errand or contact someone on her behalf, she could fit it in around meeting this guy.

"Yes, I'll come with you," she told her sister.

"Excellent. I'll text you later about it. I've only just got off the phone with Dustin and I wanted to let you know the developments straight away. This could be it, though. The proof we've been looking for. I'm excited."

"Yes, me too," Jade said. *Excited and terrified.*

"I'll speak to you soon. Love you."

"I love you too."

She hung up and got to her feet, flushing the toilet for good measure in case someone saw her enter the bathroom. Slipping the phone back into her pocket, she unlocked the door to the stall, eager to get back to her desk and reply to Rebecca's flurry of emails.

"Shit!" she yelped, pressing her hand to her chest. Nicole

was standing by the sinks. "You made me jump. I didn't know anyone was in here."

The expression playing across Nicole's angular features was haughty, bordering on smug. "Didn't you?" she said. "Oh, I've been standing here a while."

23

Nicole's ice-blonde hair was scraped back in a high ponytail and the bathroom's fluorescent lighting highlighted her razor cheekbones and wide jawline. Coupled with her pale skin and the crisp white shirt and grey utilitarian skirt she was wearing, she looked vaguely Gestapo-esque. Intimidating.

"I never heard you come in," Jade said. Her voice wavered as her mind raced on ahead of her.

Had Nicole heard her talking with Sofia just now? Had she said anything incriminating? She couldn't remember.

"My eye was sore. I came in here to take my lens out," Nicole said. "I really should get disposables. These gas-permeable buggers give me nothing but grief."

"Right. Yes." Jade hadn't moved. "I don't wear lenses. Or glasses."

Nicole raised her chin, elongating her already swan-like neck. "Lucky you."

"I was just on a call," Jade said, pointing her thumb over her shoulder at the recently exited stall. "A personal call. A bit naughty, I know. But it was sort of important and I didn't want to take it at my desk."

Nicole twisted her mouth to one side, like a bad actor selling the fact that they were thinking. "I thought you told everyone you didn't have any family?"

Shit!

What had she said?

"How do you mean?"

"I shouldn't have been listening," Nicole said. "But I couldn't help it. You said something about your mum just now. Yet I'm certain you've been telling everyone both your parents are dead."

"They are," Jade lied, her mind spinning at a hundred miles an hour. "But you're right, I did say mum. Because that's what I call her. It's my friend's mum really, but she's been like a mum to me. I call her mum, but it's like a nickname. A pet name."

Nicole didn't look convinced. "Where did you say you were from again?"

"I was born in Bromley, but I grew up in North London. Chalk Farm."

"Right, yes. And you went to Saint Martins. Graduating... when? Two-thousand and eleven?"

Jade nodded. This was all true, but she didn't like where it was going. "Then I worked as a buyer and then a junior assistant at Gartons, before getting the fashion assistant job at Tres Chic and moving to New York." She raised her chin. "I can email you a copy of my resume if you're interested?"

Jade held Nicole's gaze as prickly heat ran down her arms. Keep it together, she told herself.

Nicole smiled. "Don't be silly. I was curious, that's all. It must have been amazing working at Tres Chic."

"Yes. It was." Jade moved over to the sink and turned on the hot tap. Her reflection in the mirror appeared calm and friendly, but inside she felt like a coiled spring. "I loved working there. But I also know I've made the right decision to move back to England. This is my home."

"Yes. And you've got your surrogate mother here."

"Absolutely." She tapped some soap into her palm from the dispenser and washed her hands, all the while sensing Nicole's icy stare burning into the side of her head. Twisting off the tap, she shook the excess water off her hands before straightening up and turning around. "Listen, Nicole, I can't help but feel we got off on the wrong foot, you and I. But I'm here to stay, so I really would like it if we could try to move past it."

She reached for a paper towel and dried her hands as Nicole bucked and spluttered in response. "I don't think we—"

"How about we go for a drink?" Jade said, tossing the used paper towel in the bin. "We can wipe the slate clean. Start again. I think we'd get on well if we gave each other a chance."

Nicole's eyes remained as cold and searching as they'd ever been, but her mouth arched into a wide smile. "Sounds like fun."

"Friday, after work? There are a couple of little cocktail bars down towards Soho that I've not been to. We could check one of them out."

Nicole didn't respond, just kept staring at her in that same way. Jade held her nerve, not taking her eyes from hers. Finally, Nicole's shoulders dropped and she let out a silent chuckle as forced as her smile.

"Drinks? On Friday?"

Yes. That's what I said.

"How about it?"

Nicole tilted her head from side to side as if considering the question. "I'll have to check my diary."

Of course, she couldn't agree to the idea straight off. She was too involved in this power play for that. But so what? If

Nicole's cattiness simply stemmed from a bruised ego, Jade could cope with that.

"No problem," she said. "Why don't you check and get back to me? But it'll be nice, I think. It'll be good for us."

"Hmm. Yes."

That was about as good as she was going to get for now. Jade side-stepped around the side of Nicole and exited the bathroom. As she walked down the corridor to the main office, she noticed her heart was beating loud and fast behind her ribs.

That was far too close.

24

Rebecca beckoned the wine waiter over. Despite it only being Monday afternoon, she'd already decided on her way over here she'd forgo her no-alcohol mid-week rule in favour of a little tipple. Because why not? She was Rebecca Burton-Webb. She was a maverick. A rebel. A disrupter of culture. In her youth, she'd used a few glasses of wine as a way of opening up her creativity. Just because she was now older and wealthier and with much more responsibility, couldn't it still be used as a tool to help oil her imagination and inspiration? She certainly needed the help.

"I ordered the last bottle," she said, handing the wine list to Jade. "Why don't you get the next one?"

"Oh? Okay." she looked positively dumbstruck as she peered at the extensive selection.

Rebecca had messaged Jade late morning, telling her to meet at Garfunkel's for a lunch meeting to talk through some ideas. But it was now almost two-thirty and Rebecca figured they might as well make an afternoon of it. Not only could they get to know each other a little better, but for the first time in a while, she had some exciting ideas forming and found her new assistant to be more than an agreeable sounding board.

"What wine do you prefer, red or white?" she asked, offering Jade an easier question.

"Usually I drink red, but white is fine too."

"How about a bottle of the Rosso Piceno?" she said, leaning over and pointing. "It's rather cheeky and very easy drinking." As the waiter approached the table, she gave him the order herself, saving Jade embarrassment.

"An excellent choice," he said, jerking his torso forward in acknowledgement before gliding away.

Rebecca had been frequenting Garfunkel's for longer than she could remember. Since before Beautiful You! had even started. With its cosy lighting and high-backed leather booths offering privacy and comfort, it was the ideal place to hold court and talk over new concepts and plans.

"I'm glad we came out," she told Jade. "I feel sometimes it's better to get away from the office environment."

Jade smiled. "Yes. And it's a lovely little place."

"Isn't it. I've been coming here for years. It's here where I first came up with the idea for Beautiful You! In this very booth!"

Jade's eyes widened. "Really? Wow! This is where you were sitting?"

"Indeed. A long time ago now."

"Were you on your own?"

Rebecca paused. It was a valid question, but it threw her a little. "No. I was with an old friend," she replied. "She actually helped me come up with the concept. There was a time when I hoped we'd run the business together..." Rebecca trailed off at the hint of a wobble in her voice.

Why the hell was she telling Jade these things?

But not for the first time recently, she'd found herself

thinking of Mags and the early days. They'd been so full of dreams, so eager to make their mark on the world. Before it all went sour and the worst thing in the world happened. She sniffed and shook her head, focusing her attention back on the present before thoughts of Flick bubbled up and knocked her completely off track.

"But, in the end, it wasn't to be," she said.

She sat upright. There was no point in focusing on the past. It was over. Dead and gone. More than likely, she was only pining for the past because she missed the person she was back then. The young Rebecca was fierce and confident and certain of her worth. There would be no way she would have let Seb treat her the way he did now.

"Ah, here we are, perfecto." She sat back, thankful for the wine waiter's return.

For the next forty-five minutes, they drank and laughed and talked about fashion and culture and Rebecca's hopes for the next decade. Jade, in turn, listened intently, asking pertinent questions and commenting wisely. Rebecca spoke of her goal, to make Beautiful You! the biggest health and wellness brand in the world. She even touched on the possibility of scaling down the fashion and cosmetic side of operations in favour of more digital output. Meditation apps, wellness tracking software, even a self-hypnosis and motivational lecture series.

They'd finished the second bottle of wine before she knew it and Rebecca ordered herself a shot of sambuca to end the meal. Like she would have done in the old days. The alcohol was going down well, suitably lubricating the conversation as she'd hoped, and even though she was feeling somewhat light-headed, she didn't want to stop. Jade was funny and bright and Rebecca liked the way she talked about things. It might have been rather cliched to think it, but Jade reminded her so much of herself when she was her age. She had such vitality and self-assuredness. It felt like two lifetimes ago she'd held such poise.

"My marriage is a fucking wreck; do you know that?"

She'd downed the sambuca when the words fell out of her mouth. She hadn't intended on bringing Seb up - she made a point of never talking about her private life - but there was something about Jade's warm nature, coupled with the wine that made her want to open up. For the last few weeks, her marriage woes had never been far from her mind and she needed to vent. But really, she needed a friend.

Jade was sipping at her last glass of wine and now lowered it to the table as her expression wilted into a mixture of embarrassment and concern. "I'm sorry to hear that."

Rebecca curled her lip. "Shit. I'm sorry. I shouldn't bother you with this. It's unprofessional." The alcohol had just hit her hard. She went up into her head to do a quick recap of how much she'd drunk. Was it four or five glasses of wine? Or six? Jade had kept topping up her glass, so it was hard to work out. However much it was she'd drunk, it was enough to breach the defences of her inner world.

After all the shit and misery she'd gone through, Rebecca had spent the last three decades constructing powerful psychological fortifications around both her head and heart. But these things were only as strong as her steadfastness and ability to stay focused.

"We can talk about it if you like?" Jade reached across the table. Her fingers hovered over Rebecca's hand for a second before she thought better of it and pulled her hand back, placing it in her lap. "Only if you want to. If you think it'd help."

Rebecca looked down, trying with everything she had not to cry.

Damn it!

She shouldn't have drunk so much.

"I don't know whether it will help." She sighed and didn't look up. "I feel like I'm losing the plot. Seb keeps telling me I should go see my doctor. He also tells me I should change my will and give him the power or attorney, so I don't know what to think. He's cheating on me. I know that much. But that's not a new development." She shut up as she saw the look on her assistant's face. "I am sorry, Jade. I shouldn't be telling you these things. It's not fair."

"No. It's fine," she said. "It's a lot to take in, that's all."

Absolutely it was! She'd just spilled her guts to a relative stranger! Voiced things she'd never actually articulated to herself until this moment.

Bloody hell.

Why had she ordered that second bottle of wine? And then the sambuca!

Idiot!

One bottle at lunchtime was a bad idea. Two was downright destructive. But maybe, subconsciously, that had been why she'd done it. There was a nihilistic energy in her belly. When things were going this bad, it was human nature to want to burn it all down. If she destroyed herself, the world wouldn't get the chance.

No.

She was being ridiculous.

There was still lots to play for. She had to pull herself together.

"This old friend you mentioned," Jade said. "Do you still see them?"

Rebecca shook her head. "Not for many years."

"That's a shame."

"Yes. It is. It was. A lot of things happened back then that could have destroyed me, but they didn't. I have to be thankful for that."

"What sort of things?"

Rebecca gazed into the younger woman's large brown eyes. At that moment, she so desperately wanted to tell her everything. But even drunk and despondent as she was, a deeper sense of reason and self-preservation pulled her back from the brink.

"It is not something I like to talk about," she said. "It's in the past and that's where it should stay."

Jade gave her an empathetic smile. "I understand. It's sad you're not in touch though, if she was that important to you. It's good to have friends, someone to talk to, to share things with..."

Rebecca gasped. It felt like her chest was about to explode with emotion. She swallowed and blew out a slow breath to compose herself. A lone tear ran down her face, which she wiped away in an instant. "Friends can be good. But they also complicate matters," she said. "Especially in business."

"Do you think so?"

"In my experience, friends never last and they always let you down."

Bloody hell.

She sounded drunker and more woeful by the second. She glanced around as a hot flush overcame her. Was she going soft-headed in her old age? Or was it worse than that? Maybe Seb was right and she was losing it. Her father's sister had gone into a home when she was in her early sixties and they did say it was genetic. The family line, back then, was that she'd become 'a bit forgetful' and needed to be looked after, but today the diagnosis would have been early onset dementia.

"Well, I think you're great," Jade said. "Anyone would be glad to have you as a friend. You're an inspiration. I'm sorry you're feeling this way but I know if anyone can get over this slump, it's you. Hell, you're Rebecca Burton-Webb. You're the most—Oh! Shit! Sorry!"

Rebecca had tried her best, but the tears were now falling wantonly from her eyes and she didn't think she could stop.

"Do you want to go to the bathroom?"

Rebecca waved her away. "I need to leave. I'm sorry." She raised her hand to get the waiter's attention.

"Is everything all right?" he asked, coming over.

"Beautiful as always," Rebecca told him, but the words came out slurred. She coughed to rouse herself before continuing. "Can we have the bill and can you order me a taxi? As soon as possible."

"Of course," he hurried away, leaving an awkward silence hanging over the table.

Rebecca could sense Jade desperately thinking of something useful to say, but was glad when she remained silent. There was nothing to say. She was a mess and she had to get out of here. She saw the waiter approaching with the card machine and pulled her purse out of her bag. As she thumbed through her selection of credit cards, her vision blurred and she had to close one eye to focus. Not a good look. She pulled out her American Express and a twenty as he got closer.

"Put it on this, please." She held the money and credit card up but didn't look up at him. She didn't want him to see her puffy red eyes. "And this is for you."

"Thank you very much. It was lovely," Jade said, stepping in as a worthy distraction.

The waiter did his thing and left them to it, but not before thanking Rebecca for the tip and informing them that her taxi was outside.

"Okay, I need to go."

Rebecca shuffled along the bench seat, but as she got to her feet, her legs buckled beneath her and she cried out.

"Rebecca!" Jade was up and beside her in a second. She snaked an arm around her back and placed her other hand on her arm. "Don't worry," she whispered. "I've got you. Do you want me to take you home?"

Rebecca looked up into her kind, concerned face and it was all she could do not to erupt into more tears.

"Yes," she muttered. "Thank you, darling. That would be most helpful."

25

Jade had been careful to appear like she was matching Rebecca glass for glass. But by sipping often and taking on the role of topping up their glasses, she'd orchestrated it so her boss had quaffed the lion's share of the wine. Rebecca had been distracted, so hadn't noticed. Now, as they sat in the back of the taxi on their way to her house in Chelsea, it was clear the alcohol had taken its toll. The tears that had been elegantly brushed away in the bistro were now a stream of unrepentant sobs. It wasn't loud, or attention-seeking, but seemed to arise from a sense of deep sadness.

Jade made all the right noises. Telling Rebecca it was 'fine' and she 'shouldn't worry about it' as she patted her hand reassuringly. But inside, she was proud that she'd prompted such a dramatic fall in her boss. Proud and also angry.

What was it she'd said about friends?

They never lasted...

They always let you down...

How dare she? It was Rebecca who was the bad friend. All for her own gain. So let her cry and feel sorry for herself. She deserved to feel bad. She'd brought this on herself.

"Do you want me to come in with you?" Jade asked as the taxi pulled up outside Rebecca's white, three-storey townhouse.

Rebecca mumbled something that Jade couldn't make out, but which she took to be a yes. Handing the taxi driver a twenty-pound note from her purse, she climbed out of the car and walked around to Rebecca's side to help her out.

"Come on, I've got you," she told her, having to drag her up out of the seat. As the taxi drove away, she put her arm around her boss and walked her as far as the set of stone steps that led up to the front door. "Do you think you can make it?"

Rebecca snorted. "I'm fine. Leave me alone." She nudged Jade off of her but had only managed the first step when she stumbled to one side and let out a cry.

Jade grabbed her in time, holding on to the back of her coat and pulling her close to steady them both. "Okay, let's try that again."

"Oh, Christ! What's happened?"

Jade looked up, pleased to see Seb standing in the open doorway. His hair was wet and he looked as if he'd pulled on the first items of clothes available: a pair of black jeans and a creased Ralph Lauren polo shirt. He looked good, though. He always looked good.

"Can you help?" Jade asked, somewhat redundantly, as Seb was already on his way down. He got on the other side of Rebecca and wrapped his arm around her shoulders.

"Piss off. I'm fine," she slurred.

"I'm sure you are, darling. But we all need a little assistance sometimes." He caught Jade's eye and shook his head. "What happened?"

Jade grimaced. "We had a lunch meeting and I think we might have had a few too many wines."

"Fuck me," Seb grumbled. "It's just one thing after another."

Together, they got Rebecca up the steps. Once inside, she

appeared to rouse a touch, insisting that she was fine and that she didn't need to sleep it off, as Seb was suggesting. But as she made to go into the kitchen, she lost her balance and spun around almost a full turn before stumbling into the wall.

"Right, that's it. Bed for you." Seb grabbed her and manhandled her up the stairs, leaving Jade standing in the hallway, unsure of what to do.

"Do you need a hand?" she shouted after them.

"I can manage," Seb called back. "Wait there. I'll be down in a minute."

Jade didn't respond, but instead wandered into the front room, marvelling at the tasteful cream and natural wood décor and the enormous-leafed plants on either side of the large bay window. The room wasn't to her taste exactly, but it worked and fitted in well with the Beautiful You! brand. That was the thing about Rebecca. She lived and breathed her creative vision. Jade couldn't help but respect her for that if nothing else.

"She fell asleep the second I laid her down." She jumped at the sound of Seb's voice and turned around as he entered the room. He'd changed out of his top and was now wearing a tight white sweater that accentuated his olive skin. He'd also combed his hair back from his face and put some product through it. Not bad going, considering he'd been gone only a few minutes. He must have dumped Rebecca and left. "How much did she have to drink?" he asked.

Jade gave him a thin-lipped smile. "We shared two bottles of wine, and then she ordered sambuca. I'm sorry. Are we disturbing you?"

Seb rolled his head around his shoulders. "It's cool. I just got back from the gym. I've got a script I need to have a look at. But it's not urgent."

"A new part?" Jade asked, slipping into a more flirtatious spirit. "That's amazing. Well done."

"I haven't got it yet, but it sounds decent. It's for the leading role in a dystopian time-travel thriller. The budget isn't huge, but my agent reckons they've signed Jason Statham on to play the bad guy. It'd be my first lead in about ten years if I get it."

"Fingers crossed, then."

"Thanks." They faced each other. The air between them fizzed with electricity and Jade sensed her cheeks burning. But then Seb looked away and sighed. "And thanks for bringing Rebecca home, too. I don't know what's wrong with her lately."

He walked over to the couch and slumped on the side closest to her. Leaning back, he puffed out his cheeks and exhaled before lifting his hands to rub at his face. It was all very dramatic and over the top. Probably why he hadn't landed a lead role in so long.

"You poor thing," she said, remembering she was involved in a performance of her own. "It must be hard for you. Do you really think she's... you know...struggling with her memory?"

"Yes. I do. I'm worried about her." He was staring off at a point on the far wall. Jade watched him as he chewed on his lip. She didn't believe a word of it, of course. From what little she knew of the situation, she'd say he was gaslighting Rebecca for his own gain. For this reason alone, she felt a little sorry for her. She clearly loved the man and not only did he not love her back, but he treated her like shit.

"Do you think you could help me out?" Seb asked, sitting up and fixing her with a penetrating stare.

"What do you mean?"

"Sit down, will you?" He shunted over on the couch and patted the space beside him. "Go on."

Jade hesitated for a moment before acquiescing. Seb shifted around as she sat, so they were sitting at right-angles to one another.

"Will you keep an eye on Rebecca for me? At work and

elsewhere, when I'm not around. I don't mean you should spy on her, but let me know if you notice her doing anything weird. Or if you have any concerns."

Jade placed her hands in her lap and as she looked down, she saw they were clenched tight. She hadn't realised she was that tense.

"I suppose I can," she told him. "If you think it would help."

"It would. Thank you." His demeanour shifted. His eyes had the same sparkle of intensity, but now there was lust in his smile. "We should exchange numbers. You can text me if you have anything you need to tell me."

Jade fought back a wry smile. Was he seriously using his wife's supposed illness to get her number? She wouldn't put anything past this guy, but even for a man as privileged and egotistical as Seb Turner, it was audacious.

"If you think that would help," she said, reaching into her the pocket of her coat and pulling out her phone. "What's your number?"

"Here, let me do it." Jade gave him her phone and he thumbed in his number before tapping the screen with a flourish. A shrill ringtone reverberated through the silent house, possibly coming from the kitchen. "There, now I've got your number too."

Jade smiled as he handed her back the phone. "Thanks. Now what?"

"Why don't you stay a while? We could have a drink. Chat."

"Doesn't Rebecca need you?"

Seb snorted. "She'll be dead to the world until morning. Besides, she hasn't needed me for years. That woman doesn't need anyone but herself."

"Are you sure about that? What about her memory?"

"Oh, yes, that." He sat upright and cleared his throat. "That's a different matter. Anyway, let's not talk about Rebecca.

I'm still yet to hear the Jade Fisher story." The look he gave her was obviously well-rehearsed, but she couldn't help but feel a stir of something in her belly as he did. He was full of brooding masculinity and desire.

She looked away. "You know most of it. I grew up in London and then around six years ago, I moved to New York to work at Tres Chic. My mother died last year and her passing caused me to reassess my life. To the point, I returned to England and applied for a job at Beautiful You!"

She drew in a deep breath. Seb wasn't the only one who was well-rehearsed. It was the speech she'd gone over ad infinitum with Sofia to help solidify her backstory in her mind.

"And here you are." Seb purred.

"Yes. Here I am." She turned away as nervous excitement tipped over the edge into trepidation. "But I should go home."

"Stay a while. It's only early."

"No. I don't think I should..."

"It's fine." He placed his hand on her thigh. "No one has to know." The position of his thumb on her inner thigh told her exactly what he meant by this statement. As her eyes found his, he stroked his hand further up her leg.

"No. Please. I can't." She got up, shaking him off. "I'm sorry, this is wrong."

Seb was on his feet immediately. "Hey, it's fine. Please don't misunderstand me. I was just being friendly." He stepped back and raised his arms out by his sides. "Rebecca and I really appreciate what you did for her today. I thought you might want to stay and have a drink, that's all. But if not, that's totally fine." He smiled at her, but this time his eyes were friendly and his expression warm. Maybe he was a better actor than she'd given him credit for.

"Yes. Of course. I know," she said, scanning the room for anything she might have left. She had her phone, her coat, her purse. It was all good. She paused, composing herself as she regarded Seb. "Thank you for the offer, but I'm rather tired and I think I should go home."

"I get it," Seb said. "Let me call you a cab."

"No. It's fine." She was already side-stepping over to the door. "I'll walk up to the King's Road and get one easily enough."

"If you're sure."

"Yes, I am." She scurried out into the hallway and towards the front door, with Seb following her.

"Here, allow me." He leaned around the side of her, sticking his broad chest in her face as he unlocked the door. He smelled like he always did. A musky mix of natural body odour and cologne. She was thankful for the cool, fresh breeze that took it away as he opened the door. "Are you sure you'll be all right?" he asked.

"Don't worry." A shudder of relief ran down her spine as she stepped out into the early evening air.

"I'll tell you what. Give me a text when you get home. Yeah?"

She swallowed, nodded. "Okay."

Seb smirked, seemingly pleased with himself. He held up a hand to wave her off as she turned and hurried down the steps to the pavement. She could feel his eyes on her as she made her way to the end of the row and took a left along Oakley Street. It would take her about twenty minutes to get up to the King's Road from here, but the walk would do her good. Hopefully, by the time she got home, she wouldn't feel so grubby and nasty. All she wanted to do now was have a long bath and climb into bed. It had been a strange day and she had a lot to process.

26

Nicole had been watching Jade all morning. She'd seen her when she'd got the call and scurried out of the office just after twelve, without saying a word to anyone. After that, she'd note every hour that ticked by. Two hours, three, four... By the time the sky had turned from washed-out blue to grey, to dark grey, it was clear Jade wasn't returning to the office.

Where the hell was she?

Where had she gone?

If it had been Kristen, she wouldn't have batted an eyelid. It was usual for Rebecca's PA to be away from the office for days at a time, accompanying her on trips or running important errands. Yet Jade wasn't Kristen, and Nicole was adamant there was something not quite right about the new girl.

And despite what people might assume, her wariness of Jade Fisher wasn't just because she'd waltzed straight into the role of Rebecca's right-hand woman after only being here a few days. Although, it wasn't *not* that. Nicole had made it clear on more than one occasion, and to anyone who would listen, that she thought herself perfect for the PA role. After Kristen left, she'd expected it to be only a matter of time before she was called into Rebecca's big glass office and offered the job. Hell, she deserved it. She'd given her twenties and most of her soul to Beautiful You! But no. Jade bloody Fisher turned up and any dreams of promotion she'd harboured flew out the window.

As 6 p.m. rolled around, Nicole wandered over to Marsha's desk.

"Do you know where Jade is today?" she asked, keeping her tone casual.

Marsha looked up from her screen, screwing her face up as if she was trying to hold on to whatever thought she'd been concentrating on. "Sorry? Erm... No. I don't. Is she not in? I need to speak to her, actually."

"Oh?"

Marsha cricked her neck to one side. "It's nothing. Admin stuff."

"She seems to be doing well," Nicole said. "Rebecca clearly sees a lot in her. Where was it she came from again?"

"Tres Chic. She was a fashion assistant."

"That's right. She did tell me. Great. They must have been sad to see her go. I'm assuming they gave her a good reference." She didn't look at Marsha as she spoke.

"Yes, they did. Why do you ask?"

Nicole pouted her lips. "No reason. Just curious, that's all. She seems to have come in from nowhere and jumped straight into Kristen's shoes. It seems a little fast to me. But I'm assuming everyone is happy about her appointment."

She let the words hang in the air. She and Marsha had never been that close, but they respected each other's work and they knew how each other ticked. Nicole suspected Marsha found Jade's appointment as troubling as she did.

"She seems like a nice enough girl and she knows her stuff."

"Sure." Nicole lowered her head to look at her. "I'm sensing there's a *but*..."

Marsha groaned. "I don't know. I've still not seen her passport so can't fill in her right-to-work forms. It's not for want of asking. But now Rebecca needs her twenty-four-seven. I feel like she's going to keep fobbing me off. I don't know what's going on."

"Really?" Nicole whispered. "That's bad, isn't it? But I'm sure there's a perfectly reasonable explanation for her not bringing it in."

"Apparently her papers are at a friend's house and she keeps forgetting to get them," Marsha went on, lowering her voice as she eyed the other people still in the office. "But how forgetful can one person be?"

"Indeed."

Marsha shuddered her shoulders as if shaking off an invisible cloak. "I shouldn't be talking about this, Nicole. Mum's the word, okay?"

"Absolutely!"

But Marsha had confirmed what she'd already supposed. The new girl wasn't as golden as she had made out. Now, she felt justified in carrying out her next move, the one she'd been stewing over all day.

She walked back to her desk and, once settled behind her screen, opened up Instagram on her phone. Scrolling through her list of followers, she found who she was looking for in a few swipes. She opened the profile and read the bio.

Shona Masters. New York.
Freelance designer / Junior digital editor at
@TresChic Magazine

Nicole had met Shona three years ago at the Balmain after-show as part of Paris Fashion Week and they'd hit it off immediately. Back then, Shona had been part of the influencer marketing team at Metropunx, a digital magazine based out of Manhattan's Lower East Side, but they'd stayed in touch and last night Nicole had sat bolt upright in bed on remembering Shona had started work at Tres Chic at the end of the last year. Her and Jade's time there would only have crossed over a few months, but Tres Chic's employee list wasn't large. They'd have known each other. If, indeed, Jade worked there at all.

Nicole waited until late in the day to message in the hope she'd catch her in a live DM session. It would be around two-thirty in the afternoon in New York, the perfect time. She tapped out a quick message asking Shona how she was and if she could help her out before placing the phone down on the desk in front of her.

She waited. Running her tongue around her mouth as the minutes ticked by. It would be silly of her to expect Shona to message back straight away, but she hoped she'd see the message and reply soon enough. When her phone buzzed only a few minutes later and the notification on the screen told her she had a message on Instagram, her heart leapt.

Good bloody result.

She swiped open her phone and read the message. It was from Shona. She was doing good; she said. Busy as all hell, but good. And what did Nicole want help with?

With her breath tight in her chest, she typed out a reply.

> Bit of a weird question - but Jade Fisher has
> just started working here. I wanted to know
> what she was like...x

She hit send and waited, staring at the screen now, not able to put down her phone. The reply came straight away.

Who?

Nicole inhaled deeply, holding her breath to calm herself. *Whoa.*

This was massive. Not totally unexpected. But massive all the same. She glanced around the office - apart from Marsha who was still squinting at her screen, engrossed in whatever she was working on, there were just three other people left in the office, Lauren and Anita, the junior designers, and Sammi in purchasing. None of them was looking her way.

She tapped out another message, giving more detail. Just making sure.

Jade Fisher. She worked as a fashion assistant at BC up until the start of this year. English girl from London. Attractive. Dark hair.

She hit send once again, gnawing at a piece of skin on the side of her finger as she waited for Shona's reply. When it came, she felt like throwing her phone in the air.

A few English girls here. And, PLEASE, everyone who works here is attractive, sweetie (LOL) But no one called Jade Fisher. I just asked my colleague who's been at BC forever. She's never heard of her! What's going on there?

Nicole could hardly contain her excitement as she typed out a reply, thanking Shona and telling her she might have got mixed up. She finished saying she'd do more investigating and let her know before flinging her phone onto the desk. Her cheeks ached from the wide grin spreading its way across her face.

But what to do with this new information? Her first instinct was to march into Rebecca's office first thing in the morning with Marsha in tow and tell her what she knew. But as she considered her options, she decided to sit on it for a few days. This information was potentially damaging to the entire brand and she had to be clever about what she did with it. Used correctly, it could be the leverage she needed to propel herself to the top. But be too rash and eager, it could blow up in her face just as easily.

For now, she would keep it close to her chest. She'd keep her head down and observe. But whatever happened, she knew Jade Fisher was an imposter. Whatever her game, Nicole wasn't going to let her get away with it. The new girl was going down.

27

J ade felt wretched as she sat down at her desk and leaned around the back of her computer screen to switch it on. She'd had a shower this morning, but she could smell the rotten wine oozing out of her pores. How gross. How absolutely rotten of her.

Why had she done it? She'd been all but sober after returning from Rebecca's house. She had planned to have a long soak in the bath and then an early night. But as she was finding out, recently, there was certainly something in that phrase about best-laid plans...

After her bath, she'd eaten a bowl of soup which left her feeling satisfied and wholesome. But as the night had drawn in so had a host of worrisome thoughts and niggling doubts. She knew taking back what was rightfully theirs was justified, even if their approach was a bit underhand. Yet, seeing Rebecca today, so distraught and upset, had been hard. When she and Sofia and been planning their revenge, she'd viewed Rebecca Burton-Webb as a symbol of the unjustness of their situation, a foe that needed to be destroyed at any cost. But since then, she'd sat with her, talked with her, seen through the bluster and

180

bravado. Rebecca put on a good front, but it was clear to Jade she was as broken and messed up as anyone. Yes, she'd screwed their mother over and she owed them the recompense. But was there an easier way of getting it?

It was a tough question to answer and the more it played on her attention, the more she'd felt drawn to the bottle of Pinot Grigio in the fridge. An hour later and she'd drunk the entire bottle whilst watching some crappy tv show.

Sat here now in the Beautiful You! office, she couldn't even remember what the show had been about. She remembered laughing at some joke, but it could have been anything. That wasn't good. She had to get a grip. Especially as they were meeting Sofia's contact after work. If her sister detected she was floundering and getting herself messed up again, she'd be down on her like a tonne of bricks.

Reaching for her water bottle, she glugged back half of it before logging onto her screen and sitting back to wait as her system loaded. She had sixteen unread emails to deal with, plus another twenty-three she'd flagged that needed a follow-up. She couldn't face any of them right now. Finishing the rest of her water, she got up and headed to the cooler to get more.

Thomas had just got in and was taking off his jacket as she passed his desk.

"Morning," he said, before smiling mischievously at her. "Bloody hell. Are you feeling all right?"

Jade stopped and curled her lip. "Do I look that bad?"

"No. Just a bit...tired. Was it a late one?"

"I had lunch with Rebecca. It turned into a bit of a session."

"No way," he whispered, eyes wide, urging her to divulge more. "What happened?"

Jade grinned and ran her tongue over her top teeth. She was all ready to dive into a little office gossip, but she stopped herself. A voice in her head that sounded a lot like her sister reminded her to step carefully. She still had alcohol in her system and this, coupled with her latent desire to be accepted by her peers, could get her into trouble.

"I'm kidding," she told him. "I didn't have a great night's sleep is all. And I think I might be a bit iron deficient." This wasn't a lie. She'd been taking iron tablets for a few years after reading an article on anaemia. "I'll have an early night tonight."

Thomas pulled a disappointed face. "Spoilsport. Though, to be fair, she looks fine."

Jade followed his eye line over to the main entrance in time to see Rebecca flouncing through the door.

What the hell?

She looked radiant. Her skin was practically glowing as she strode across the office, smiling and waving at her staff as she went. Seeing Jade, she made a beeline for her, stopping a few feet away and hitting her and Thomas with the cheeriest of smiles.

"Good morning," she sang. "And how are you both today?"

"Great, thanks," Thomas said.

"Yes. Good," Jade added.

Rebecca shifted her focus to Jade. "Thank you for yesterday. You were an enormous help."

What was she playing at? Jade hadn't even expected to see her in the office today. And here she was looking and acting as if she'd just got back from a week-long spa break.

"I feel we broke some new ground," Rebecca went on. "Very useful.

Jade felt herself nodding, far too eagerly. "Yes... Sure..." She stopped and composed herself. "I did too."

"Actually, do you have a minute?" Rebecca asked. "I need to talk to you about something."

"Yes. Of course."

Jade smiled at Thomas before putting her head down and scampering after Rebecca as she opened the door to her office.

"What time did you get in today?" Rebecca asked, holding the door for Jade.

"I've only just got in myself a few minutes ago," Jade said, letting the door swing shut behind her.

Rebecca removed her coat and hung it on the stand before walking over to her desk. "Can you take a few notes for me? I've got a meeting across town in an hour with Lydia at Showgirls and I need you to send a couple of emails on my behalf."

Jade didn't move. Once inside her soundproof office, she'd expected Rebecca to apologise for getting drunk or, at the very least, acknowledge what had transpired yesterday. But she wasn't letting on at all. Did she even remember what had happened? Or was this her playing it down, rewriting the narrative to keep face?

Rebecca sat and waved her over. "Come along, dear. Sit down. There's a pad there you can use."

"Yes, of course."

Jade sat on the chair in front of Rebecca's desk and did as instructed, scribbling down in shorthand as Rebecca dictated the content of the emails she wanted her to send. Once finished, the muscles in Jade's hand and wrist ached from where she'd been gripping the pen too tightly. She examined the pad in her lap. She had three pages of notes. They were extensive enough and seemed to make sense as she scan-read the top page. Yet for the last five minutes, her mind had been elsewhere.

Rebecca must have woken up feeling at least a bit miserable and hungover. Surely, she'd have remembered some of what happened. Or, if she hadn't, surely Seb would have delighted in notifying her of her chaotic behaviour. Unless he hadn't and was playing some kind of weird game she wasn't privy to. There was a lot to consider and it only added to Jade's agitation. For

Rebecca to not comment at all on how she'd acted seemed odd. Unsettling, even.

Although maybe it made perfect sense. If this was Rebecca's way of dealing with situations that didn't fit her brand or the version of herself she wanted the world to see, then what she'd done to their mum made more sense.

"Do you have everything you need?" Rebecca asked with a smile.

"I think so," Jade replied. "It's just..."

Rebecca frowned. "Yes?"

"I was just wondering how you were feeling. After yesterday." Even with indignation as her primary driver, she couldn't deny the crushing anxiety that overcame her as she asked this.

"I feel fine," Rebecca said. "Absolutely fine."

"Oh. Right. Good."

"We had fun, didn't we?"

Jade blinked. "Yes. Sure."

Jesus.

She was a fucking narcissist. This was what it felt like to be gaslit in real-time. And to think she'd even started to feel sorry for this woman.

But no more. The sincere, accessible persona Rebecca put out there was a total sham. She was as cold and calculating as Sofia had always insisted she was. Her sister's words echoed in Jade's throbbing skull.

Five-hundred-and-thirty-eight million dollars...

Rebecca owes us...

Took advantage of a sick woman...

She got to her feet and held up the pad. "I'll get on with typing this up."

"Great. See you later."

Jade left Rebecca's office and walked back to her own desk,

muttering to herself as she went. She felt sick and angry and rather stupid, but at least now she had no doubt in her mind that they were doing the right thing.

But first, however, she had work to do. Rebecca might have fallen a long way in Jade's estimation, but she still had to convince her and the rest of the office that she was a loyal and worthy assistant. She signed back into her computer, ready to type up the first email when she sensed someone approaching her desk out of the corner of her eye.

Her heart sank as she looked over to see it was Nicole.

"Hey, hun. How are things with you?"

"I'm good," Jade said, tilting her head back to take her in. "And you?"

"Wonderful. I was just thinking about you."

"Oh?" She was being far too friendly. It made Jade's stomach twitch.

"I've got a week off next month and I was thinking about heading over to New York for a bit of a vay-cay. The last time I was there was almost seven years ago. Can you imagine that? How terrible! So, I wanted to pick your brains about cool places to go. Nice bars, restaurants, clubs. But nothing too hipster. You know my taste."

"Right. I'll have a think and get back to you."

"Excellent." She was staring at Jade far too keenly.

Bloody hell.

Her head was pounding and her mouth tasted of metal. She didn't need this today.

"Whereabouts did you say you lived when you were over there?"

Jade sighed out a silent breath of acceptance. Nicole was testing her. "I don't think I did say," she replied. "I lived in Williamsburg for the first two years and then moved to Greenwich once I'd established myself a bit more."

"Awesome. I bet it was great living there."

"It was."

"And you worked at Tres Chic the entire time? Until the start of this year. Is that correct?"

Jade folded her arms, teeth grinding together behind her smile. "Yes. The entire time."

"Hmm." Nicole made the sort of confused face a small child might make. "That's strange."

"Why so?"

"Oh, nothing. Forget it. It's me. I'm all over the place right now." She leaned forward and held her hand out; fingers splayed. "Thank you for that. If you could come up with a few suggestions of places to go, that would be wonderful." She rolled her shoulders back. "Must get on."

She spun on her heels and strutted back to her desk, hips swaying aggressively as she went.

Damn it.

Jade had assumed she'd made peace with Nicole, but clearly not. She was up to something, or she thought she knew something. Jade sat back in her chair. Life. It was never easy. Right now, all she wanted to do was go home and curl up on the couch, or her nice warm bed. Screw the insomnia that had been twisting at her nerves ever since she'd agreed to take on the role of Jade Fisher. She wouldn't have any problem falling asleep tonight. It would be bliss. A full eight hours of benign nothingness, with nothing to think about but...

Shit.

She was imagining how nice it would feel to have a soft, heavy duvet wrapped around her when the realisation smacked her in the soul.

Sofia's contact.

They were meeting him this evening. She groaned, wondering if she could back out of it somehow. But even as she thought this, she knew Sofia would never let her. Besides, the guy had important information for them and she needed to know what it was. Even if that meant more work and stress, more anxiety and deceitfulness to get her head around.

Sitting up, she began typing out the first of Rebecca's emails. It was true what they said. There was no rest for the wicked. Or the just. But which of those things she actually was, she was no longer sure.

The lines were getting more blurred as time went on.

28

Sofia was leaning against a tree outside Berkshire Road station when Jade arrived in Hackney Wick that evening. Dressed as she was in a long beige rain mac, and with a wool scarf wrapped around her neck, she certainly looked like an investigative journalist. Albeit a rather cliched version of one. She didn't smile or greet Jade as she got close.

"Come on, we're going to be late," she said, shoving off from the tree

"Is everything all right?" Jade asked, quickening her pace to keep up as Sofia marched off down Felstead Street, before crossing over the busy carriageway to join Trowbridge Road. Her hangover had diminished somewhat but her nerves were frayed.

"Why wouldn't it be?"

"You seem tense. That's all."

Sofia snapped her head around to glare at her. "I am tense. This is an important meeting, Justine. A lot is riding on it."

They walked on in silence for a few minutes, down to the end of the road before taking a right onto Chapman Road.

"How's it been, the last few days?" Sofia asked not turning around.

Jade let out a bitter laugh. She didn't know why. "I had a lunch meeting with Rebecca yesterday. She got so drunk and messy."

"Yeah? Did anything come out?"

"Not really. She was knocking back the wine like she didn't care. We got through two bottles but I was taking it easy, hoping she might get so drunk she let something slip. I was asking her about the past, trying to coax something out of her, but didn't get anywhere. She got really upset at one point and started crying. I had to take her home."

Sofia scoffed. "You sound like you feel sorry for her." When Jade didn't respond she glared at her again. "Fucking hell, J. You do?"

"No, I don't. I hate her for what she did. But...I don't know, Sof. There are still parts of this I'm unsure about. It's not that I feel sorry for her. But maybe I pity her a little. Seb Turner treats her like total shit but she loves him. I get how that feels." She held her hand up to Sofia, instinct telling her she was about to cut in. "Listen, I'm not saying we shouldn't be doing this. What she did to mum was wrong and today I saw a part of her I didn't like. But if we treat her like she's a movie villain without wants and needs and fears of her own, we risk underestimating her."

Sofia stopped and turned fully to face Jade. "What are you saying?

"I don't know! Only that there might be other ways to get what we want from her. I still wonder if we opened up to her, she might—"

"Jesus. You don't get it, do you?" Sofia stepped forward, leading with a sharp finger and prodding it into Jade's chest. "She doesn't deserve your pity. You say we shouldn't vilify her. I'd suggest she already did that herself when she screwed mum over. If she was that bothered about her being involved, she could have made her a silent partner, given her some decent shares at least. But no, it was a quick payout and 'see you later'. Now the money's gone and mum's ill."

Jade held her ground. "I know all this, Sofia. I get it. But I'm the one on the front line—"

"I'm the one caring for mum! Bathing her! Taking her to the toilet three times a day! Don't forget everything I've given up for this family, *Jade*. Don't forget what mum has done for us both. You need to stop getting your head turned by that bitch and focus on what's important."

"I am!"

"Are you?"

Sofia stormed away, leaving Jade standing on the roadside. She gnashed her teeth as an impotent rage burned in her chest. Although Jade appreciated what her sister had given up for her and the family, her constantly being reminded of it wasn't helpful. But this was Sofia all over. Jade had bowed down to her most of her life. It was one of the reasons she'd been so drawn to the job in New York. For once she could stand on her own two feet, away from the long shadow cast by her older sister. When she'd left for America their relationship was the worst it had ever been and the subsequent years apart had healed some of the rifts, but as she watched Sofia strutting away down the street, coat flapping dramatically behind her she couldn't help but feel a twinge of unease. As she followed on behind more troubling thoughts swirled in her head.

Was Sofia driven purely by a need for justice?

Or was it something else?

Despite her intelligence, Sofia had always jumped to conclusions about people, and there was no way spending hours and hours on the internet reading spurious online articles had assuaged the more paranoid and indignant elements of her personality.

Jade caught up with her on the corner and Sofia pointed to a pub across the road, The Blind Beggar.

"That's where we're meeting him," she said, stiffly. "Are you ready?"

Regardless of her doubts, Jade raised her chin. "Absolutely," she said. "Let's do this"

Dustin had arrived before them and was sitting in the back corner of the old-fashioned pub. He nodded in acknowledgement as Jade followed Sofia over to his table.

"I was starting to think you'd stood me up," he muttered.

"Never," Sofia said, wringing her hands together with the cold. "This is my sister, I told you about.

He gave Jade a cursory glance up and down but didn't go to shake her hand. "Charmed, I'm sure."

"And you," she said. "Thank you for meeting with us."

Dustin shrugged but as he caught Sofia's eye his face softened. "No worries. All for a good cause. And nice to see you again, Sofia."

"Do you want another?" she asked, pointing at his glass.

"Go on then."

He looked as if he'd been sitting in the pub all day and exuded a certain type of masculinity that Jade felt uncomfortable around. Perhaps she was being unfair and he was a lovely guy under the grizzly façade, but she was too frazzled to care. She guessed he was in his early forties, but the bags under his eyes and patchy stubble made him look older. He was wearing a dark green misshapen jumper over a cream shirt.

"I'll go to the bar," she said, putting her hand on Sofia's shoulder. "What do you want?"

Her sister shot her a look. "Vodka and soda."

"Dustin? Same again?"

He grinned. "Amstel, I think it is. Thanks."

She headed for the bar. Being early evening and the start of the week there was no one waiting to be served. She ordered the drinks - opting for a vodka and soda herself also, hoping it might help her get over the last vestiges of her hangover – and took them back to the table in two trips, Dustin's pint first and then the vodkas.

When she finally sat down Dustin and Sofia were deep in conversation, discussing mutual friends and old acquaintances. It was clear Dustin had feelings for Sofia, but Jade found something sinister in the way he looked at her. She'd seen that look before. It was as if he knew Sofia would never feel the same way about him and so hated her for it.

Jade sipped at her drink as they talked. She couldn't taste much vodka but it was refreshing. After a few minutes of listening to the two of them reminisce, she kneed Sofia under the table to spur her on. At first, she ignored it but then sat upright and clapped her hands together.

"Gosh, I could talk forever," she said, glancing at Jade and then back to Dustin. "But you said you had important information for us. We're both keen to know what it is."

"I bet you are." Dustin poured the remnants of his first pint down his throat, placing the glass to one side before sliding the fresh drink in front of him. He sat back and smiled lasciviously, relishing the power he held. Under the table, Jade gripped her thighs, nails digging into the flesh above her knees to keep herself calm. If this guy was playing bullshit games they would get up and leave. She'd had enough for one day.

"Come on, mate," Sofia said, speaking over gritted teeth. "Out with it."

Perhaps sensing both women's unease, Dustin held his hands up. "Fine." He leaned forward and lowered his voice. "Does the name Jonathan Samuels mean anything to you?"

Jade looked at Sofia. Sofia shook her head. "No. Should it?"

"I'd say so." He chuckled to himself, still enjoying holding all the cards. "He's the key to all this. He's what you've been looking for."

"How do I find him?" Sofia asked.

"You don't. He's dead." Another chuckle. "But if you uncover the truth *behind* his death, then Rebecca Burton-Webb is finished. Forever."

29

Prickly heat blossomed in Jade's chest as Sofia pointed a finger at her old colleague. "Enough with the theatrics, Dustin. Just tell us who the fuck this guy is and why you think he's so important. I know you're loving this and I appreciate your help. But I need you to tell me what you know. Without the hyperbole and grandstanding."

"Grandstanding? Moi?" Dustin blew air over his lips, making a rasping noise. "Whatever."

"Who is Jonathan Samuels?" Sofia tapped her finger on the table, emphasising each word.

Dustin gave her a toothy grin. "What's this information worth?"

Jesus.

Jade leaned into her sister, letting her know she was there. But Sofia was rigid with anger and didn't need the support.

"Are you fucking serious?" she hissed. "Come on, Dustin. I knew you'd grown disillusioned. But remember what you used to stand for. You were a damn good journalist. You still are. What was it you used to say? The truth is all that matters. Facts. Tell me what you know. Please."

His eyes dropped to the pint glass in front of him. Holding it in both hands he spun it around on the beer mat, thinking. When he looked up his previously smug expression had turned dark and serious.

"Jonathan Samuels was a freelance journalist," he said. "He prided himself on investigating corruption at all levels of society. A piece he wrote in the late eighties, about sitting MPs accepting cash bribes from Saudi investors sparked off his career. The client journalists of Fleet Street hated him but to us fledgling reporters he was a bit of a folk hero."

Sofia had been sipping at her drink but now placed her glass on the table. "What's his link to Burton-Webb?" she asked. "You said before there were rumours of a scandal. Something about the brand not being as eco-friendly as she made out."

Dustin held his hand up to slow her down. "Before I continue, you need to know this comes from a worthy source, but I've not corroborated it. It's almost impossible to find anything written down about what happened, for reasons which will become clear soon enough."

"Yes. Fine. Go on."

Dustin glanced around the room before ducking forward. Jade did the same as he continued.

"As I already mentioned. Samuels had found out Burton-Webb's products and production line were nowhere near as ethical or ecologically friendly as she claimed. But it gets worse. Samuels had been digging around for months and had a source who told him the company had been using slave labour and sweatshops over in Myanmar to keep costs down. Not just that but they were paying off corrupt government officials to keep it all quiet. Samuels was getting his ducks in a row, making sure he had the legal aspects of his article cast iron but from what I can gather, was all ready to spill the beans. Somehow, he got into a charity ball Burton-Webb was attending. My guess is he was after a comment from her. But he never got it. He never left the party alive."

"Shit," Sofia whispered."

"Who told you all this?" Jade asked.

"I can't divulge that." Dustin raised an eyebrow at Sofia before shifting his attention to Jade. "But the person who told me used to work with Samuels. They were friends. Sort of."

"What happened to him?" Sofia asked.

"Poor bastard fell over a balcony and broke his neck," Dustin said. He gulped his beer, allowing the words to sink in. "The official ruling was death by misadventure. Eyewitness reports from the party said he was acting drunk and obnoxious, then wandered out onto the balcony for a cigarette and tripped and fell over the side. But that's bullshit."

"How do you know?" Jade asked.

"Because it is! Because he could take his drink and he was a professional. And also, because there were other eyewitness accounts - early on - that said he'd been arguing with someone out there. No prizes for guessing who."

"You think Rebecca pushed him over the balcony?" Sofia asked. "She's not a big woman. Are you sure?"

"If not her, then someone on her payroll. People don't trip over balconies. Plus, those eyewitnesses that saw him arguing with someone suddenly changed their minds about what they'd seen, and once the inquest happened, no one was talking. It was all covered up." He glanced from sister to sister, eyes widening as he went on. "Rebecca Burton-Webb is the only person who would have gained from that story disappearing. She's the only person who gained from that poor bastard's demise."

"Did your source mention anyone else?" Jade asked. "A business partner of Rebecca's?" She jumped as Sofia elbowed her in the ribs, but she needed to know. "Was it just her involved, do you think? Or were there others?"

Dustin frowned. "I don't know. But if you ask me, Burton-Webb killed Samuels or had him killed, and then paid for a cover-up. She could afford it, even then, and it was a small price to pay to stop him from exposing her dodgy business dealings. If that article had come out, it would have ruined her."

"Thanks, Dustin," Sofia said, picking up her glass. She finished her drink in one swig and waved the glass at him. "This is golden. We've got the bitch."

"Yes," Jade added. "If we tell her we know about Samuels, she'll have to give us what we want. Whatever her involvement in his death, she won't want this story to see the light of day. There's no smoke without fire and all that."

"She's guilty," Sofia said. "I know it.

"But you'll need proof," Dustin said. "Even if just for insurance purposes. If she did kill a man to stop the truth from coming out, you could put yourself in danger without proper clout behind any accusations you throw her way."

He was right, of course, even if it was difficult for Jade to see Rebecca as a cold-hearted murderer. But the way she'd acted this morning – gaslighting Jade, acting as if nothing had happened yesterday - it put a different spin on things.

"What now then?" she asked, addressing her sister.

"We stick to the plan," Sofia said. "There has to be proof somewhere. Bank statements, lawyers' fees, the name of a fixer on her books, even an old diary entry. There's got to be something in one of those safes we can use."

Jade nodded. That was what she was expecting her to say, but it didn't make her feel any less nervous. Because this was it. There was no more messing around. Despite her trepidation and uncertainty, she had to see this through to the end. She reached for her drink and downed it in two gulps. No matter how frightening and horrible things might get, she had to return to Rebecca's house and find some way of opening those safes.

30

That night in bed, Jade tossed and turned for hours. Her mind was busy with half-thoughts and unhelpful ideas that never really took form but left behind a nasty feeling all the same. The name Jonathan Samuels reverberated in her head. The second she'd got inside her flat, before even taking off her coat, she'd opened up her laptop and searched for his name. But except for a brief mention at the bottom of a couple of online articles, citing his work as a reference point, there was nothing. No obituary. No reports of his death. No reference to him ever really being alive. He'd died before the internet went mainstream, but there would have been something online about him. The only explanation she could come up with, sitting alone in her dark living room, the walls illuminated blue from the screen, was that someone had indeed covered up his death. Rebecca. And if she was capable of that, what else was she capable of? This question alone troubled Jade. It troubled her a great deal.

Nevertheless, she must have fallen asleep at some stage because the next thing she knew, the sun was filtering through her window and the birds were chirping their morning song in a nearby tree. She rolled over and grabbed her phone off her bedside table. It was only a few minutes after five.

Bloody hell.

She must have been asleep for two hours at the most.

Closing her eyes, she wondered if she might fall back asleep, but the birdsong irritated her and the spectre of Jonathan Samuels was back and looming heavy on her mind. After a few minutes of trying to sleep, she accepted she was wide awake and, throwing back the covers, she got up and walked to the bathroom. Rubbing at her eyes, she made a beeline for the walk-in shower and twisted it on. Shards of ice water speared at her skin and made her yelp, but she forced herself to remain in there, placing her head under the jets as they turned from cold to lukewarm to hot.

Once showered and dressed, she made herself a slice of brown toast with honey and ate it whilst looking out of the window, washed down with a mug of instant coffee. The next few days were going to take a lot out of her, but she could do this. Or, at least, Jade Fisher could do this, even if Justine Taylor had her doubts. Because Jade Fisher was a badass. She was tough, cool and driven. She did what was needed, regardless of the circumstances. The greater good mattered more than her sensibilities. There was a strong possibility she was going crazy, but it helped to think of herself this way. The Jade persona was more than a cover, it was also a shield.

That's what she told herself, anyway.

Yet, despite her renewed vigour and determination, the clock above the cooker told her it was only 5:45 a.m. There was little point in setting off for work for at least an hour and she worried if she stayed in the flat, her positive outlook might crumble to dust. Grabbing her jacket, bag and phone, she locked up and headed out onto the main street. It was a crisp, autumnal morning, the sort of morning that made you glad to be alive. She walked to the end of her street and then onto Regent's Park Road. The sun had yet to come up and the area was deserted except for a few people walking their dogs. Keeping her head down, she pressed on, crossing over the bridge, and following the road as it curved around to join Primrose Hill Road. From here it was another five minutes of incline before she got up to the bench where she and Sofia had sat with their mum a few years earlier. Coming to this specific spot hadn't been a conscious decision, but now she was here it felt right. The last time they were here, their mum had received her diagnosis and was becoming forgetful, but she still knew her daughters' names and who they were. They could still laugh together. It helped to remember her like this, rather than the husk of a person she'd visited a few days ago.

It was at moments like this – stolen moments in time when she slowed down enough that her thoughts could fully form – that she couldn't quite believe her life had turned out this way. If you'd asked her five years ago where she'd be at thirty-two, she'd have told you she'd be in New York, married to Jacob and with a baby on the way. She'd be happy and content and without a care in the world.

She shook her head as another thought came to her.

What would life have been like for her and Sofia if Rebecca hadn't screwed over their mum?

Margaret Taylor would have been – *should have been* - as rich and influential as Rebecca Burton-Webb. Justine and Sofia would probably have grown up as complete brats because of it, but it would have been the life they were owed. Her mum most of all. From what Sofia had discovered, it sounded as if she'd been integral to the business in the early days. Had she known about the problems with the products and supply chains? Their whole lives she'd been deeply concerned with social and ecological issues, boycotting many brands and companies she didn't think were ethical. Had she found out about the nefarious practices? Was that the reason why Rebecca pushed her out?

She got up from the bench and stretched her arms wide. Below her, the capital was waking up and if she looked over to the East, she could see a sliver of the sun making itself known over Westminster and Mayfair. It was going to be a good day and Jade Fisher was ready to grab it by the horns. No more messing around. No more doubt.

———

Six hours later, however, the determination Jade had experienced up on Primrose Hill had begun to fade. Given the bright day and excellent air quality, she'd had the idea to walk to work, but by the time she'd arrived, she was hot and sweaty and had to go to the bathroom to dab her armpits with balled-up tissue paper. After that, she'd opened up her computer to find thirty-six emails waiting for her, including one from Rebecca, which contained a ten-point list of things she wanted Jade to complete before the day was out. What made it worse was that most of the items on the list were inane, admin-based tasks - ordering new plants for her office, creating an up-to-date list of their French suppliers – things that Rebecca would have jotted down to get the thought out of her head, rather than needing them doing urgently.

Rebecca had mentioned in the email she'd be in the office 'some time' that afternoon. It was now close to one and Jade wondered if she'd have time to nip out for something to eat before Rebecca arrived. The last thing Jade wanted was for her boss to arrive and for her to be away from her desk. It might have been her projecting, but she'd detected a coldness in Rebecca yesterday and in her email. She needed to get back in her good books if she was to stand a chance of finding the proof she needed. Or maybe it was somebody else's good books that she should focus on?

She picked up her phone and was about to sign off her computer when Nicole sidled over to her desk.

"I love what you've done with your hair," she said.

Jade touched her hand to her head. "I've not done anything with it," she replied. "It could probably do with a good brush, to be honest."

"No, no, it looks great. Really grungy. I love it!"

Jade leaned back in her seat. *What did she want?*

"You're looking good," she said. "As always. Nice blouse."

Nicole's smile was full of impatience, the sort of smile one might give an old lady after you spent ten minutes behind her at the check-out whilst she located her purse. "I was wondering if you fancied that drink. Tomorrow night?"

"That would be nice." The truth was, it was the last thing Jade needed, but Nicole still seemed suspicious of her. Anything to get her off her back. "Do you want to check out Soho?"

Nicole's smile turned from impatience to one of pity. "Perhaps not Soho. I know a lovely little bourbon and oyster bar just off Kensington High Street, though. It's perfect for a few drinks and a bit of goss." She let out a high-pitched laugh. It sounded false, but it was the first time Jade had heard her laugh.

"That does sound good. I'll bring a change of outfit."

"Wonderful. See you later."

Nicole sauntered back to her desk and Jade waved as she glanced back with another fake smile. Her soul felt empty with lack of sleep, but tomorrow was a new day and it would be helpful to clear the air with Nicole. Glancing at her phone, she saw it was almost 1:30 p.m. Her stomach rumbled as if to spur her on, as she logged off her computer.

"Jade? Do you have a minute?"

Bugger.

She took a deep breath and forced a smile. "Hi, Marsha. I was about to get some lunch."

Marsha came right up to her desk. "I don't suppose you've got those documents for me?" She grimaced as if she felt awkward about asking, but the hardness around her eyes and the way she was standing told Jade otherwise. "I do need them quite urgently."

"Yes. Sorry. I get it. I've not had time yet to pick them up." She stood, alleviating the power balance between them. In her heels, she was half an inch taller than Marsha. "I will get them, though."

"It is very important, Jade. I know everyone thinks of HR as being pernickety and a pain in the arse, but without us, everything grinds to a halt."

"Oh, God! I know!" she said. "I respect what you do a huge amount and I don't want you to think for one second I'm dismissing your request as being trivial. But you must understand, it's been a whirlwind for me since I got back from New York and started working here. From intern to Rebecca's PA in a week. My head is all over the place. I just haven't had the chance to get them. But I will." She shut up and pulled in another long breath. The words had come out of her fast and garbled, but as she gave Marsha her best smile, she hoped they'd done the trick.

But perhaps not. Marsha shook her head. "If I don't get them soon, I'm going to have to suggest to Rebecca that you don't come in until we have your file up-to-date. We're putting the entire company under threat by having you working here illegally."

Jade pulled a face. "It's not illegal. Is it?"

"It is illegal, Jade. We're breaking the law."

"Oh come off it, Marsha. Who's going to know—"

"I'll know! This is my job. You say you appreciate what I do and then dismiss this as just—"

"Hey! Ladies! What is going on here?"

They both turned to see Rebecca standing at the other side of the desk. She was wearing a long white coat and had a camel Mashu tote bag hanging in the crook of her arm.

Marsha cleared her throat. "I was reminding Jade that I still need to see her passport for her right-to-work documents," she said.

Rebecca tsked, but looked at Jade. "Do you have them?"

"Yes! I was telling Marsha. I'm going to bring them in."

"There we go then," Rebecca said, flicking Marsha a sharp look. "Nothing to worry about." She stared at her until Marsha nodded.

"Fine. Thank you."

Marsha walked away and, once she was out of earshot, Rebecca let out a heavy sigh. "Don't worry about her," she said. "Now then, how are you today?"

"I'm good, thank you."

"Excellent. Can you please book me on the first available flight tomorrow morning to Paris? Business class. I'm needed Thursday until Monday afternoon, so any return flights after six are okay. I have meetings the whole time so I won't be contactable much. You'll probably be glad to get rid of me for a few days, I imagine." She laughed at this last part, back to her warm self.

Jade returned the sentiment. "Not at all! But I'll get on that straight away. Do you want me to book you some accommodation as well?"

Rebecca's mouth twitched. "No, that's not needed."

No. Of course she didn't.

Idiot.

Rebecca owned an apartment in Paris. She knew that.

Along with the one in New York and the villa in the Maldives. While their mum faded away in a two up two down in North London.

"I'll get on it now," Jade repeated. "Shall I email you the booking reference once done?"

"Perfecto." Rebecca beamed. "Now I must make a call. See you later."

Jade nodded and smiled before turning back to her computer screen. Her stomach was rumbling louder than ever, but she had no time to eat. Besides, there was something other than hunger twisting her stomach now.

Rebecca was going to be out of town for a few days.

This was her big chance. It would be a long shot and would take all her mettle and resolve, but she could do it. She had to. Despite the anxiety and dread spreading through her system, it was her only option.

For her family.

For her mum.

31

The next day brought with it more anxiety and unrest. In fact, for most of the day Jade felt as if she might throw up at any second. At some point before Rebecca returned from Paris, she had to get into her house and find proof she'd not only screwed over a sick woman but had killed a man and paid to have it covered up. It was no mean feat, but this wasn't the cause of her nausea as much as the insidious realisation – creeping up from the depths of her awareness and weighing heavily on her shoulders - that to succeed in her plan, she'd have to do something completely against her character, both spiritually and emotionally.

Could she do it?

And if so, what did that make her?

She was staring at her computer screen and contemplating these questions when her phone rang.

Bloody hell.

She scooped it off the desk to see it was Sofia calling. Typical. It was as if she'd been reading Jade's thoughts just now. They did say sisters could have an almost telepathic bond, but Jade didn't believe in ESP or any of that nonsense. More than likely, Sofia had picked up on her concerns the other night.

"Ringing me at work, *again?*" she whispered down the receiver on answering. "Do you not care if I get into trouble?"

"Bit late for that. But it's fine, isn't it?"

Jade glanced around. "Yes. I suppose so."

"Cool. So, you texted me last night, saying you had some good news."

"Did I?" she genuinely didn't remember. But she'd been completely exhausted when she'd got home from work and didn't remember eating or getting undressed.

"Yes. And you said you might have an idea."

"Right. Yeah. I think I might." She turned to look as Lauren burst out laughing at something Thomas had said. Jade couldn't help but smile herself, half-wishing she was still sitting with those guys. At a different time, in a different world, she'd have loved to work at Beautiful You! It was pretty much her dream job. That part wasn't a lie. She shook the thought away and returned to the call, speaking in a low whisper. "As of this morning, Rebecca is in Paris and will be there until Monday."

She paused to let the statement land and for her sister to appreciate what it meant. "That is good news," Sofia said. "And what's your big idea?"

Jade raised her head over the top of her computer. It was just after ten and the office was filling up. Victoria, one of the buyers who sat on the desk closest to Jade, had just arrived. "Hang on," she said, getting up. It was a long walk to the bathroom and she didn't want Nicole to discover her in there a second time. But Rebecca's office was empty. "Two seconds. I'm going somewhere more private."

Lowering the phone, she strode over to the big glass office, hoping the air she gave off was one of confidence and purpose. On the way, she made a show of frowning and nodding to herself, as if remembering she needed to fetch something. Without looking around but with a prickle of goosebumps running down her arms, she opened the door and entered Rebecca's office.

"Okay, I can talk now," she said, lifting the phone to her ear as the heavy door sucked shut behind her.

"Come on then. Spill. Will it work? Is it safe?"

Jade sniffed. "That depends on how you look at it."

She walked over to the bookcase that spanned the back wall and, whilst pretending to search for something, told Sofia what was on her mind.

"How do you feel about that?" Sofia asked once she'd finished.

That was the question, wasn't it?

"Not good, if I'm honest. But what other options do we have?"

"What about the safes? How will you get inside them?"

Jade pulled out an old copy of Vogue from October 2003. It had 'the actress' on the front cover, Rebecca's nemesis. Perhaps not her only one.

"I'm not sure," she replied. "But I've been doing some research on those types of safe. They require you to programme in a six-digit code and my guess is most people would use a date format to fit those parameters. I've started making a list of any dates I can think of that are relevant for Rebecca. I'm hoping one or two of these will work. If they don't, I've no idea what we do. This will all be for nothing. But this is as good as we're going to get."

"I agree."

"I am terrified, though." The phone went silent for a moment, and Jade lifted it from her ear to check they were still connected. "Are you there?"

"Yes. I am. I'm just concerned you're not up to this."

The unease that had been nibbling away at Jade's soul since she realised what she had to do gave way to a rush of indignation.

"Wouldn't you be terrified? Bloody hell, Sofia. You seem to think you're the only one of us who's suffering. I was happy in New York. I had a life, a career. I came back for you and mum. Because I know how important this is. So please don't question my motivation or loyalty. I'm living every day on my wits, and when I think about what I'm about to do, it makes me want to throw up with nerves. But I am going to do it. For us. Okay?"

She spun around, scared that she'd been speaking loud. But it was fine. The room was soundproof and no one on the other side of the glass was looking her way.

"That's good to hear," Sofia said, but there was a curtness to her voice. "Keep me updated."

"Will do." Jade hung up, resisting the urge to fling her phone against the wall.

She took a moment to compose herself before heading for the door and opening it out to the main office.

Bloody hell.

Nicole was standing next to Jade's desk.

What did she want this time?

As Jade walked over, Nicole made a point of looking down at her computer screen, a wry smile playing across her dark red lips.

"I say. Bit of a fan, are we?"

Jade frowned. But as she moved around to see what Nicole was referring to, her heart dropped into her belly.

Shit.

Shitting hell.

With all the stress and distraction, she'd forgotten to lock her screen. A recent browser window was still open and the screen was full of photographs of Seb Turner. Not able to form words, she scanned the string of open tabs along the top of the screen, hoping these wouldn't be as incriminating. But no such luck. It was clear from the visible text the adjoining pages were also Seb-related. Three interviews and two articles, along with his IMDB and Wikipedia entries.

"Oh, shoot," she said, laughing to cover the nerves. "I bet you're thinking I'm a complete psycho stalker, but it's not what you think." She laughed again, this time to buy her some time, whilst she came up with a believable explanation.

Nicole sucked her cheeks in, eyes still on the screen. "He is a bit of a hunk, isn't he?"

"I don't know. Yes. I suppose he is." Jade screwed her eyes up. Come on. Think. "But he's Rebecca's husband, so I don't think about him like that. It's their tenth anniversary coming up. Rebecca has asked me to come up with some gift ideas. That's what this is. I'm researching him in the hope an old interview or article might provide me with some ideas."

She swallowed, not daring to breathe, but pleased with her fast thinking. It sounded feasible enough.

"Doesn't Rebecca want to get him something herself?" Nicole asked, tearing her gaze from the screen at last. "It's a personal thing, no?"

"She'll have the final say. But she is very busy, as you know. And quite stressed, just between me and you." She hoped this was another savvy move on her part. Sharing a little insider gossip should endear Jade to her unyielding colleague

"The life of a PA, hey?" It seemed to do the trick if the brief, high-pitched chuckle from Nicole was any indication.

Jade lowered her head. "You said it."

A silence fell between them. Jade shuffled her feet.

"If I think of anything suitable, I'll let you know," Nicole said. "In my experience, men like Seb Turner are hard to buy for. They have everything they'd ever need on a plate."

"Yes. I suppose you're right," Jade said, sliding a foot towards her chair. "And thank you. I appreciate that. But I should get back to it."

"Of course. We can talk more tomorrow evening."

Shit!

With everything else going on, she'd forgotten all about going for drinks with Nicole on Friday.

She rolled back her shoulders and coughed. "Yes, about Friday. I'm so sorry, Nicole, but I'm going to have to cancel. My friend has just got out of an abusive relationship and I need to help her move house. It's very last minute, but she's got no one else. It has to be before the weekend."

Whoa. That was a good one.

Nicole's perfect eyebrows sloped to a point over her slender nose. "Oh? How awful for her. I hope she's okay. We can rearrange, of course."

"Thank you for understanding." Maybe if Jade had a friend in an abusive relationship, she'd feel bad about using her as an excuse. But she didn't. She didn't have any friends. None except Sofia. Which was why she was unfaltering as she sat and closed the browser window. "I'll have a look in my diary and throw some dates your way. But soon."

"Not a problem," Nicole said. "I'll see you later."

The expression on her face as she turned around sent a shiver down Jade's spine. But screw her. She had nothing.

"Oh, by the way," Nicole said, stopping and glancing back. "It's tin."

Jade startled. "Sorry? What?"

"For a tenth anniversary. It's tin. You know, for your gift ideas." She smiled, but it was far too sweet for it to be genuine.

"Thanks," Jade muttered as Nicole walked back to her desk. "I'll keep that in mind."

32

L ooking for gift ideas for Seb from Rebecca?
    What a lot of crap.
    Nicole sat, drumming her long nails on the desk in front of her as she played back the last five minutes in her mind. She'd known there was something off with Jade Fisher from the start and after Shona at Tres Chic had confirmed it, she'd now experienced it first-hand. What was it she'd said? She wasn't a psycho stalker.

We'll see about that.

The pieces of the puzzle were all coming together, but the bigger picture still eluded Nicole. There were obvious reasons Jade would lie on her resume, such as her not being qualified or experienced enough for the job. But it felt to Nicole like there was more to it than her simply sexing up her resume to get her foot in the door. And if she expected her to believe all that guff just now about her researching Seb Turner so Rebecca could buy him a suitable gift, then the stupid girl needed her head looking at.

No way. Not a chance.

So, was that it? Did she have her heart set on Seb? Is that why she was here? It would explain the lies and secrecy. And Nicole had seen the way Jade had acted when Seb was last in the office, giggling and playing with her hair while they talked, like a pathetic teenager.

Something close to excitement stirred in Nicole's loins. What if something had already happened between the two of them? If they were having an affair behind Rebecca's back, and she could prove it, the new girl would be out on her ear quicker than you could say Coco Chanel.

Finding herself smiling at the thought, Nicole wondered what she might do to make her dream a reality. If she could catch them in an illicit tryst, say - and get photographic evidence - then Rebecca would destroy the traitorous bitch. Factor in that Shona at Tres Chic had never heard of Jade Fisher, and that Jade had obviously provided Marsha with a dodgy reference, and Rebecca would make sure she never worked in this industry again. That would teach her to step on people's toes.

She craned her neck over the banks of desks, seeing Marsha across the other side of the office, beavering away as usual. Nicole sneered at the sight of her. It was like her father used to say, *a lot of activity, but not much action going on with that one.* She was the head of HR. She should have done her job and not let Jade fob her off so easily. But like many people in this office, in this industry, she was frazzled and disorderly and somewhat of a people pleaser.

A lot of activity but not much action...

Nicole folded her arms across her chest and smiled, not having thought about her father for a long time. He'd been a hard taskmaster, especially after her mum had left, and had offered little reward or affection in return, but these days Nicole was glad he'd been that way. She'd had to grow up fast, but in doing so had become strong and independent, able to cope with whatever life threw at her. Indeed, if her father was still alive, she might even have thanked him. He'd made her confident and hard-working. Not like Jade Fisher and her ilk. Those simpering, overly smiley types of people, who seemed to do as little as possible and somehow always came up smelling of roses.

But not anymore. Not her.

Jade Fisher would rue the day she ever walked into this office. She'd regret ever setting eyes on Seb Turner.

A smile spread across Nicole's face as a plan formed. If she caught them at it, she'd ruin them both and be there for Rebecca to help pick up the pieces. Once she'd made herself indispensable and proved how dedicated she was, the PA role would be hers. No question.

She dropped her shoulders and let out a contented sigh. It was all falling into place. Across the office, she could see Jade leaning over her desk, her pretty little face illuminated by the computer screen.

"Helping a friend out tonight, are we?" Nicole whispered. The story sounded believable enough and Jade had almost sold it. But, on reflection, she now suspected it was another lie. She ran her tongue across her teeth, stopping herself short of actually licking her lips. But that's how she felt. Hungry and eager. Like a horny cartoon wolf. Only the object of her desire wasn't Betty Boop, or Bugs Bunny dressed up as a female rabbit. It was revenge. Payback.

Her plans for drinks after work might be scuppered, but she knew exactly what she was going to do instead. She knew Marsha kept hard copies of everyone's personnel files locked in the cabinet next to her desk. She also knew that, for ease, she kept the key to said cabinet in the desk tidy next to her computer. Something told Nicole she might have to work late tonight. Until she was the last one in the office, at least. Jade might yet not have provided Marsha with suitable documentation, but she'd have filled in her new starter paperwork, including her current address. That was all Nicole needed. She sat back and folded her arms. It was only a matter of time before Jade Fisher fucked up. And when that happened, she'd be there to capture the moment for everyone to see.

33

othing looked right. Nothing fitted the way she wanted it to. Jade climbed out of the vintage Valentino dress, the black one she'd bought with her first paycheck from Tres Chic, and flung it on top of the pile of clothes on her bed.

Bugger.

All these outfits and not one of them did the job. But then, maybe it wasn't the clothes. Finding an outfit that would provide her with an all-encompassing feeling of confidence was probably asking too much of some nicely stitched-together material. She slumped on the edge of the bed and sneered at her reflection in the mirror.

Who was she kidding?

She wasn't cut out for this.

Once she was in play tonight, there was no going back. She would return home tomorrow a changed woman. Her reflection offered no answers or advice. But she did notice her hair looked good and that buoyed her a little. Two hundred and seventy-five pounds well spent at a boutique salon in Mayfair for a cut, colour and blow-wave.

She tossed her thick locks over her shoulder and sat up straight, sticking out her breasts and sucking her cheeks in at the same time.

Jade Fisher could do this. Because she had to. Justine Taylor had messed around for too long. She'd been selfish. She'd left her family when they needed her the most. Yes, the job opportunity at Tres Chic had been too good to turn down. But her mum was already becoming forgetful and a part of her knew even then she was running away from her responsibilities. She was young and ambitious and full of passion. She didn't want to watch her poor, beautiful mum fade into a shadow of her former self. Her mum didn't want that either. That was what Justine told herself, at least.

So she'd moved across the world regardless, having only needed the vaguest of blessings from her sister to accept the job and buy herself a one-way ticket to New York. But because of this decision, Sofia had to give up her career. After the money ran out and Sylvia left, one of them had to. It was the least either of them could do after everything mum had done for them. But only one of them did it.

Justine had promised to visit often and told Sofia she'd spend her Christmas and summer vacation back in the UK. But that had lasted exactly one year before the excuses started. She had to work. She'd met a man. She and Jacob were going away together. She'd thrown herself into New York life and hardly given her family a second thought.

But that was then. She was older now and Jacob was gone. Family was what remained when everything else was stripped away from you. No matter how uncomfortable or scared she felt, the next few days had to happen. It was her penance and her duty. Not to mention their only chance of achieving justice.

She got to her feet, ready to go another round with her

outfits when her phone rang. She walked over to the dresser and picked it up. It was Sofia.

She swiped to answer. "Hey."

"Hey. How's it going?" Sofia's voice sounded unusually calm and warm.

"Not bad. I'm looking for something suitable to wear."

"Did you find anything?"

Jade cast her gaze over the mound of clothes on the bed. "Not yet. But I will do."

"You always look good. Don't worry."

"Easy for you to say."

"I see. You're still having second thoughts, then?"

Jade let out a huff. "Something like that."

"I thought you might be. I don't blame you."

Jade detected the smile in Sofia's voice but also the hesitation. She wasn't calling to give her a pep talk.

"What is it?" she asked.

"Can you come over to the house?"

Jade lowered the phone to check the time. "It's almost eight. I was going to get an early night..."

"I know. But this is important. I don't want to say it over the phone. Please, J. Get a taxi and we'll go halves on the fare. Just get here. I need you."

A new prickle of anxiety blossomed in Jade's chest. "Okay. I'll be there as soon as I can."

Sofia opened the front door before Jade had even made her way down the path. She smiled a thin-lipped smile, the sort of smile you might see on a police officer who'd knocked on your door at 3 a.m. or on a surgeon right before they told you they'd done all they could.

Something was wrong.

Very wrong.

"Is it mum?" Jade asked as she got up to the house.

Sofia shook her head and stepped back into the hallway so she could enter. "No. She's fine. She's asleep."

She let Jade enter and then reached around the back of her to shut and bolt the door. "Come through to the kitchen," she said.

Jade followed her down the dark corridor in silence. Sofia's laptop sat open on the kitchen table, alongside an empty cafetière and a chipped mug with the words *World's Best Journalist* printed on the side.

"What's going on, Sof? You're scaring me."

Sofia pulled in a deep breath, holding it in her lungs as she gestured for her to sit. Jade did so, opting for her usual chair in front of the cooker. Sofia sat in front of the laptop. Her eyes were glassy and unblinking. She looked as if she hadn't slept for days.

"What is it?" Jade asked again.

"Okay, here goes," Sofia said, placing her hands, palms down, on the table. "You know how Dad was killed in a car accident when I was three and you were just eighteen months old?"

Jade nodded slowly. "Yes."

Sofia bit her lip. "Fuck. I can't believe I'm saying this, but I don't think that's true. In fact, I'm certain it isn't." Jade sat forward, but Sofia held her hand up to her. She looked down as she continued. "It was something mum said a few days ago. I've been sitting with her every day, asking her questions about the past in the hope some memories from that time are still in there somewhere. I figured the right question might unlock them and they might help."

"Makes sense," Jade said, working on staying present rather than letting her imagination race ahead. "What did mum say?"

"It wasn't much and it was kind of muddled like usual. But she distinctly said something about 'her Clive' and that he shouldn't have done what he did. She said he left us when we needed him most." She chewed on her lip, still not meeting Jade's eye. "At first I didn't think much of it, because it still fits what we knew, right? But her words began to play on my mind and so I started researching it. I don't know why I never did before. I'm wondering now if maybe subconsciously I feared what I might find. It took me a while, but I found the name of an old neighbour of ours. Do you remember her - Emily? We knew her as Mrs Carter. She lived next door to us until you were about six. Nice lady. Used to buy us each a bag of sweets on a Friday."

"I've got vague memories," Jade replied. "Did she wear glasses?"

"Yes and she had big curly hair. Anyway, I found her. On Facebook, of all places. She's in her late seventies now and lives in Eastbourne, but she's still got all her faculties. She gave me her number and I rang her. We were on the phone for about an hour. She remembers us both, she remembers everything." She looked up finally and her eyes were wet.

Jade knew where this was going, but she had to ask. "And she confirmed dad didn't die in a car accident?"

She nodded. "He hung himself in the top bedroom. Where mum is asleep now. Emily said he must have been planning it for a while. It was a Saturday afternoon and Mum had taken us to the playground in Talacre Gardens like she often did."

"He committed suicide."

"He lost his life to suicide."

Jade sat back. "Fuck off, Sofia! Call it what it is for Heaven's sake!"

"It's how you should refer to what he did. 'Committed' implies it was some sort of crime. It's archaic and wrong."

"Fine. Whatever," Jade said. "You've been spending too much time in front of the internet if you ask me."

"Well, I didn't.

Jade glared at her sister. She could sense both of them were on the verge of tears. She looked away. "I'm sorry."

She'd wanted to say more, but it wasn't the time. Plus, she was reacting to the news rather than her sister's use of language. A heady maelstrom of confusion, anger and sadness enveloped her. She took a moment to compose herself before adding, "Poor Dad."

Being still a baby when he died, she had no actual memories of her father. But her mum had told her and Sofia enough stories about him over the years that she felt she knew him. He'd grown up in a rough part of Croydon but was clever and driven and had managed to make something of himself. He'd been studying to be a lawyer when he died. There'd been plenty of photos of him, too. He was a big guy from Irish stock. Their mum always said how he loved his family, playing rugby and drinking whiskey. In that order. In every photo Jade had seen of him, he looked happy, smiling at the camera or joking with whoever he was with. She knew that didn't mean much and people were very good at masking their pain – yet it didn't feel right. For him to take his own life, or whatever the correct term was, it was against who he was.

"Are you certain?" she asked, wiping a tear from her cheek. "Is Mrs Carter certain?"

Sofia nodded. "Mum took us around to her house after she found him. And in the weeks after she was with us a lot, lending a hand, being a shoulder to cry on for Mum."

"Did you ask her about Rebecca?" Jade asked.

"Of course. She said they didn't talk about it much because

Mum was very upset and any mention of her old life only upset her more. But Emily confirmed what we already suspected. She and Rebecca started Beautiful You! then Mum had you and six months later she was gone from the company. Emily thinks the stress of it all was a factor in why Dad died. She said there were lots of fights immediately after mum left work. She could hear them through the walls. So we can add our Dad's death to the list of things Rebecca needs to atone for."

Jade could barely take it all in. "Why did Mum stay here, do you think?" Jade asked. "In the house where...you know...it happened."

"I don't know. She had a support network here. She wasn't well, remember? Maybe she felt close to him here. She's the only one who can answer that question and now she can't. But this only makes me more determined, J. And you know what? This isn't about the money for me anymore. Yes, I want to get Mum the best treatment we can afford, but more than anything I want to destroy Rebecca Burton-Webb. The world needs to know what she did. That woman is a liar and a charlatan, not to mention a murderer. She cares more about profit than people's lives. She left her best friend to wallow in pain and obscurity whilst she swanned around the world, building her empire."

Her voice broke with emotion and she wiped at her eyes. "Sorry, it's just a lot."

"I know. I get it."

Jade stuck out her chin. A few days earlier, Sofia's words might have given her cause her concern, but now they were rousing. They'd awakened something inside of her. Because she was right. Directly or indirectly, Rebecca had destroyed their family. She'd taken away their legacy and screwed her mum over when she needed her the most. It was despicable what she'd done and she had to pay.

Jade reached out for her sister's hand. "It's okay, Sof. We're going to make this right. I'm going to make this right. Whatever I have to do, we'll show the world who Rebecca really is. For Mum. And Dad."

The smile Sofia gave her was full of love. "You can do it," she whispered.

And she was right about that, as well. She could.

Tomorrow night.

She was going in.

34

The Baccarat Club looked to be just the right side of busy as Seb Turner entered through the door held open for him by Lewis, the doorman. Seb thanked him with a wink as he stepped into the warmth of the club. Despite being the start of the weekend, it was still relatively early for The Baccarat's usual clientele and his hope was he'd have a few quiet drinks at the bar before it got busy.

Standing at the top of the steps that led down to the main space, he breathed in the rich smells of wood and leather, of luxury and expense. He went through this short ritual every time he entered The Baccarat Club. His way of reminding himself that, whatever the critics might say, he'd made it. Seb Turner had arrived. The room in front of him was dark but not gloomy, panelled almost entirely in rich mahogany with booths along the right-hand side and a sea of round tables spread across the extensive floor space. Most of the booths were already occupied but in the subtle orange glow cast by the hanging wall lamps, he could see his favourite barstool was free.

Moving slowly and confidently, Seb walked down the steps and over to the bar on the far side of the room. He could sense people watching him but kept his head up and didn't let on. He did pout, however, like he always did in public, knowing the effect made his lips look fuller whilst also tightening the skin on his neck and emphasising his cheekbones. Reaching the bar, he undid the bottom button of his Tom Ford suit jacket - a birthday present from Rebecca – and sat on his stool. He enjoyed sitting here because it was against the wall and he could lean back and get an almost three-sixty view of the venue. But also, propping up the bar in a private member's club, rather than sitting at a table, made him feel both eminent and louche. In his head, he was part of a long lineage of hard-drinking hellraiser actors that started with Burton and took in Reed, Harris and O'Toole. Getting further into character, conscious of every movement, he rested one elbow elegantly on the bar top before raising a finger to get the barman's attention.

"A Yamazaki, double," he said as the neatly dressed young man ventured over.

"Very good, sir. Ice?"

"Two chunks." He nodded him away and turned back to get a better look at the other clientele. Mainly, they were men around his age, city boys from the looks of them. You could just tell. But occupying two of the booths were separate groups of women. One group, the ones nearest the bar, were a little older than him and dressed in smart skirts and blouses, no doubt having come here straight from work. The other group, however, wore tight dresses and had their hair and faces made up for a night out. Despite the laid-back demeanour he was projecting he couldn't help but grin to himself. A few whiskies and maybe he'd saunter past their table. One of them was bound to recognise him. Once that happened, it was usually a foregone conclusion that he'd be having some fun later. Although, he couldn't help noticing one of the older women from group one kept glancing over at him. And he did have somewhat of a penchant for the older lady.

"Here we are, sir. Do you want to pay now or...?"

"No. Start me a tab." He spun back around to face the barman and reached into his jacket pocket for his wallet. Flipping it open, he slid out his Amex Centurion card, handing it over in such a way that anyone looking this way would notice it.

"Big spender, hey?"

"That's me." Seb turned towards the source of the voice, at the same time tilting his mouth into the crooked half-smile that had always worked so well for him. A half smile, half smirk. But when he saw the woman sitting on the stool next to him, his façade dropped. "Jade! What are you doing here?"

It wasn't a line. It genuinely surprised him to see her. The Baccarat Club was an exclusive establishment, frequented mainly by media types and bankers. Jade might be accepted for membership now she was working for Rebecca but the last time he checked, the waiting list was two years.

She arched an eyebrow. "I have my ways."

"Is that so?" he replied, slipping effortlessly back into his sophisticated barfly persona. "It's good to see you. Do you come here often?"

Jade gave him a look as if to say 'that's original', but he ignored it and held her gaze.

"It's my first time. But I've always wanted to try this place. And I was in the area. So, here I am."

"Did you know I was a member here?" he asked, before realising. "Ah, that's right. I was coming here when I dropped you off that time."

"Oh? Was that this club? I wasn't really paying attention."

Seb narrowed his eyes, trying to read her expression. She was here for him, wasn't she? She had to be. A warm feeling ran up the backs of his thighs into his groin and he felt his entire body swell with lusty conceit.

"Can I buy you a drink?" he said.

"I thought you'd never ask."

He hailed the barman over. "Can the lady have a..." He held his hand out for Jade to continue.

"A dry Martini, please. With an olive."

As the barman bowed his head and scuttled away to prepare the cocktail, Seb picked up his glass of Japanese whisky and leaned back against the wall to take her in. She was wearing a metallic grey mini dress with dark tights that highlighted her slender but shapely legs, topped off with a pair of ball-breaking black heels. Nice. He'd always appreciated women's clothes, even before he met Rebecca, but he appreciated what was in them most of all. Jade looked more than fine this evening. She looked ravishing. Her thick wavy hair had been pinned up to expose the tanned skin of her neck and with her smoky eyes and red lips, she'd nailed it in terms of his ideal look for a woman.

"You look amazing,' he said, leaning in. "Are you going somewhere later?"

She shrugged. "Not especially. It's Friday night and I'm young, free and single. I'll see where the universe takes me."

"Love it!" he said, wagging a finger at her. "Same here. Well, sort of young, sort of free..."

Jade's red lips opened into a perfect 'O', but he could tell she was only playing shocked. Flirting. "You're terrible," she said. "What would Rebecca do if she knew you were telling women in bars you were available?"

"Rebecca knows what I'm like," he said. "She doesn't mind as long as I'm careful and discreet about it,' he lied.

The barman brought Jade's drink over, cutting short that conversation. Probably for the best. She was Rebecca's PA, after all. But, hell, what he wouldn't give.

"Put it on my tab," he told the barman, waiting until he walked off before leaning in closer to Jade. "What are you really doing here?" he asked.

She'd been taking a sip of her Martini and almost spat it out at the question. "I told you," she said, laughing. "I was in the area."

"Yes, sure." He flicked up his eyebrows and grinned. "And how is life treating you now that you're back in London? It's got to be a bit of a shock to the system."

"Yes and no. This is my home. And I love working at Beautiful You!"

"That's great to hear. And what else do you like to do? I know nothing about you. What do you do in your spare time, for instance?" It was a lame and unimaginative question, but he wanted to move the conversation away from work and Rebecca.

"I like going out dancing," Jade said, in answer to his question. "I like reading, watching movies, shopping. The usual stuff."

Seb sipped his drink, watching Jade as her eyes flitted around the room, taking the place in. She was so attractive. He had to have her. So what if she was Rebecca's assistant? If they did fuck, she wouldn't tell anyone. In fact, her working for Rebecca was almost the perfect insurance. It was in her best interests to stay quiet.

"What movies do you like?" he asked.

Jade smiled at him over the top of her glass. "Oh, you know, any that have this handsome actor in them. Seb Turner, I think he's called."

It was all he could do to stop himself from grinning like a randy simpleton. "Is that so?" he purred.

"Yeah. He's all right."

They both drank, eyes fixed on one another. Seb couldn't

stop smiling. It was clear where this one's fidelities lay, and it wasn't with his wife.

When he'd first met Rebecca, she was hot and feisty - and being ten years his senior and at that 'special' age for a woman - was almost as randy as him. But, as the years passed, the stress and strain of being Rebecca Burton-Webb had begun to show on her face and body. She was still an attractive woman, but she wasn't the person he'd married and for the last few years, she'd seemed uninterested in sex or even closeness. The way he saw it, it was her fault he was like this. She didn't appreciate him.

He caught Jade's eye and winked, sending her turning away as her cheeks flushed. She recrossed her legs and her already short dress rode up higher on her thigh.

Lovely stuff.

It was game on. Without a shadow of a doubt. If she'd come here specifically with the hope of bumping into him, then there was nothing to worry about. She clearly didn't care about Rebecca as much as she'd made out.

In fact...

He smiled and took another sip of whisky, his mind suddenly racing with possibilities and ideas. Could she help him? Would she go for it? It would take some manipulation on his part, but his mother had always said he could charm the pants off anyone. With his baby blues and chiselled features, he could sell ice to the Eskimos. It was all just a matter of waiting for the right moment. But he had time. With Rebecca away, he had all weekend.

His gaze lingered on Jade's slender neck and perfect jawline. What a weekend it was turning out to be.

35

J ade turned and held Seb's gaze. The night was going
better than she'd imagined, but that brought a deeper
sense of uncertainty. She smiled regardless, giving the
man sitting next to her the requisite amount of eye contact,
letting him know she was interested in him, without being too
forward. It was a fine line, but with Seb Turner she didn't think
it mattered. He didn't strike her as the type of man to be put off
by much. She could probably pounce on him, straddle him right
here at the bar, and he'd have gone for it. Still, it was important
to remain focused, which was why she was only sipping at her
Martini and would be careful not to drink too much, despite the
unease still bubbling inside of her.

Relax, she told herself.

Try to enjoy it.

Luckily, sitting here now in the decadent surroundings of
the private members' club, warm and with an ice-cold Martini
in front of her, she couldn't help but feel a little proud of herself.
If tonight went to plan – and it was certainly looking like it
would – then her role would be complete. She could go back to
being Justine Taylor once again. Although, after everything that

had happened, who that person was was another question altogether.

Her morning had been wrought with threat and annoyance. She'd sensed Nicole watching her from the moment she arrived at the Beautiful You! offices and her narrowed-eyed stares hadn't let up for most of the day. Jade couldn't tell whether she was merely pissed off that she'd cancelled their date or if there was more to it. But she told herself it was just her paranoia getting the better of her. With Rebecca out of the country and in meetings for most of the day, she'd had a relatively unencumbered day work-wise but that had only meant she had eight long hours to contemplate what she had to do this evening. After everything she now knew, she was adamant she'd go through with the plan. But it didn't stop her from feeling sick with anxiety.

Those eight distraction-less hours had also provided ample time to think about her father. She'd always thought he'd died in a car accident. That was what her mum had told her when she'd been old enough to understand. She didn't remember him, but she loved the memory of him. People had told her how he loved his family more than anything in the world. It made her sick with sadness to think how bad things must have got for him to do what he did. And that was why she was here tonight, ready to do whatever was required of her to avenge him and her family.

So, she laughed along, rolling her eyes playfully at Seb as he told stories of his acting days.

"I didn't think you were like this," she lied.

"Like what?"

She didn't take her eyes off his. "I don't know, so easy to talk to. So much fun. I mean, I knew you were handsome and charming, but most actors can be very full of themselves. I don't think you are." She drained her glass, letting the olive slip into her mouth and rolling it around on her tongue. It was a tacky move but had the desired effect. Seb's lascivious smile widened.

"I am a very sensitive guy, truth be told," he said. "Most people don't realise that about me."

"And smart too."

He frowned. "Don't I come across as smart?"

"Yes. You do. Sorry, I didn't mean that. But someone so handsome and talented - and intelligent too - it's almost like... *come on, mate, it's not fair to the rest of us.*"

He cocked his head back and laughed. "I think you're doing okay in the looks and brains department. But you're quite correct. People misjudge me." As he said this, she detected a glimmer of something unpleasant and troubling behind his eyes. She looked away and blinked.

Ignore it.

You've enough to deal with this evening.

"I'm still curious about how you got in here," Seb said. "Lewis, on the door, is a friend of mine. I've never known him to let anyone in without membership, no matter how clever or good-looking they are."

Jade flashed her eyes at him. "I told you already. I have my ways." The truth was Sofia had been a member of The Baccarat Club since her days writing for The Times and Jade had used her pass. But she couldn't tell him that.

"I see. Still playing the dark and mysterious card. I like it." He smirked. "I wondered whether you'd commandeered Rebeca's membership card while she was out of town."

Jade opened her mouth wide in shock. It was a put-on expression, but she also wanted him to know the comment had upset her. "I would never do that."

"Really? I would. I wouldn't have blamed you."

"Is that so?" She looked away and ran her finger around the rim of her empty glass. The energy between them was shifting, and not for the better. "I thought we weren't talking about Rebecca tonight." As she spoke, she looked back at him with what she hoped was a smouldering look.

"Rebecca who?" he said.

She wrinkled her nose at him; the heat rising once again. "Why don't you tell me more about you? I know Seb Turner, the famous actor, the celebrity. But I want to know the real Seb."

"Anything specific?" he asked, leaning in a little more.

"Did you always want to be an actor?"

He dipped his head, still gazing into her eyes. "I think so. My mum died when I was nine and I went a bit off the rails. I fell out with all my friends. I wasn't interested in school. But I had this one drama teacher, Miss Rusby, who took me under her wing. She was as strict as all hell, but I needed that. She taught me how to channel all my rage and emotion into my craft."

"I'm sorry about your mum," she said. "My dad died when I was a baby. And my mum, she's dead too now."

"Yeah. It's rather shitty losing a parent so young, isn't it?"

"Yes." She reached out her hand and placed it on top of his. "It is."

He tilted his head to one side. "It's funny. My therapist thinks my mum dying at an impressionable age explains why I'm drawn to older women." He shook his head and laughed. "Sorry. That was probably too much information."

"No. It's fine." She kept her hand on his. Leaning in, she dropped her voice to a low purr. "I am a little upset you prefer older women, though."

His eyes shot up to meet hers. "That was in my younger days," he replied, not missing a beat. "I'm not like that anymore. I like all women."

"All women?" she repeated, moving closer. "Is that so?"

"Well, not all women."

233

"Oh?"

They were just inches apart now, their eyes darting to each other's lips as they spoke. Words were just sounds, conduits to the inevitable. It felt like one of those moments that Jade had always felt was far too cliched when they happened in Hollywood movies. But maybe not. She had to concentrate hard on not dropping out of the moment. Because this was it, her plan playing out in real-time.

"What sort of women do you like?" she whispered.

"Beautiful ones. Clever ones."

Jade closed her eyes as their lips touched. Seb's hand grabbed the back of her head and pulled her towards him. They kissed forcefully and passionately with open mouths and pounding hearts, their tongues winding together in a war dance as old as time.

"Do you want to get out of here?" he growled, pulling away slightly but resting his forehead on hers.

"Absolutely," she replied.

"I know this wonderful boutique hotel in Knightsbridge. We can—"

"No!" Jade said. "Let's go to your place."

"My place?" Seb pulled back some more. "But that's— really? You want to go there?"

She nodded. "Don't treat me like one of your other women, Seb. I don't want to be taken to a hotel, like some cheap whore." She lowered her head, gazing up at him through her eyelashes. "Let's go to your place. She's not back until Monday. I promise you won't regret it."

Seb hesitated for all of three seconds. He couldn't argue with the look she'd given him.

"Okay," he said. "Let's go."

36

The sex was good. Jade couldn't deny that. But she'd expected nothing less from Seb Turner. There had even been moments over the last two hours when she'd actively enjoyed the experience. Seb was a passionate and generous lover and as she lay back and let him take control, she found a release for all the anxiety and tension she'd been carrying with her.

They did it three times and once it was finally over; she lay spent and breathless, staring up at the ceiling and fighting the pull of post-coital sleep with every bit of energy she had left. Which wasn't a lot. She waited, pensive and silent, trying to make sense of what had just happened, until she was certain Seb had fallen into a deep sleep. The weird thing was, she didn't feel too bad about what she'd just done. Maybe it was because she was in control. Or maybe she'd lost her soul a long time ago.

She guessed it was now around half an hour since Seb had returned from the bathroom and climbed into bed beside her, giving her ass a firm squeeze before nuzzling his face into her neck and falling asleep. They were in the largest of Rebecca and Seb's guest bedrooms. Jade's insistence on coming back to the house notwithstanding, she'd insisted they do the deed here rather than in the marital bed and Seb had promptly agreed. He might have been an ego-driven lothario with dubious principles, but he drew the line somewhere. And Jade needed that top bedroom unoccupied.

Keeping one eye on Seb's naked form, she leaned over the side of the bed and grabbed up her handbag from where she'd flung it. Unbuckling the clasp, she reached inside for her phone, swiping it open to see it was 3.06 a.m. Time for Jade Fisher to go to work. Turning on the torch app, she peeled off the duvet cover and sat up, knocking her handbag onto the floor as she did.

Shit.

She froze, her face clenched in a grimace. Slowly, she turned, unblinking eyes exploring Seb's face for signs that she'd woken him. But she needn't have worried. He was sound asleep and snoring softly. In the moonlight filtering through a crack in the blackout blinds, he looked very handsome and, dare she think it, almost innocent lying there.

Did he know about Rebecca's past?

Did he know what she'd done?

She doubted it. Rebecca had completely erased that part of her story. It didn't fit her narrative. She was the eco-friendly fashion giant. The ethical influencer. Add ruining her best friend's life, and the very real possibility she was a murderer, to that bio and suddenly Rebecca Burton-Webb was a very different person from the one she purported to be.

But wasn't everyone?

Jade swung her legs onto the thick carpet and eased herself off the bed. As she did, Seb groaned and mumbled something unintelligible.

"Shh," she whispered, reaching out and placing her hand on his. "I'm here. Go to sleep." She remained like that for a few seconds, not daring to move away until she was certain he'd succumbed once again to slumber. Satisfied he wouldn't wake, she shone the torch around the room, locating her black lace panties in the far corner and her bra and cocktail dress lying in a heap at the end of the bed

Moving with stealth, she scooped up her clothes and tiptoed out of the room onto the expansive first-floor landing. Dashing for the bathroom, she switched on the light and closed the door silently behind her before getting dressed. A deep wash basin stood in front of an enormous mirror that spanned the back wall. Turning on the cold tap, she scooped a palmful of water into her mouth and gulped it down. She was feeling dehydrated and a little light-headed and needed to rouse herself. She'd been careful with her alcohol consumption this evening, only having the one Martini in the club and hardly touching the Chablis Seb had opened after their first round of sex, but it was getting late and she was tired.

Looking up at her reflection, she wondered if tonight would be the last time she would ever call herself Jade. If things went according to plan, that person would no longer be required. Would she miss her? She was certainly stronger and more ballsy than Justine Taylor.

Turning from the mirror, she left the bathroom and walked across the landing towards the staircase she knew led up to Rebecca's master bedroom. Leaning into the handrail, letting it take her weight in case a creaky step gave her away, she made her way up. Once there, she flicked on the light and exhaled the long breath she'd been holding in her chest since beginning her ascent.

Rebecca's bedroom looked as it had when she was here a few days earlier, only without the plethora of expensive outfits strewn around. Not wasting any time, she strode over to the middle wardrobe and carefully slid open the heavy wooden door, parting the clothes to reveal the three metal safes. They stood in front of her like three stocky security guards, indifferent and unyielding. Kneeling in front of the first one, she tapped her finger on the touchpad, tensing as the screen awakened and let out a high-pitched beep.

It was fine. Seb was fast asleep on the next floor. There was no way would he have heard anything.

She went to her phone and opened up the notes app. A list of dates and possible number combinations flashed up on the screen as she tapped the top entry. She'd gone deep in her research. The first lot of numbers were the birth dates of every person Rebecca had ever been close to, then twenty-six date combinations that related to important events for both Rebecca personally and Beautiful You! Knowing Rebecca was also interested in numerology Jade had also come up with a list of numbers that related to wealth, success and happiness, as well as ones that were supposed to offer protection. The last lot of numbers on her list were alphanumeric combinations of pertinent six-letter words she'd transposed into numbers, A being 1, B-2, etc. Amongst others were 'Chanel', 'design', 'Lauren', 'Jacobs' and "RBWBYI' which stood for 'Rebecca Burton-Webb Beautiful You! Incorporated'. It was a long shot, but anything was worth a try.

There were around sixty number combinations in total and her hope was one of them might unlock at least one safe. With adrenaline surging through her veins, she typed the first set of numbers into the keypad. As she hit the last digit, a red light came on and a low and disgruntled buzzing noise sounded.

Not a problem.

She wasn't expecting it to be that easy.

Shifting over to the next safe, she tried the same combination and got the same result. Undeterred, she pressed on, working systematically down her list, trying each number combination in all three safes before moving on to the next one.

It took longer than she'd expected and with each unsuccessful attempt, she grew a little less confident and a little more perturbed.

What if none of the numbers worked?

What then?

There was the office down on the second floor but there were so many box files and folders fighting for space down there, without knowing where to look, it could take her hours to find anything. If there was anything of worth down there at all.

No. If there was proof in the house of Rebecca's crimes, then it would be in one of these safes. She ran her finger down the screen of her phone, finding the next number and shuffling back over to the first safe. She typed it in and was instinctively moving over to the middle safe when a green light flashed on the keypad and the lock released.

Shit.

She'd done it.

Glancing down the list of numbers she saw it was the date that Rebecca had first registered Beautiful You! as a limited company – the first of May nineteen-ninety-one. From her research, Jade also knew it was the first time Rebecca was listed as the sole director. It must have been one of the first things she did after getting rid of her mum. The fact Rebecca had used the date of this callous act of self-interest as the combination to the safe told Jade she was doing the right thing.

With her heart pounding, she pulled open the safe door.

"Jade? What the fuck are you doing?"

Shit!

She shot a look over her shoulder to see Seb standing at the top of the stairs. He was naked except for a pair of white boxers and his perfect eyebrows hung heavy with confusion.

Bloody hell.

She'd been so engrossed in what she was doing, she mustn't

have heard him coming up the stairs. Either that or he'd crept up without making a sound.

"Seb, hey," she gasped, getting to her feet. "This isn't what it looks like."

"Really?" He stepped forward, his confused expression morphing into something approaching rage. "Because it looks to me like you're breaking into Rebecca's safe."

"No. I mean, yes. I mean... Shit! I'm not trying to steal anything. Please, Seb, let me explain."

"Fair enough," he said. "You've got exactly two minutes to tell me what the fuck is going on before I call the police."

Jade held her hands up, suddenly feeling more exposed than she had done the entire evening. "Don't call the police. Please. I swear to you I'm not a bad person."

Seb's full lips twisted into a cruel sneer and he tsked angrily. "I don't care what sort of person you are. What are you doing in here? And how the hell did you get that thing open?"

Jade kept her hands raised, but Seb's change in tone confused her. Now he sounded riled rather than enraged. "I tried a few dates of interest. The one that worked was when Beautiful You! was first registered as a company."

Seb scoffed bitterly. "Bugger. Should have known."

"You've tried to open them?"

"It's my house as well as hers," he said, walking over to Jade. "And you've still not told me what the hell's going on. What are you looking for? What's in there?"

Jade swallowed. "Do you not know?"

Seb shook his head, before leaning around the side of her and squinting into the safe. "She's always been so fucking secretive," he said. "She said it was just boring legal documents,

240

but I never really believed her. Looks like she was telling the truth."

Jade risked a glance behind her. Inside the safe were two shelves piled high with files and folders and old manila envelopes. There was so much paper crammed together it was impossible to see what anything was. She puffed her cheeks out, suddenly feeling empty and lost. Even if Seb hadn't discovered her, it would be like looking for a needle in a haystack.

"That's a lot of paper," she whispered.

"What are you looking for in there?" Seb growled. "Because I still don't feel you've provided me with any good reason I shouldn't call the police."

"Fine. Call them," Jade told him, buoyed by a realisation. "But if you do that, Rebecca will know I was here tonight. She'll know what we did. What you did. Last night you said she doesn't mind what you do as long as you're safe and discreet, but I don't believe a word of it. I know it breaks her heart to think about what you get up to behind her back. I'd say having it shoved in her face would be the last straw. And with her PA too." She was thinking fast, saying anything she could think of to ease the situation. "Rebecca loves you, Seb. But she won't lie down and let you walk all over her. If this gets out, she'll protect her status over her heart. Do you want to risk losing everything?"

Seb waved his finger in her face, but the rigidity of his jaw and the hatred in his eyes had diminished since he'd burst into the room minutes earlier. "You're a devious bitch," he sneered at her. "But I like your style. You've got balls. So fair enough, I won't call the police. But I still need you to tell me what's going on. Right now."

There was something in the way he was staring at her that made Jade incredibly uncomfortable. He was no longer exuding sexual desire or even rage. There was something more sinister behind his eyes. She could almost see the cogs turning as he stepped back and rubbed at his chin with the side of his thumb.

"Please don't hurt me," she whimpered. "I'm so sorry..."

"Fuck me, I just realised," Seb said, huffing out a bitter laugh. "You used me. You knew where I was going to be and you came in all legs and smiles. I get why you were so desperate to come to the house. You slept with me so you could get up here. Jesus. What is in those safes?"

An icy shiver ran down Jade's back. The man in front of her was like a different person from the one she'd been flirting with all evening. Her guts were telling her to run, but her legs weren't listening. She sniffed as a wave of emotion shuddered through her.

"Don't you fucking dare," Seb snarled. "Tears do nothing for me. Now spill."

Jade glanced at the open stairwell behind him. Could she make it out of here without him catching her? Maybe. But if so, what then?

"Okay," she said, gesturing over to the lounge area at the far side of the room. "Can we sit down? And I'll tell you everything."

Once sitting, on opposite ends of the plush velvet couch, it took Jade less than five minutes to relay to Seb everything she knew about Rebecca and her mum and what she was looking for in the safes. Initially, she wasn't sure if it was a good idea to tell him everything, but at this stage, there was little point in holding back. The plan was dead. She'd failed. At least if she made Seb understand why she'd done what she'd done, he might go easy on her.

She told him everything, her real name, about her mum and

dad and Sofia. About how they'd initially planned on blackmailing Rebecca before discovering she had a secret more scandalous than they'd ever imagined.

"Bloody hell," Seb exclaimed, once she'd finished. "You really think Rebecca pushed that journalist over the balcony?"

Jade nodded. It was rather disconcerting talking to Seb whilst he was sitting in his underwear, but she remained stoic. "If she didn't, one of her people did. And either way, she was behind the cover-up. She was ruthless back then. She got rid of anyone standing in her way. Including my mum, her supposed best friend. You see, that's why I did this. It's why I have to get inside those safes. We figured there had to be something in one of them that linked Rebecca to Jonathan Samuel's death or to the people who cleaned up the mess afterwards. Follow the money. That's what they always say in the movies, isn't it?"

Jade had sort of hoped the reference might appease the famous actor, but from the harsh look he gave her, that was wishful thinking. He didn't speak for what seemed like forever. When he did his voice was cold and without emotion.

"What would you do with this evidence," he asked, "if you found it?"

Jade folded her arms across her chest. "I don't want to say."

"You should. I might be able to help."

"What do you mean?"

Seb sniffed. "If Rebecca's done what you say she has, then she deserves it. And the rest." As he spoke, he stared off into the middle distance.

"Do you love Rebecca?" Jade asked him. When he didn't answer, she changed the question. "Did you ever love her?"

That snapped him from his thoughts. But where she'd expected him to appear reticent to answer, he seemed to find the question amusing. "Once," he said with a sly smirk. "Maybe. A long time ago."

"But not anymore?"

His smirk grew wider. "I know you're the one using me, darling. But I did just fuck your brains out, three times. Do you think I'd have done that if I loved my wife?"

"I don't know." A rush of shame made her drop her gaze. It only made Seb scoff louder and more forcefully.

"Oh, come off it. Regardless of your intention, you enjoyed it. No one is that good an actress, Jade. Or whatever your name is."

"Jade is fine. But I don't get it. What are you saying?"

"I'm saying I can help you. But first, I want to know what you plan to do."

Jade sat upright. "I'm not sure. Initially, we wanted evidence that Rebecca made my mum sign over her half of the business when she was ill and not thinking right. We figured we'd force Rebecca's hand, get her to pay us off to keep quiet. We need the money for my mum's care, plus there's a place in America that has developed a new drug—"

"Yes, yes, whatever," Seb cut in. "Get to the point. What are you going to do if we find proof she was involved in this guy's death?"

Jade swallowed. "I was coming to that. You see, since we found out about Jonathan Samuels' death, I've felt conflicted. My sister still wants us to get what we're owed from Rebecca and I told her we'd do it her way. But I'm torn. I wonder if we should expose her. Show the world what she did."

"I see. But to do that means you'll probably ruin her and the market share in Beautiful You! to boot."

"Possibly."

"Yeah, I prefer the first idea."

"What do you mean?"

"I mean, you're not the only one who wants what's rightfully theirs. Ten years I've given that woman, and for what? She treats me like a child. She doesn't respect me. Most of the time, I feel like I'm just another accessory for her. A nice-looking appendage." He shook his head. "Ten years. Ten fucking years. But she's clever, I'll give her that. She made me sign a prenup before we got married, the crafty cow. I didn't understand what it was at the time. I was young and eager. And like I say, I did sort of love her back then. So, I signed it. But as it currently stands, I have to stay with her until she dies or I won't get a penny of her fortune. I've been waiting down the clock for what seems like forever, hoping she might drop dead. But she's still going strong. I was working on her, trying to get her to give me power of attorney for her estate. But she wasn't buying it."

Jade drew in a deep breath as she considered the extent of what Seb was telling her. "And you still won't get anything if we expose her."

"Exactly. But I know Rebecca. If you believe there's evidence that she killed this guy, she'll do anything to keep it quiet. Her brand and her public persona are everything to her. If we stick to your original plan and blackmail her, we'll both get what we want."

"Yeah. I get it but—"

"Do you, Jade?" He leaned forward. "Do you get it? Because I'm not asking you. I'm telling you. This is the way we play it. Otherwise, I call the police and you get nothing."

"Neither do you."

"Maybe. Maybe not." He pouted. "What do you say?"

What could she say? He had her.

"Fine. We play it your way. But without evidence, this is all irrelevant. Let's find what we need and we can discuss the details later."

Seb arched an eyebrow. "We've plenty of time. Rebecca isn't back for two days.. Why don't we go back to bed and we can start afresh in the morning? I don't know about you, but I'm pooped."

Jade raised her head. "Come on, Seb. We need to do this. Now."

"Ugh." He huffed out a dramatic sigh and sprang to his feet. "Fine. Let me put some clothes on and we'll start looking."

37

Whilst Seb got dressed, Jade made a start on the first safe. She removed all the files and folders from off the shelves and placed them on the carpet in ten piles. Each one was at least four inches high, and it would take them hours to sift through everything. She was unsure if there was anything of merit here, but as she flicked through the first pile - seeing invoices, receipts, typed notes, minutes of business meetings and even printed-out email correspondence – a renewed confidence surged through her. Rebecca was indeed as meticulous, bordering on pernickety, as she'd hoped. There had to be some damning evidence in here. Otherwise, why invest in three safes that your husband didn't even know the combinations for?

Although that too had been a savvy move on Rebecca's part, it seemed. Jade had always suspected Seb Turner to be untrustworthy and selfish but hadn't realised until now how narcissistic and treacherous he was. A niggling voice in her head told her to be wary of him, but for now, she had little choice but to work with him.

"Wow. Very methodical." She looked around as he entered

the room. He was wearing dark grey jogging bottoms and a black t-shirt and carried a steaming mug in each hand. He held them up. "Strong coffee. To keep us going."

Jade took the offered mug, nodding in appreciation and taking a sip. He wasn't kidding about the strong part; it was thick and bitter and rather unpleasant. But he also wasn't kidding about them needing it. Dawn was making itself known through the glass patio doors. The new day's sun, starting its ascent over the rooftops of Chelsea.

Seb stood over her, sipping his coffee and casting his eye over the stacks of paper. "There's a lot to get through."

"Indeed."

Jade coughed and pulled her shoulders back, trying to stay calm, telling herself there was nothing to worry about. But, with his cards now on the table the affable and charming Seb Turner had vanished. Taking his place was someone much colder and mean-spirited. It felt as if he'd got what he wanted from her and now didn't care what she thought of him.

"Have you found anything?" he asked.

"Not yet." She shifted around, walking on her knees to give him space. "We're looking for bank statements or documents dated around August ninety-one. Or a contract or anything that mentions Margaret Taylor. That's my mum."

She looked up at Seb, trying to work him out as he rubbed at the back of his neck. His expression remained stony and his eyes dead. But the muscles around his temples and his jaw were twitching, highlighted in the shadows cast by the stark spotlight above his head. He was thinking hard about something.

"It looks as if she's kept everything," he said. "She usually does. Every bloody receipt. Every invoice. I can't enjoy a meal without her getting proof of what I had for dessert. You'll probably find paperwork for my nose job somewhere."

"That's what I'm hoping," Jade said. "That she's kept

everything. Not your corrective surgery. It looks good, by the way. You'd never tell."

She smiled. Seb didn't.

Turning her attention back to the contents of the safe, she flipped open a beige dog-eared folder and pulled out the stack of papers from inside. As Seb knelt opposite and picked up a file of his own, she examined each document, scan-reading each piece front and back, and then placing it in a new pile to one side. It took about a minute or two per document depending on the amount of text and detail contained within, and there were at least two or three thousand documents in front of her. A full day's work. At least.

For the next hour, they searched through the piles of documents in relative silence. The only sound in the room came from the heating system turning itself on and the odd sneer and tut from Seb as he shook his head at what he was reading.

"Do you have access to the other safes?" he asked after another half hour had passed by.

Jade looked up from the printed emails she was clutching - a lengthy thread of correspondence between Rebecca and a supplier in Germany.

"I'm not sure. I've got a list of possible combinations. I thought we could work our way through this one first and then..."

"Do it now," Seb said. "Open the other safes."

Jade lowered the papers to look at him. "We don't know if any of the other number combinations work. Don't you think we should—"

"Now." He glared at her, solemn and unblinking. "Do it now."

"Okay."

She picked up her phone and got to her feet. Sensing Seb watching her, she walked back to the wardrobe and tapped out the same code that had opened the first safe, into safe number two. As she entered the final number, she tensed, praying it would work. But the buzzer sounded and a red light flicked on. Wrong code. No access.

"What does that mean?" Seb asked.

Jade bit her lip. What the hell did he think a red light meant?

"It means I carry on down the list," she replied, not turning around but holding her phone screen over her shoulder to show him. "I can't promise anything, though. I was lucky with that first one." She let out a nervous laugh, but it was met with silence.

Back to it.

Keep your head together.

Lifting her phone next to the keypad, she tapped out each combination, speeding up as she went. The further she got down the list, the more unsettled and dejected she felt. If she couldn't get this safe open, or the next one, all her efforts and sacrifice could be in vain. But it wasn't only that. It was doubtful Seb's reasons for wanting to find dirt on his wife were the same as hers, but he seemed as committed as her in finding a smoking gun in one of these safes. How would a man like him - arrogant, privileged, incapable of accepting the word no - react if he didn't get his way? His conduct, since dropping the charming Lothario act, was worrying.

"Have you tried my birthday? Or the date we got married?" Seb called out.

"Yes. Tried them both."

She gritted her teeth. She was almost at the end of the list. As she tapped in the final few number combinations, she knew in her heart the safe wasn't going to open.

Bugger.

She turned around to see Seb on his feet, staring at her. His full lips were pursed in a sharp pout and as their eyes met, he lowered his chin and raised his eyebrows. "You can't get it open?"

Jade shook her head. "Not unless we keep trying new combinations."

"Shitting hell!"

"Let's get through these," she said, shuffling over to the nearest pile of papers and picking up a few sheets from the top. "If there's nothing here, I'll try number safe three and if that doesn't open, we'll have a rethink and..."

She trailed off as she shifted her attention to the top piece of paper she was holding. The paper was thin and yellowing in places but it looked to be a bank statement. But that wasn't all.

"What is it?" Seb asked.

Jade held a hand up to him as she scanned the paper. Rereading what she'd seen. She flipped the paper over to see there was nothing written on the back and then looked up. "I might have something here. What do you think?"

Seb walked over to peer over her shoulder "A bank statement?" he asked.

"Yes. But, look, that's Rebecca's handwriting, yes? At the bottom here, a line from this amount of ten grand and then a name, P. Sawyer and a number. And look at the date; the second of September nineteen-ninety-nine. Not long after Jonathan Samuels died."

"May I?" Seb took the piece of paper from her. He was right.

"Do you think this P. Sawyer is a fixer?" Jade asked. "Do those sorts of people actually exist?"

Seb sneered at the mere suggestion. "Some of the rumours I've heard about people in my industry that never made it into the papers. Jesus, it'd make you physically sick. So, yes, fixers exist. And I'd say ten grand is a nice round figure one might pay to cover up a murder. What do you reckon?"

A shiver ran through Jade. "This could be it," she whispered. "P. Sawyer. Do you think we should ring the number? It was thirty years ago, so it's a bit of a stretch, but if we can link the line to whoever this person is, then we might have her. Can I?" She got to her feet and reached for the statement, yelping as Seb snatched it away from her. She grabbed for it again, but Seb held on tight. "Hey! Give it here."

Seb's eyes were wide and steely and his jaw rigid with effort. He didn't speak as he tugged at the paper.

Shit.

As the realisation hit home, it felt like her heart had dropped into her stomach. She felt dizzy and sick with adrenaline overload as Seb yanked the document from her grip. At the same time, he shoved her away, sending her stumbling back against the wardrobe.

She cried out. "What are you doing?"

But it was obvious, wasn't it?

Why had she been so bloody stupid?

Of course, Seb Turner didn't want to expose his wife. If the truth about Jonathan Samuels came out, Rebecca would be ruined, and his meal ticket gone. Not to mention he was due to inherit the business when she died. But what business? Beautiful You! couldn't survive its CEO and founder being labelled a murderer.

"Oh, come on, Jade," Seb said. "You're a clever girl. Isn't it obvious what I'm doing? I've invested far too much in Rebecca to have her lose everything." He walked over and placed the telltale statement on the bed before walking back and kneeling in front of her. "I'm afraid I can't let any of this come out, Jade. And I can't have you meddling any more in our affairs." His smile prickled the hairs on the back of her neck.

"I want justice for my mum." Her voice sounded weak and youthful. Like she was a little girl. She didn't take her eyes off Seb. "We can work something out. You won't lose anything."

"You're damn right I won't."

"Fine. We'll play it your way. I won't say anything. I'll tell Sofia we didn't find anything. That'll be the end of it." She was grasping at straws, barking out anything she could to placate him. A deep, unflinching terror had gripped her, but with it came frustration and anger. She'd underestimated Seb Turner and what he was capable of. She swallowed, tensing her face and mouth to hold it in, but it was no good. "Please, don't hurt me," she whimpered as a tear ran down her cheek. "I'm sorry."

"You will be."

She shuffled backwards, scrambling to her feet as he moved closer. Her phone was lying on the floor next to the bed. Too far away to reach. She held her hand out to him. "I'll scream."

Seb laughed. "Go on, then. Scream. No one's going to hear you."

She scanned the room, searching for something she might use to distract him. Or even as a weapon if it came to it. Seb was blocking the only exit, but she was fit and spritely and surprisingly strong, people had always told her. If she could ward him off, even for a few seconds, she could—

They both froze as a noise like a door opening drifted up from downstairs. Jade met Seb's horrified gaze as she heard a woman's voice.

It was Rebecca.

She'd returned early from her trip.

38

Sitting on a park bench on the Chelsea Embankment, with a clear view of Cheyne Walk and the front door of Rebecca Burton-Webb's house, Nicole smiled to herself. A minute earlier the woman herself had just got out of a taxi and entered the building. Back from her trip to Paris early.

This was a plot twist she hadn't seen coming.

Wrapping her coat more tightly around her she craned her neck to see through the tall windows. But it was useless.

Still, any minute now...

Tick-tock, bitch.

Nicole had known Jade was lying to her the moment she'd opened her mouth. That pathetic story about helping her friend move house stank to high Heaven. Even if she hadn't been giving off so many tells - rubbing at her neck, eyes looking up and to the right - there was no way someone like her was that selfless. But she was up to something. Nicole was certain of that. So, she'd followed her. Why not? It was Friday night after all, and her plans were ruined.

She didn't have to wait long outside Jade's flat before she came out, dressed to the nines and with her hair and make-up done. Seeing her like that Nicole could hardly contain her excitement. She had her. She knew it. Hanging back, but matching her step for step, she'd followed her down to Chalk Farm tube station and jumped on the next carriage along to hers, keeping one careful eye on her through the doors and getting off at Embankment when she did. The station had been busy with people so it was easy for her to remain out of sight as she followed Jade over to the District Line and onto an eastbound train towards Upminster. When Jade got off six stops later at Tower Hill, she knew exactly where she was heading.

Having finally been granted membership of The Baccarat Club at the start of this year Nicole was able to follow Jade inside and found a table in the far corner, away from the bar which provided a perfect vantage spot for her to watch as Jade threw herself at Rebecca's husband. She'd even got photographic evidence of the seedy rendezvous. A photo of Seb breathing down Jade's neck and a slightly blurred one of the two of them kissing.

She could hardly believe what she was watching. She knew Jade was bad news, but she'd thought her conniving and clever rather than impulsive. Surely, she knew she wouldn't get away with this. If not Nicole, then someone would have seen her and Seb together. The circles Rebecca moved in were exclusive and thus small. Even if Nicole hadn't just seen her walk in through her front door, the news of her husband and her new PA's betrayal would get back to her, eventually.

Especially if Nicole had her way.

Still, she'd almost messed it up, having been so engrossed in an imagined scenario - where Rebecca was telling her how valued she was, and that she would love her to be her new assistant – that she'd almost missed Jade and Seb as they slipped off their stools and headed for the exit, giggling like naughty children. Thankfully, however, she'd snapped out of it in time and jumped into the cab after theirs, feeling like a sexy femme fatale as she instructed the driver to 'follow that car'.

It was a cool night but thankfully she'd dressed for a stakeout and, despite having been sitting outside on this punishing wooden bench for the last four hours, she was relatively warm in her thick woollen Camia coat and a long Jacquemus scarf. She'd not had any sleep, but she'd catch up. Something told her once Jade Fisher was out of the picture, she'd sleep a lot more soundly.

She sat up and rocked her weight onto her feet as she saw all the lights were now on in Rebecca's house.

How delicious.

That meant she would have found them at it. How Nicole wished she could be a fly on the wall right now, but she'd have her fun soon enough. Rebecca would be upset, of course. But with the right help and support, it would be easy to turn her sorrow into anger and hate. Swiping open her phone, Nicole flicked through the photos she'd taken that evening. The ones in the club were a little grainy. But the ones she'd snapped as her taxi had pulled up behind theirs – of the two of them scurrying up the steps to Rebecca's front door, then entering the building together – were crystal clear. Once she'd paid her driver and they'd disappeared inside, she'd even walked around the side of the building and managed to snap a photo of Seb topless at the window as he reached up to close the curtains. Her heart skipped a beat as she enlarged the photo and realised Jade was visible behind him, wearing just her bra. She was cast in shadow, and it was a little blurry, but anyone who knew her could tell it was Jade.

"Got you. Little bitch."

Even if, by some miracle, Jade and Seb had heard Rebecca entering the house and had managed to not only get dressed but come up with a reasonable excuse why Jade was there, they couldn't talk their way out of these photos. They were both finished.

The clock on her phone told her it was almost six. Too early to be making a house call, especially on a Saturday. But late enough, perhaps, for a visit from a troubled colleague, a concerned friend. She'd give it another five minutes, then walk up to the front door and ring the bell.

Getting up off the bench, she stretched her arms. Poor Rebecca. One had to feel sorry for her. She didn't deserve this. She didn't deserve any of it.

Jade Fisher, on the other hand.

She deserved everything that was coming to her.

39

Jade scrambled to her feet as Seb paced the room, rubbing at his forehead. "Shit. What are we going to do?"

"What are *we* going to do?" Jade repeated. "That's rich. A second ago, I thought you were going to kill me."

"Kill you!?" Seb laughed. "Don't be stupid. I was just worked up, that's all. I know I come across as rather aggressive when I'm stressed. But it's all bluster, I assure you. I'm working on it with my therapist."

Jade frowned, going over the last few minutes in her head. It was true she was also tired and stressed, and probably not thinking straight. But she'd genuinely feared for her life. The way he'd looked at her...

She observed him now as he nodded at her and smiled. Like one might do to a small child you were encouraging to eat their vegetables.

"I didn't mean anything by it."

No. She wasn't having it. She'd seen behind the façade. Seb Turner was a nasty, self-obsessed brute. This was the act. This was the fake Seb.

"Get away from me," she hissed as he held out his hand to

her. "You shoved me into the wardrobe. You said if I screamed it wouldn't matter, implying you wanted to get rid of me. Was that just bluster?"

Seb opened his mouth to answer before a noise from downstairs made him stop. It sounded like Rebecca was filling the kettle with water. The thought came to Jade she should shout down to her, admit what was going on and tell her to phone the police. She would never get what she wanted from her, but Rebecca could be her saviour.

"Listen, Jade. I swear to God, you're mistaken. Bloody hell." He screwed his face up, rubbing at his eyes with his thumb and forefinger. "Look, I'm sorry for pushing you. I don't know why the hell I did that. I was upset and confused about the letter. I only meant to swipe you away." He opened his eyes and hit her with that crooked half-smile. "Something else for me to work on, I guess. But I swear I would never hurt you. We just made love, for Christ's sake. I like you. A lot. I'd like to see where we could take this once all this is over and—"

"Fuck you," Jade spat. "You might be able to gaslight your wife, but it won't work on me. You're a fucking narcissist, out for himself and whatever he can get. I don't trust a thing you've said all night."

She stepped back as Seb advanced towards her. "Come on, Jade. This is silly. We need to do something. She'll be up here any minute." He was talking fast, without breath. Genuinely stressing out, rather than just pretending to as an excuse for his violent behaviour. "We can't be found together. Hide in the wardrobe. She'll run a bath. She always does after a flight. Once she's in the bathroom, you can sneak out."

"No," Jade said, shaking her head. "It's over Seb. We're done. Both of us."

"It doesn't have to be that way, Jade. We agreed. We'll work together. Find the evidence and blackmail her.

Whatever we get, we'll split it fifty-fifty. But now we have to do this my way. So, get in the wardrobe. She's coming up. I can hear her." He gritted his teeth. "Get in the fucking wardrobe."

"Are you serious? What about all this?" She gestured at the files and stacks of paper in front of the wardrobe.

"I can sweet-talk her. I'll tell her she gave me the code and asked me to tidy it up or something. I have a way with her."

"I bet you do..."

"Jade."

She tensed; she was almost vibrating with anxiety. Could she still pull this off? If she got out of here without being seen by Rebecca, she might make a deal with Seb. But would he go for it?

She jerked her gaze away from him, hoping the erratic movement might reset her ridiculous thought processes.

Don't listen to him.

He's bad news.

She was about to tell him as much before a scuffling noise and footsteps on the stairwell made the words dry up in her throat. A second later, Rebecca was standing in the doorway.

"What the bloody hell is going on?"

Seb spun around. "Rebecca! Hi! You're home early. Bugger. We were hoping to surprise you with this."

Rebecca stepped into the room, eyes darting to the contents of the safe, all over the carpet, and then to Jade and back to Seb. A sharp frown worried the Botox and fillers in her forehead.

Jade glanced at Seb. He was glaring at her as if trying to control her with his mind. "Listen, Becca. It's not what it looks like, I swear it—"

"Really?" she spat. "And is the mess in the guest bedroom not what it looks like either? The used condoms? The half-drunk glasses of wine? Was it an attempt to recreate Tracey

Emin's bed, perhaps?" She laughed bitterly. Jade looked at her feet.

"Becca, please..."

"How dare you!" She turned on Seb. "In my own home. Do you really think that little of me? Do you hate me that much?"

Jade didn't look up but could hear the emotion wavering in Rebecca's voice. The initial shock and anger she'd exhibited on entering now made way for hurt and anguish.

"Needless to say, Jade, you're fired. And as for you, my darling husband, what an old fool I am. I knew, of course, what you were up to on those nights you spent away from home. Or I suspected, at least. Perhaps I didn't want to believe it."

"Or he made you question yourself," Jade muttered into the carpet. "Made you believe it was all in your head."

"You can shut your fucking mouth!" Seb snarled. "I mean it! This is all her fault, Rebecca. I'm so sorry, darling. I was drunk and stupid and I let my dick get the better of me. But it would never have happened if she hadn't seduced me and tricked me."

Jade looked up to see Rebecca glancing between the two of them, a mixture of disgust and confusion twisting her usually placid expression. "Really? You're putting this on her?"

"It's true," Seb went on. "Tell her, Jade. TELL HER!"

She tried to swallow, but her throat was dry and she had no saliva, anyway. "Seb and I, we bumped into each other and—"

"No! Not that! Tell her why you're really here. Tell her how you used me to get into our bedroom, and our private things. She wants to ruin you, Becca."

Jade froze. It felt like the entire universe was rushing towards her. In a second, her head was going to implode in on itself and she'd go pop. She didn't think that wouldn't be a bad thing. She held her hands up to her face.

"Seb, please. I don't know what you think you know, but you're mistaken."

"Bullshit. Tell her. I want to know what she has to say about these ludicrous claims you've been making all evening. Tell her, *Justine.*"

Rebecca snapped her head up. "Justine? What?"

A sudden calm washed over Jade. Or maybe it was a sense of finality. Either way, she wasn't agitated any longer. It was over. There was nothing else to worry about.

"Fine, I'll tell you everything, Rebecca." She gestured to the bed. "But you might want to sit down first."

40

Rebecca didn't say anything for almost a minute after Jade had finished talking. She just sat on the edge of the bed, staring into the middle distance. At first, Jade wondered if she'd gone into shock, but then Rebecca shook her head and let out a low laugh.

"Well, well..." she whispered into the carpet.

Jade hadn't felt the need to hold anything back. What was the point at this stage in the game? Starting at the beginning, she'd told Rebecca who she really was, who her mother was and what she suspected Rebecca to have done. She explained about her mum's illness and how she and Sofia had orchestrated her appointment at Beautiful You! so she could gain more information and evidence. She even told her about their plans to blackmail her, before they discovered the story of Jonathan Samuels, and their plans took a new turn.

To her credit, Rebecca listened without comment, only making the merest of gasps at pertinent points. She did, however, look down and away at the mention of Samuels, before sniffing back a tide of emotion. That told Jade everything she needed to know.

When, at last, Rebecca spoke, her voice was soft. "I can't believe it. You're Justine. Maggie's girl. The last time I saw you, you were only a year old. I remember holding you in my arms."

"You saw me?" Jade asked. "After I was born?"

"Yes. I came often. The last time was soon after Clive - your father - died."

Jade looked away, trying to make sense of what she was hearing. "Why would you? Why would Mum let you? You screwed my family over. It was because of you my dad ended up... doing what he did."

When she looked back at Rebecca, it shocked her to see a resigned smile on her face.

"It wasn't like that. That's not what happened."

Jade stepped closer to her. "What do you mean?"

Rebecca sighed and, slapping the tops of her thighs, got to her feet. "I need a bloody drink. I think we all could do with one. Why don't we go downstairs and get one and then I'll tell you my side of the story? I think you'll find it illuminating."

There was still anger and hurt in her voice, but her overall demeanour was calm. The effect was both unnerving and puzzling.

"Isn't it a bit early for alcohol?"

Rebecca puffed out another bitter laugh. "I'm not so sure. But coffee then. Whatever." She turned and headed for the stairs, but Seb stepped in her way.

"No one's going anywhere," he said, holding his hands up.

"Excuse me?" Rebecca snapped. "What the hell are you talking about? Don't be ridiculous. After what I've just walked in on, I need a damn drink!" She made to swerve around the side of him, but he moved with her, still blocking her exit.

"I can't let you do that, Becca. Not until I've worked out what's going down."

Rebecca scoffed and waved her hand at Jade. "You heard

what she just told me. And now I'm going to explain to everyone what actually happened. But first I want to calm my nerves a little. Okay? This is a lot. A hell of a lot!"

"He doesn't mean that," Jade whispered. Then, when Rebecca and Seb both glared at her, she said, louder. "What he means is, he wants to work out what he's going to do with us. Isn't that right, *Seb*?"

"What is she talking about?" Rebecca asked, turning back to her husband.

Seb didn't respond, just shook his head and sneered.

"Sebastian? Please. Let me pass." She made another break for the stairs, but like before, Seb got in front of her. This time, however, she doubled back on herself and tried to side-step around the other side of him. Seb grabbed her by the arm and swung her away. Rebecca cried out.

"I said no one is leaving this room," Seb growled. "And do not call me Sebastian. You know how much I hate it. But this is what you're like, isn't it? Treating me like a child. Fuck me, I know you always wanted kids, but it's pretty messed up to transpose that pathetic need into the guy you're screwing. Or used to, at least."

"The guy I'm screwing? You're my husband. We've been married ten years for God's sake."

"Yes. Don't I know it? Ten years of waiting, thinking sooner or later you might trust me enough to dissolve the prenup you got to me sign. Or give me a seat on the board at least. But, no. You keep me dangling on a leash, like a fucking plaything. Another good-looking accessory for you to show off. I'm right. I know I am."

Rebecca glanced around, open-mouthed. It was an over-the-top gesture and could have been for effect, but Jade didn't think so. "I love you, Seb. I always have. I only want you to be happy. Goddamn it, I pay for everything for you, provide you with this lifestyle. I even turn a blind eye to you..." she gritted her teeth and gestured violently to his crotch and then to Jade. "...doing this!"

"Oh, aren't you a fucking saint," Seb spat, his tone and expression hardening. "But, screw it, why not? Jade or Justine or fucking Jiggly tits, here, is right. This is a real mess, but I'm going to make it go my way."

Rebecca eyed Jade, the realisation of what her husband was saying was dawning on her.

"You wouldn't."

"Watch me. What have I got to lose? You'll probably want to divorce me now and I won't get anything. After all these years, pretending I enjoyed fucking your dry withered body, whilst I prayed the stress and strain of your work might manifest in a fatal stroke or cancer."

Jesus.

His words hit Jade like a stomach punch. She could only imagine what they'd done to Rebecca. She made a strange, warbling sound, like an alley cat, and leapt at Seb.

"Bastard!" she screeched. "After everything I've done for you." She slammed her fists into his chest, pounding away until he grabbed her wrist.

"You've done nothing for me." He snarled, lowering his head to look at her. His eyes were wild and, at that moment, Jade knew he was capable of doing exactly what she feared he might. "But don't worry. You will do. Now I'm taking control of the situation."

"Let go of me," Rebecca yelled, swiping at him with her free hand. She caught him on the side of his neck, her long, perfectly manicured nails clawing at his skin and drawing blood.

Seb flinched but kept hold of her wrist, striking her with a vicious backhand across the face and shoving her away. Rebecca screamed as she stumbled backwards and banged into the wall. Seb followed her over, moving away from the top of the stairs.

And now Jade saw her chance.

Time slowed down. It felt as if her legs didn't belong to her. Yet they were doing what she needed them to do as they propelled her across the room. All she could see was the doorway to the stairwell. Two more strides and she'd reach it. If she made it to the ground floor, it was only another few feet to the front door.

"Get back here!"

She had her hand on the handrail and was leaning into the turn when a hand on her shoulder snapped her back to the terror of the moment. Seb's fingers clasped the material of her dress, pulling her back. She gnashed her teeth, struggling against him with every ounce of energy she had left. She heard Seb yell. She felt pressure on her face. Then the world turned into a blur of white and grey as her feet lifted off the ground. It felt as if she was flying. Her stomach flipped over and she reached out to steady herself, arms flailing but finding nothing. She heard someone cry out. It could have been her. Next, her face collided with something hard that wiped out her vision and sent a sharp pain spiralling deep into her sinuses. Bouncing from surface to surface, she came to a stop on a different plane. This one was soft and made of fabric, but no less jarring as her head slammed against it. The last thing she heard as a heavy blackness took all her senses away was Seb Turner's voice.

"That's what you get. Stupid cow."

41

As the room stopped spinning and the swirling cyclone of colours formed into shapes and then objects, Jade gasped awake. Her awareness spread further and she found herself sitting on a wide landing, with her back against something hard.

Where the hell was she?

What was going on?

She blinked, conscious as she did of a dull pain that spread down from her temple into the roots of her teeth. In front of her were two doors, one closed and the other open a few inches. Through the gap, she could see the room beyond, an office space with rows of shelves full of box files and paper folders. She blinked again, to focus her vision. She recognised that room. But this wasn't her house. Or her mum's. And why couldn't she move her arms?

Shit.

It was because her hands were tied behind her back. She struggled at whatever was binding them. It felt like sticky tape. She glanced around her some more as her memory came back online. She was sitting on the first-floor landing of

Rebecca Burton-Webb's Chelsea townhouse. Rebecca herself was sitting a few feet away against the same wall but in front of a large vintage radiator. The skin over her left eye was cut and bruised, and her lip was bleeding. There was no sign of Seb.

"What happened?" Jade whispered.

"You fell down the stairs and banged your head."

"Fell, or was pushed?"

Rebecca sniffed out a curt laugh. "Does it matter?"

"We need to get out of here," Jade said. But, sitting upright, she saw her feet, too, were bound together. Thick brown parcel tape had been wrapped around them many times and the more she tugged, the tighter it gripped. She rested her head back against the wall. "Shit. Where is he?"

She rolled onto her side to try to get up, but the pain in her head and side pinned her down. A wave of dizziness blurred her vision.

"Take a minute," Rebecca said. "You hit your head quite hard."

Jade rolled back and got herself upright. "Can you move?"

"No. He's tied me to the pipework." She leant forward to show her. "He was going to do you as well, but he ran out of tape. That's where he is, I think. And he said something about making a phone call."

"What's he going to do with us?" Jade asked.

Rebecca shook her head. "I've no idea. I've never seen him like this before. He's gone crazy."

"This is bad," Jade whimpered. "Really bad. He's going to hurt us. If he's tied us up, he's going to—"

"I can talk to him," Rebecca snapped. "He's making a big mistake and he'll see that. He's not a monster."

"He's a narcissist and he's violent."

Rebecca looked away. Her lip trembled. "He wouldn't be

doing this if you hadn't got your claws into him. I don't understand what you think you were going to achieve."

"You destroyed my family." Despite all the scheming and planning over the last year, she'd not factored in what she'd say to Rebecca when it came down to it. As she heard the words coming out of her mouth, she felt a shiver of nervous energy. "I know all about your dodgy business practices," she continued. "I know my mum didn't like it and you screwed her over. You made her sell her half of the business to you when she was too ill to know what she was doing. How could you?"

Rebecca let out another bitter laugh. "Is that what you think, that I got rid of her because of what was going on in our factories?"

"And the rest. I know you had Jonathan Samuels killed and paid for the cover-up." She jutted her chin at Rebecca, but she didn't respond or even react. "You couldn't let it come out and ruin your business, so you got rid of everyone involved. Bought your way out of it. Only my mum never got over your betrayal. She's going to die in obscurity, not even remembering her own name. That's why we were doing this. We needed money for a new drug that's just come out in America."

"For heaven's sake, girl. Why didn't you come to me and ask? I'd have gladly helped. And for what it's worth, the deal Maggie and I made was consensual and the amount paid was more than generous. As for everything else, you couldn't be more wrong."

"Is that right?" Jade asked. She was feeling less woozy and the pain in her head was subsiding a little. She tugged at her hands, trying to free them from the tape. "Well, why don't you enlighten me?"

Rebecca closed her eyes and let out a sigh. It sounded like it hurt her. "We were in our third year of trading, already doing better than I'd ever imagined, when Jonathan Samuels first contacted us. By that point, we had two stores open and were getting attention from all the influential magazines. We even had endorsements from the likes of Kate and Linda. Everything was going to plan until we received that phone call. Jonathan said he'd been digging around the company's practices and had a source that claimed we were using slave labour in our Myanmar factories, and that the raw materials we'd sourced came from a company with ties to an insurgent group."

Jade stopped trying to free herself. "So, it's true."

"That part is. Yes. Jonathan accused us of greenwashing, of lying about where our products came from. But you have to understand, we didn't know. In those days, it was hard to know for certain what was going on in these faraway factories."

Jade startled at a sound from downstairs. It sounded as if Seb were opening drawers and then slamming them shut. She shot Rebecca a look and they waited in silence for a few seconds. But when nothing happened, Rebecca continued.

"Before Jonathan contacted us, we had no idea of any wrongdoing. I swear. We were young. Naïve. We had a local man over in Myanmar, a man called Ufi, who was dealing with the production side of things. We trusted him. He reported back weekly and always told us everything was above board. We later discovered that Ufi was completely corrupt. He was cutting corners, skimming money where he could. But he was sloppy, too. It would have come out eventually, even if Jonathan hadn't been so determined. He told us he was going to write the article and asked us if we wanted to comment. At first, I said yes. I wanted him to write the story, but with us closely involved. We'd grant him interviews and first-hand accounts. So we could control the narrative, as we say these days. Jonathan was keen on that idea. He believed his article would have more power as a balanced investigative piece rather than a tabloid-style exposé. In turn, I convinced myself it would be a way of wiping the slate clean. We were still a young company and this was before the internet and social media. With the right spin, we could have used the issue to rebrand and start again. Perhaps it was me being youthful and idealistic, but I thought it would be a positive step. We'd admit we'd been duped and, by being so transparent, would retain most of our fanbase and customers. But your mother, Maggie, was more business-minded than me. She thought doing the article was a bad idea, that it would be the end of us. We'd both put so much of ourselves into the company and she couldn't bear to think it might all be in vain. Plus, she had a young child and was already pregnant with you. She didn't want to take the risk. She said we should get our lawyers involved and try to stop the article that way. In the end, I agreed with her."

Jade frowned. "I don't understand. My mum would never... She said it was all your fault. You killed Samuels to stop the piece coming out and then paid to cover it up. I saw your handwriting. P. Sawyer"

Rebecca let out another long sigh. "Just what is it you think happened? Hey?"

"I know that there was some sort of charity event. And Samuels fell over a balcony to his death."

"It was a fundraiser for Water Action. But I wasn't in attendance that night." She raised her eyebrows as if to emphasise the statement. "It's true. I wasn't even in the country. I was in Germany meeting potential new merchants."

Jade had been ready to say more, but words failed her. She twisted her feet around to try to work them free, but it was useless.

"But I do know what happened that night," Rebecca went on. "It's true that Jonathan sneaked into the fundraiser looking for trouble. He found your mum having a cigarette outside on the balcony and confronted her. This was after we'd already told him we weren't going to cooperate with his article and had our lawyers reach out to him to scare him off. From what I was told, he became angry and abusive. Until..."

She trailed off, perhaps hoping Jade would fill in the rest. "You're saying my mum pushed him?"

"No dear. Not your mum. Clive was there too, you see. He was a big man, your dad, and he had a short fuse, especially with people he thought were a threat to his family. He and Jonathan had words, there was a scuffle." She tilted her head back so her crown was resting against the wall, staring at the ceiling. "I never got the exact details; I think it all happened so fast. But it was your dad, Justine. He was the one who pushed Jonathan over."

Unblinking, Jade stared at Rebecca, searching the side of her face for any obvious signs this was a lie. She didn't see any.

Rebecca ran her tongue over her top lip. "I know it's hard to hear. But it's the truth. The way he and Maggie told it, it was an accident and I believed them. But he'd have got manslaughter at the very least, and there was no guarantee he wouldn't have stood trial for murder. The motive was clear. Jonathan Samuels was going to destroy everything we'd worked so hard for."

Another bang came from downstairs, but Jade hardly acknowledged it. She stared into the carpet as if she was going to find the answers there. But she didn't even have the questions.

"My dad killed Jonathan Samuels," she mumbled.

"Yes, dear. And it is true, we did pay for a cover-up. We discussed it and we knew we had too much to lose. There had been no witnesses to the fall other than your mum and dad, and through a mutual friend, I met with a man who said he could make it all go away. Peter Sawyer. He told me he used to work for MI5 and I was never sure if that was true. But he was shrewd and he knew what he was doing. He convinced everyone Jonathan Samuels had been drunk out of his mind and had toppled over the balcony unprovoked. A tragic accident. We made a substantial donation to the organisers of the ball to keep it out of the papers and that was that. It's amazing what you can make disappear with the right people and enough money."

"I can't believe it," Jade said. She felt numb. So much so that she'd almost forgotten where she was or that she was trying to free herself.

"It's a lot to take in, I know," Rebecca said.

"But I don't understand what happened to you and my mum. If you'd just gone through all that together, why did you pay her off?"

"I didn't want to lose her. But Maggie was already struggling with what had happened - guilt, I suppose - and then you were born and her hormones went haywire. She lost all sense of herself." She tutted as if she couldn't believe what she was saying. "It was a few months after that your dad killed himself. I knew he was racked with guilt also, but I never expected him to go that far. He was drinking heavily too, which didn't help. It was just an awful, awful time. I was running the business single-handed, whilst trying to keep your mum afloat mentally and help with you and your sister when I could. I wanted her to hire a nanny, but she refused. She refused a lot of help and support. It was like she'd shut down and wouldn't let anyone in. Then one day she told me she wanted to go to the police and confess everything. Tell them what happened to Jonathan and what he was about to reveal. I told her no, that it had gone too far and we had no other choice but to keep going. I know that was terrible of me, but you'd already lost your father. If we told the truth, we'd have both gone to prison and they'd have put you into care. We couldn't have that. Plus, we'd parted ways with Ufi by that stage, and I'd set up a more robust system for doing background checks on every supplier used. It's the same system we have today. We were completely legit. No more skeletons in any closets. Eventually, I convinced Maggie it was in everyone's best interests to never mention what had happened. But by that point, she wanted out. Of the business, of our partnership, of the industry."

"So, you did buy her out?"

"Because that's what she wanted! And it was a fair price that I paid. We stayed in touch afterwards. I loved coming to see you and Sofia, but your mum was still struggling mentally, and after a few years, she cut me off. She told me to never darken her door again. Said it was all my fault what had happened. I knew she wasn't well and I hoped once she got help, she might get back in touch. But time moves on and before you know it thirty years have gone by."

Tears were rolling down Jade's face. She couldn't stop them even if she had her hands free. "Are you telling the truth?" she asked.

"Yes. I am. And, now you know I'm not some evil witch, we need to work together to get out of here."

As if to highlight their plight, they heard another crash coming from downstairs.

"What can we do?" Jade asked. "Do you have your phone nearby? If we can get our hands on it, we might—"

"He took both our phones," Rebecca whispered. "He's a lot cleverer than he makes out. When he comes back, let me do the talking. Maybe I can get through to him. He's not a bad man."

Jade wanted to tell Rebecca she was wrong, and that she'd spent so long in a toxic relationship that she had no idea what her husband was really like. But the sound of footsteps on the stairs stopped her.

A second later Seb appeared from downstairs, smirking as their eyes met. "Ah, you're awake," he said, stepping up onto the landing. "I was wondering whether it was all over for you. So glad you're still with us."

"Fuck you!" she spat. "You need to let us go. Now!"

He chuckled at her outburst. "I don't think I'll be doing that. Sorry. You see, I've just come up with an absolute humdinger of a plan that gets me exactly what I want. Honestly, I think I might be a bit of a bloody genius."

Rebecca lowered her head. "Darling, come on, you don't need to tie us up. We can talk about this. Now that I know you're unhappy, we can discuss where we go from here. There's always a way, sweetie. Whatever you want. We can make it happen."

"You said it," he replied, pointing a roll of parcel tape at her. "But I don't need you to help me. Not as such, anyway. You see, as I was looking for more tape, I realised Jade here has provided me with the perfect opportunity."

Jade leaned forward to pull at her ties. "What do you mean?" she asked, as he caught her eye.

"I mean that the best lies are always those with as much of the truth in them as possible." He placed the parcel tape down on the handrail that ran around the top of the landing. "Now, bear with me here. But I think this is rather brilliant."

"Get on with it," Jade yelled, using the surge of emotion to yank harder at her ties.

There was still no give.

Seb laughed and held up his hands. "Okay, so this is how it goes. Jade here, knowing Rebecca was in Paris, broke into our house to find evidence that she planned on using to blackmail Rebecca. But what she didn't know was that Rebecca was about to arrive home unexpectedly and catch her in the act. *Oh dear*, we all say. And now here comes the clever part, where the narrative changes to my advantage. Jade is about to kill Rebecca – let's say by strangling her to death – and then she'll escape with the contents of the safe. Then poor old Seb, after making sure he's seen around town all morning, will return home to discover his poor wife dead. At which point he'll call the police."

Rebecca let out a low whimpering sound. "No," she whispered. "You can't... You wouldn't..."

"He couldn't," Jade said. "He'd never get away with it. We were together last night at the club, remember?"

"We were, but I've already spoken to my good friend Lewis. You might remember him. The doorman? Unfortunately, all the security footage from last night has gone missing and he swears blind I was alone all evening propping up the bar. The barman will say the same once Lewis has had a quiet word with him." He grinned. "Sorry about that."

Jade carried on, twisting and pulling at the ties. The tape had rolled itself up into thin strands and tore at her flesh, but she kept going. "Why did you want me to get in the wardrobe?" she asked.

"I don't bloody know!" He made a goofy face at her. "I was just spitballing, thinking on my feet. But this way is so much better."

Rebecca was still muttering to herself. Jade looked over to see she was rocking back and forth like a broken toy. Maybe she was broken. It would be understandable.

"What happens to me?" Jade asked.

Seb cricked his neck to one side and then to the other. "I reckon I'll leave it a few days until the coppers mark you down as prime suspect number one. You know how the old boys in blue get once they have someone in their sights. They rarely look elsewhere. After that, I'm thinking you'll turn up in Norbury Park or somewhere, hanging from a tree."

"You evil bastard," Jade spat.

"I thought you'd like that. It's romantic, in a way. Going the same way as your old man."

Jade was surprised to find anger her primary emotion. But she'd gone through them all since she regained consciousness. Fear, confusion, sorrow. But anger was the driver now. Hopefully, that was a good thing. As long as she could keep it in check and make it work for her.

"If you kill me now, once they ascertain the time of death the police will know I've not committed suicide in some park. And then what? You'll still be the secondary suspect."

"I know!" Seb yelled. "I'm not stupid! This is why, when I called Lewis just now and asked him to supply me with some roofies. Rohypnol, Jade. Once you're out for the count and more pliable I'll take you to a flat I've been renting out in Soho for the past couple of years. Sorry, Becca. I never got around to telling you about it. For obvious reasons." The grin he gave the two of them made Jade want to throw up.

"I can keep you there for a few days, until the timeline works for me and the drugs are out of your system. Then I'm thinking a signed confession and a trip to the woods. Perfect. But, until then, who knows, it might even be fun."

"Fuck you!" Jade hissed.

Seb smirked. "Careful what you wish for, sweetie. But it's a good plan, I think. Lewis has supplied me with roofies in the past so he's almost as complicit as I am. It's why I know I can trust him. You know how it is with some of these modern women. They look easy, but then you get talking to them and they're not as agreeable as you'd like."

"You rotten piece of shit." She felt sick. Knowing what she'd done. What she'd let him do. "You won't get away with this."

"Hmm, I think I already have." He flashed his eyes at her. "Oh, speak of the devil." He held a hand up, reaching into the pocket of his jogging bottoms with the other. He pulled out his phone and answered it as he brought it to his ear. "You're here. Great. Come to the house... Fine. Yes. By the river. I get it. I'll see you in five." He hung up. "Right, ladies. Time for me to nip out for a minute or two. Don't go anywhere."

With that, he turned and ran down the stairs.

42

Nicole had left the bench and was marching across the street towards Rebecca's house when the front door swung open. Not expecting this eventuality, she leapt behind one of the thick oak trees that lined the leafy street and concealed herself there, peaking around the side to observe.

Seb appeared in the doorway.

This was also unexpected. She'd hoped it would be Jade, scurrying away with her treacherous tail between her legs and a head full of abuse. But she must be still inside the house. With Rebecca.

That didn't make sense.

Gripping the rough bark of the old tree, she leaned around to get a better look. Seb's face was red and as he cast his gaze left and right down the street, he looked angry rather than ashamed or upset. But that was understandable. His cheating ways had finally been exposed and he had nowhere to go but down. Rebecca must have heard the rumours; she must have suspected he'd been doing the dirty on her over the years. But seeing it with her own eyes was another matter. He'd be out on his ear soon enough.

But as he walked down the steps to the pavement, a smirk broke out across his lips. He'd been holding his neck the entire time and, as he reached ground level, he removed his hand and examined his fingers. There was blood on them. That's when Nicole saw the wound on the side of his throat, underneath his chiselled jawline. Three scratch marks, each only an inch long, but deep. They weren't the marks of passion.

What the hell is going on?

At the bottom of the steps, Seb pulled a phone from his pocket before marching down the street towards Chelsea Embankment.

Nicole waited, frozen, unsure what to do as a flurry of irrational thoughts whirled in her head. She watched Seb Turner until he disappeared around the curve of the road and moved out from behind the tree. As she crossed over to the other side of the street, the tall white townhouse loomed over her. Rebecca and Jade were still inside. Seb had left, nursing an injury to his neck. Any way she viewed this picture, it looked bad.

Maybe she should leave. Go home to bed. What right did she have here, anyway? One didn't go around spying on people. And what if there was a perfectly reasonable explanation for what was going on? Okay, not reasonable, not with a possible love triangle ending in one of the parties leaving with blood pouring from his neck, but what if they were all complicit in some sordid game? She imagined herself banging on the front door only for it to be opened by Rebecca and Jade, naked and wrapped around each other, asking her what the hell she was doing there. If that happened, it would be Nicole for the chop.

As she reached Rebecca's steps, she hesitated, swaying as her head told her one thing, her heart another and her guts something else. Maybe this indecisiveness was a sign. She had no idea what she would find inside the house, and maybe it was best she left right now before anyone saw her. It had been foolish of her to follow Jade. The act of a mad woman, some might say. In her mind's eye, she could already see Marsha's dour expression as she asked Nicole if they could 'have a chat?'

No.

She blinked those thoughts away, telling herself to trust her instincts. She'd been in enough toxic relationships over the years to know when something felt wrong. This situation had red flags all over it. She had to find out what was going on. For her own sanity, if nothing else.

She scaled the four stone steps in two strides, hauling herself up by the metal handrail. Glancing back over her shoulder to check Seb was out of sight, she pressed the buzzer, dancing from foot to foot as she waited for a response. When none came, she pressed it again, holding her finger down for longer this time and then putting her ear closer to the door to listen.

For a moment, she thought she could hear shouting coming from inside and closed her eyes to listen. But it was useless. The dull hum of a city waking up filled her hearing and she couldn't pick out anything else through the thick wood. She pressed the buzzer again, but only for an instant, before stepping back from the door and craning her neck to peer up at the windows. It was an awkward angle, so she ran back down the steps to get a better look. The lights were on in most of the rooms, but there was no sign of movement, no shadows cast.

Gripped with the desire to find out what was going on, she threw her attention around the area. A gated alleyway ran down the side of Rebecca's house, presumably leading to the back of the property. Throwing another furtive glance over her shoulder, she eased open the black, wrought-iron gate and slipped through before running along the dark, narrow alley until it opened out in a wider lane with a line of trees at the end.

There was a door on the right that led into Rebecca's back garden but, on trying it, she found it locked.

"Bugger."

She was about to give up, having fallen at the second hurdle, when she heard a banging noise coming from above. Looking up, she saw Jade standing in one of the windows. Or, rather, she was leaning against it, banging her head on the glass. Her right eye was swollen shut and she had a red graze running down the side of her face on that side. The way her body was twisted, it looked like she had her arms tied behind her back. She glared at Nicole with one wide, terrified eye and head-butted the window again.

"Yes. I see you," Nicole rasped. Her heart was pounding in her chest. She threw her arms out. "What do I do?"

Jade nodded at her frantically, as if trying to show her something, gesturing down. The back door? Was that it? *But it's locked.* The walls surrounding the garden were about seven feet tall, too high to scale, especially in kitten heels. But as she moved around the corner, she found a row of wheelie bins, tall enough to climb on. Grabbing the handle of one of them, she dragged it against the wall, breaking a nail in the process and scuffing the toe of her new shoes. On any other day, either of these things would have angered her, but she was now committed to her role of saviour. Her only focus was getting inside that house.

But she could do this. The world might know her as Nicole Sorbonne, beauty and wellness influencer and high-fashion princess - but that was because she'd carefully orchestrated that persona for herself. Inside, she was still the same tough-spirited girl she'd always been, who'd spent most weekday evenings and every Saturday morning being pushed to her limits at her local athletics club. She could even hear Coach in her head, telling her to watch her balance and poise as she clambered up onto the top of the wheelie bin. Once there, she grabbed the top of the white-rendered wall and pulled herself up. By the time she'd swung one leg over the top, she knew she was in, and a rush of adrenaline and pride spurred her on as she jumped down into Rebecca's back garden.

Her ankle buckled as she landed, but she held her poise, steadying herself using the trunk of a small Acer tree. Not bad going, considering she'd not vaulted a horse or walked a balance beam in fifteen years. And in a pair of Jimmy Choos, as well.

But there was no time for congratulating herself. Jade was still at the window, banging frantically like a caged animal. She was in distress and needed Nicole's help. The ironic nature of that fact was not lost on her as she ran up to the back door. It was an old wooden frame with nine frosted-glass window panels at the top and a rusty old Mortis lock. That could pose a problem, but she hoped Rebecca used it in the same way her father always had done when she was a young girl. Picking up a decent-sized rock from an overgrown rockery beneath the window, she returned to the door and smashed the rock against the lowest glass panel on the left, above the lock. With her eyes screwed up tight, it took her a few tries before she heard the satisfying sound of breaking glass and opened her eyes to see the pane had gone except for a jagged shard sticking out of the bottom of the frame. She pulled her coat sleeve down over her hand and jimmied out this last piece of glass before snaking her slender arm through the hole.

Yes! As she'd been hoping, the key was in the lock. The angle meant it hurt her arm as she got hold of it and an electric charge ran up her forearm as she turned it in the lock. It was stiff and old and for a moment she didn't think she was going to manage it, but then she heard a click. It was open. Pulling her arm out, she yanked down the handle and opened the door. She'd done it. She was inside.

43

In Seb's haste to meet Lewis, and lost in his egotistical tirade, he'd forgotten to tie Jade to the radiator. She'd realised this the moment he'd left and had struggled some more to free her hands before realising it was futile and deciding she had to go for it, regardless. Rolling around like a demented caterpillar, she'd managed to position herself with her face against the wall and used the friction of her cheek to drag herself upright. Once on her feet, and with Rebecca spurring her on, she'd hobbled as fast as her bound legs would allow over to the edge landing, overlooking the hallway below. She was standing there when the buzzer sounded.

She swung around to look at Rebecca, who had thankfully snapped out of the disassociation quagmire she'd been lost in whilst Seb was talking.

"No idea," she said. "It could be a delivery."

Jade turned back, yelling at whoever was at the door for help.

"They can't hear you," Rebecca told her. "We had the windows done last year. Triple-thick, triple-glazed with laminate layers in between. It's practically soundproof."

Jade nodded; she thought as much. But there had to be another way of getting their attention. With renewed alacrity, she hobbled across the landing and barged into the front bedroom, which looked out over the street. Stumbling over on her way to the window, she pressed her face to the glass in time to see Nicole disappearing around the side of the house.

She was the last person Jade had expected to see this morning, but she was also their only hope. Bounding out onto the landing, she headed for the second bedroom that looked out over the garden, barking out to Rebecca that it was Nicole at the door and that she needed to get her attention. In the back room, she hurled herself at the window, smacking her already pounding head against the glass and making as much noise as she could. Her heart almost exploded with joy as Nicole looked up and saw her. She watched in awe as she made short shrift of scaling the garden wall and got the back door open.

"I think she's in," Jade cried, falling out of the bedroom and onto the landing carpet in her rush to tell Rebecca. Rather than try to stand, she wriggled over to her before rolling onto her back and using her bound hands to push herself into a sitting position. "Did you hear?"

"I heard breaking glass," Rebecca replied. "Do you think she could reach the lock?"

The sound of Nicole's voice coming from downstairs answered her question. "Jade? Rebecca?"

"Up here," Rebecca called down. "On the landing."

They stared at each other, both fighting back tears as Nicole dashed up the stairs. As she reached the top, she stopped.

"Bloody hell," she gasped. "Did he do this? Seb?"

"Yes," Jade said. "And he could be back any second. We'll tell you everything, but for now, you need to untie us. Quick."

She was concerned the shock of discovering them this way

would cause Nicole to falter but she ran straight over and got behind Jade, working on the tape.

"Shit, it's all twisted." She pulled at the ties, yanking Jade's hand at the same time. It was no good. "Wait there. I'll run down to the kitchen and get a knife."

"No! Wait!" Jade cried. But Nicole was already heading down the stairs, taking them two at a time.

"Thank God!" Rebecca rasped.

But Jade wasn't ready to celebrate yet and, as they waited for Nicole to return, her fears became manifest when she heard a key in the lock downstairs. A gust of cool air whipped up the stairs as the front door was flung open and immediately slammed shut.

Seb!

He'd returned.

Jade shuffled around, getting back into the same position she'd been in before he left. She was almost there when she heard a grim chuckle.

"And what are you up to, may I ask?"

Jade looked up into Seb's smug face. "Nothing. I wasn't doing anything."

"Doesn't matter if you were. It's too late." He had one hand in his pocket and, in the other, a thin plastic medicine vial. He held it up and rattled it. "You know, I was thinking I'd give you both one. Make it painless. But, as Lewis just so kindly reminded me, I can't. It's detectable. Sorry about that, darling." He pulled a sad face at Rebecca.

"After everything we've been through," she hissed. "Everything I've given you. I love you, Seb. I always have. Please don't do this. We can talk about it. If you want more freedom, to go out, to do whatever...I understand. You're a young man and I know I've not been as forthcoming with affection as I could have been the past year. And I'm sorry about

287

that. Really, I am." She didn't blink or take a breath as she talked, not shifting her gaze from Seb. But his contemptuous leer told Jade he didn't care.

"We had some good times. Once," he said. "But I've had enough of you. Of living a half-life. Like your pet. Once you're dead and your fortune is mine, I have big plans. A production company, for starters. And I'll probably move to LA. Start again. I'm still a young man. It's time to live my life for me." He pulled his other hand out of his pocket to reveal he was carrying a glass paperweight. He tossed it in the air and caught it, puffing out his cheeks as if demonstrating its weight. "It'll be quick, darling. Jade, here, is going to knock you out first and then strangle you. It fits the narrative better; I think and will be less horrific for all concerned. One quick blow and then nothingness." He drew in a deep breath and stepped forward.

"Seb! Darling! Don't! Please! All those things you mentioned – LA, the production company. You can still do all of that." Rebecca was sobbing now, her voice shrill and wavering. "I love you. But if you really want to get away from me, then we can talk about that too. I'll speak to Gerard first thing on Monday. Have him write up a new marital agreement for if – *when* – we divorce." She gulped back air; her breathing was sharp and fitful. Panic, taking over. "Or I can make a deposit in your account today. However much you want. It's yours. It'll take me a few hours to get it finalised, but I can do it. Please, Seb. Please, don't hurt me."

Jade scowled. She got it. She was terrified just as much as Rebecca. But it was sickening to hear her pleading for her life this way. Before discovering what she'd done to her mum – or, rather, what she thought she'd done – Jade had harboured a bit of a girl crush on Rebecca Burton-Webb. Not in a sexual way. But she looked up to her. She was bold but kind. A worthy role model. Not to mention a woman at the top of her industry who was still influential, even after all these years. And now here she was in floods of tears, hyperventilating, pleading with her husband not to kill her.

But maybe she wasn't pleading.

Maybe she was buying them some time. Because Jade had just caught sight of Nicole creeping up the stairs behind Seb. Her head appeared first, eyes sharp and alert, lips pursed in a tight pout of concentration. She was moving with deep consideration and care, easing herself up onto each step without making a sound. As she got closer to the top, Jade saw the pair of metal dress-making scissors in her hand. She had them splayed open, holding them with one of the sharp points facing down.

Jade tensed, not daring to move or look directly at Nicole in case she alerted Seb to her presence. But she had nothing to worry about. Rebecca's performance was still capturing his attention. He was telling her he was sorry, but that he had to do this. That she'd forced his hand with how she'd treated him over the years. Typical gaslighting bullshit but taken to the darkest degree imaginable. *You made me kill you.* What a total fucking prick.

Jade's eye twitched. She was so full of anxious rage that she wanted to scream. It felt like time had stopped. Nicole had almost reached the landing. Another step and she'd be within arm's reach of Seb. What she did next decided all their fates.

Come on, Nic.

You can do this.

Jade lowered her head as out of the corner of her eyes she saw Nicole lift the scissors above her head. She stepped up onto the landing, ready to strike. A floorboard creaked beneath her.

Shit!

No!

Seb spun around as Nicole lunged at him. The scissors swished down in a sharp arc, but he'd seen her in time and dodged out of the way, leaving her slashing at empty air. The momentum sent Nicole staggering forward, and before she could right herself, Seb grabbed her by the throat.

"Get off her!" Jade cried out impotently, as Seb held her up in front of him. He snorted derisively before raising his fist and smashing it into Nicole's face. Jade screamed as blood burst from Nicole's nose. With a grunt, Seb shoved her backwards, following her as she teetered at the top of the stairs and slammed his fist into her stomach. As she bent over in pain, he gave her another shove, sending her tumbling down the stairs.

"Nicole! No!"

Jade looked over at Rebecca. Her expression perfectly exemplified what she was feeling. A mixture of disbelief and terror.

Was she...? Had he...?

She'd never know. Because he was coming for her now, red-faced and furious. A cold fury that turned her stomach replaced the smugness that had exuded from him minutes earlier. But if this was it, she wasn't going down without a fight. Calling forth every ounce of mettle she had left, she curled her legs back underneath her, rocked forward onto her knees and jumped onto her feet. As Seb closed in, she used the force of motion to propel herself forward, barging him with her shoulder and knocking him into the railing at the edge of the landing. He cried out as his spine smacked against the wood.

"You stupid bitch," he snarled as she staggered away from him. "Why can't you let me get this over with?! I don't want to do this! But I have to! It's the only way!" He stepped towards her and hit her with a heavy backhand that knocked her to the ground.

The blow stung her cheek and sent her head spinning. Before she could get up, Seb had pushed her onto her back and was on top of her, legs straddling her torso, knees crushing her ribs as he placed his hands around her throat.

"You've ruined everything," he spat. "But fuck this. I've had enough." Spittle flew from his mouth. He loomed over her, squeezing at her neck, crushing her windpipe with his thumbs.

Jade wriggled and bucked her hips to get him off, but she had no strength left in her and it did nothing to stop him. She tensed her throat muscles, trying desperately to hold on to consciousness as Seb tightened his grip, strangling all the hope out of her. Somewhere she could hear Rebecca screaming, but with the pressure in her ears, she couldn't make out what was being said. She felt dizzy and sick. Her entire body was rigid with panic. She knew she was going to die. It was over. She thought of Sofia and her mum. Of her poor dad, who'd lost his life in a similar way. It wasn't fair. None of this was.

"Please," she wheezed. "I can't... I don't...Please..."

Even if her words had been intelligible, it was pointless. Seb Turner had cracked. He was mad, insane. The dark mirror side of his character she'd only caught glimpses of previously had now taken over. She kicked out in one last pathetic attempt to get him off her, but it was useless. The darkness was taking hold. She could feel herself slipping away. She closed her eyes. This was it. All she could think as the life force left her was... *It's not fair.*

It's not fair.

It's not...

She gasped for air as the crushing grip on her throat loosened and then released. Opening her eyes, she saw Seb sitting back with a confused look on his face. A deep gash over his right eye was already pouring with blood. As Jade's awareness spread, she saw Nicole standing behind him, holding what looked to be some kind of award. It was shiny metal and triangular-shaped with a black marble bass. As she looked on, blood ran down Seb's face and onto the front of his t-shirt. He looked at her and opened his mouth, but before he could speak, Nicole hit him around the back of his head with the award's heavy base and he slumped off Jade onto the carpet. Nicole stared down at him for a moment before chucking the award at him.

"Prick," she spat.

Jade, panting for air, caught her eye, and Nicole gave her a sharp nod. Jade smiled and nodded back. She had no words. No words were needed.

44

Nicole used the spare parcel tape to bind Seb's hands and feet together and, once she'd cut Jade and Rebecca free, the three of them had dragged him over to the top of the landing, using the remaining tape to secure his hands to the railings. He was still there, bleeding and dazed but alive and conscious when the police arrived twenty minutes later to arrest him and take him away.

"Quite an eventful morning, all in all," Nicole said as she and Jade sipped cups of tea in Rebecca's front room a while later.

Jade laughed, but it hurt her throat, so she stopped.

"That's putting it mildly," she said, but she appreciated the gallows humour. They'd been chatting for a while and she was warming to Nicole. But when someone had just saved your life, that was understandable. While Rebecca was in the kitchen with the police making her statement, Jade told Nicole everything that had transpired. From the moment she and Sofia realised their mum and Rebecca were linked until today. It had felt good to get it all out in the open, cathartic even. And Nicole was a part of this now. She deserved the truth.

"He was going to go through with it, though," Nicole said. "What a bastard."

Jade gulped back a mouthful of sweet tea. She never took sugar normally, but at times like this, it was needed. "In the end, it was a good job you were suspicious of me," she said. "You were onto me from the start, weren't you?"

Nicole turned her mouth down and shrugged. "I've got a gift. I sometimes think I should have been a cop. But imagine me in a uniform. Ugh."

There was a pause. They both sipped their drinks. "Thank you," Jade said. "I mean it. You saved my life."

"Don't mention it. Buy me a drink sometime."

Jade smiled. "Deal."

"Hopefully this time you won't stand me up, so you can seduce someone's husband."

Jade looked away. She deserved that one. And the way she said it, there was no malice. Just more gallows humour.

"You know what, Nicole? You're not who I thought you were." As soon as she heard herself, she realised what she'd said. She smiled sheepishly as Nicole shot her a look. "Yeah, fair enough."

"But I'll take that," Nicole replied. "I guess I do take a while to settle in with new people. Who knows – *Justine* – if you stay on at Beautiful You! we might even become friends."

"I don't know about me staying on. I doubt Rebecca will want me around after what I did."

"But you've got all that history. Your mum was part of Beautiful You! And now you accept Rebecca's version of events. I reckon she'll want to keep you close. She's a good woman, and she's not got any family. Even less so now." She lowered her voice. "I always sensed she was a bit lonely."

She sat upright as the door opened and the woman herself walked in. She looked exhausted.

"How was it?" Jade asked.

"Not too bad," Rebecca said, slumping into the armchair next to the fireplace. "They're not finished upstairs, but I've told them everything I know. Everything I want them to know." She gave Jade and Nicole a stern look, which expressed all it needed to.

"So, it's all still...under wraps?" Jade asked. "Jonathan Samuels, I mean."

Rebecca sighed. "As they were taking Seb away, he was shouting and bawling, saying he was going to expose the truth and sell his story."

Nicole waved her hand in the air. "No one will believe him."

"Maybe not. But maybe it's time for me to come clean, anyway. A clean slate. Like I wanted. It won't be pretty and we'll have to take plenty of advice from my legal team, but I don't want that man to have any more hold over me. I think with the right comms team, we can get ahead of this story and spin it our way. I'm not saying our share price will hold up and we might be in the wilderness for a while, but I've got a feeling we can wear it in the long run. It's the right thing to do. No more lies. No more secrets."

"Wow, that's brave," Nicole said.

"And stupid?"

"No. Not stupid. Reckless maybe, but you've never been one to play the safe game. You're Rebecca Burton-Webb. You do things your way."

"Thank you, dear." Rebecca smiled.

Jade finished her tea, but held onto the mug, resting it in her lap. She stared down into the empty vessel, hoping she might find the strength to say what she wanted to.

"I'm sorry, Rebecca. For everything." She didn't look at her. "We should have come to you and told you what was going on.

But we were worried if we did you'd shut it down and... I don't know...I don't even know how it got to this. I'm so sorry." She chewed on her lip, focusing her energy on not crying. When Rebecca didn't answer, she risked glancing up at her. She was surprised to find her smiling. It wasn't exactly a warm or loving smile, more the sort you might offer a grieving wife at a funeral. But a smile all the same.

"It's all still very raw," she said. "What you did, what you thought I did, it hurts me. But I suppose in the long run you did me a favour. It was only a matter of time before Seb tried something like this, anyway." Her eyes crinkled at the corners. "And it is good to see you again, after all these years. I know you were only acting from the information you had and it wasn't malicious. Just misguided. We'll talk more about it once we've both rested. But I'm sure we can move past this. I would like to see Maggie again, too. And Sofia."

Jade – Justine – sniffed. "Thank you," she said, but there was barely any sound behind the words.

Rebecca slapped her knees. "Right then, I don't know about you two, but I need a stiff drink."

The two younger women looked at each other and then at the clock above the fireplace. It was only a few minutes after ten in the morning. Rebecca followed their gaze but shrugged.

"Screw it," she said. "After the night we've had, we need one. Plus, as they say, it's always five o'clock somewhere."

"True enough," Justine replied, relaxing her shoulders finally. "Thank you, Rebecca. A drink would be great."

45

A few hours later, once the police had finished and forensics had everything they needed, Rebecca said goodbye to Nicole and Justine, telling them she'd probably take the week off work, and that they should too.

After seeing them out, she closed the door and locked it before leaning back against the wood. The events of the last few hours had not yet properly sunk in. She didn't feel sad or angry or confused. She didn't feel anything.

Closing her eyes, she breathed in the large empty house in front of her. It was cold and airy and far too quiet but that didn't bother her too much. She'd always enjoyed her own company and was better off being alone. If you didn't rely on anyone else, then they couldn't hurt you. Or let you down. This had been proven to her time and time again over the years. If she wanted something done well, she did it herself.

Pushing off from the door with her shoulders, she strode down the hallway and up the stairs. She hardly noticed the police tape and the bloodstain on the carpet as she walked across the landing and up to her bedroom. The contents of the first safe had been rifled through by the police, but, like Justine and Seb, they'd found nothing of any worth. And at least they'd tidied the papers up into neat piles, ready for her to put back where they belonged. Going over to the wardrobe, she knelt in front of the middle safe, silently thanking whoever or whatever was up there watching over her, that no one had managed to get inside this one. She tapped out the access code – his birthday – and opened the door.

She hadn't had reason to open the safe in many years, but she found what she was looking for easily enough. An old brown envelope on the bottom of the middle shelf under a stack of invoices and receipts. She pulled it out and held it up. The envelope was sealed, but she didn't open it. She already knew what was written on the letter inside. More of a confession than a letter. She'd written it almost ten years earlier, on one of the first nights when Seb had stayed out all night long without telling her where he was. She'd hoped after drinking an entire bottle of wine and then moving on to vodka she might have been able to sleep her doubts and fears away, but all the alcohol had done was awaken even more terrible memories.

Holding the envelope to her chest, she closed the safe and walked downstairs and through into the office. She walked over to the corner unit and took down her old shredder, placing it down on the centre of the desk and plugging it in. She should have done this years ago - the next morning when she woke up and realised what she'd confessed to. But something had compelled her to keep the letter. Perhaps she hoped it would be found after her death. But that idea no longer appealed to her. It was time to silence the demons of her past for good.

She switched on the shredder and held the letter over its greedy mouth a moment, before lowering it down into the metal jaws, watching without expression as it sliced her confession into tiny strips.

Now no one would ever know.

She had addressed the letter to 'who it may concern' and over two pages explained how it was she who'd first discovered their production line in Myanmar was less than ethical. She'd wanted to cut all ties with Ufi immediately and own up to their mistake. But Maggie had said no. She'd said it would have ruined everything they'd worked so hard for.

Racked with guilt and unsure what to do, Rebecca had confided in a man she'd met a few years earlier whilst still at Saint Martins. An ambitious freelance reporter called Jonathan Samuels. Or Flick, as she called him, because of the way he often tossed his long fringe away from his face.

Rebecca was Samuels' source.

The two of them had got on well and met often, working out how Rebecca might admit her mistakes and come clean without losing everything. After a few months of working together, they'd fallen in love. But so that Jonathan could write the article without being accused of prejudice, they'd kept their affair secret, even from Maggie. But both of them knew, if they were to present the story the way they wanted, then they needed her engagement and consent. If it was only Rebecca's account, it would come across like she was whistleblowing on her partner and that would destroy them and their company quicker than if the tabloids got hold of the story.

Rebecca's letter went on to explain how she'd begged Maggie to come clean, telling her they could admit their mistakes in a way that might even benefit them in the long run. But she wouldn't have it. As a last resort, Flick approached Maggie at the Water Action fundraiser, and that was when Clive had thrown him to his death.

As the shredder whirred and clanked, Rebecca wiped the tears off her cheek before pulling her phone out of the pocket of her cardigan and scrolling through her extensive list of contacts. She hadn't had cause to ring Peter Sawyer in many years, but she hadn't deleted his number. She had no idea whether he was still on this line – or even alive – but after a couple of rings, he answered.

"Sawyer." His voice was gruffer, older.

"Hello Peter," Rebecca said. "Do you know who this is?"

Sawyer cleared his throat. "I didn't expect to hear from you ever again, Rebecca. I thought everything was hunky dory, and you were the uber earth mother these days."

"Something like that," she said. "But I might need your help with a few issues. Are you still in the business?"

"Of helping people out of a fix? Not for some time. But for you, I can make an exception. What's the job?"

Rebecca watched as the last bit of the letter vanished into the shredder. "I'm not sure, yet. Things I thought were long buried have risen to the surface. Margaret Taylor's youngest daughter. She knows about what happened thirty years ago. The fundraiser. Most of it, at least. Enough that she could be a problem."

The part about Maggie falling ill and Rebecca paying her off was all true. As was the part about Sawyer being paid to cover it up. But that was also the part that could cause problems for her. Big problems. Both Justine and Nicole had sworn they wouldn't tell anyone what they knew, and she supposed if she looked after them both in terms of salary and career advancements, that would remain the case. But she hated the idea of people having a hold of her. The fact she'd let Seb almost ruin her and make her believe she was losing it only solidified this sentiment.

"What are you thinking?" Sawyer asked. "Are you wanting to get rid?"

"No," Rebecca said. "I don't think so." But a part of her wondered whether it might have to happen, eventually.

"What then?"

Rebecca hesitated for a moment before replying. "I need to consider my options. But I just wanted to know you were still out there and still available if I needed you."

Sawyer sniffed. "Like I said. For you, anything."

"Thank you. I'll be in touch."

Rebecca hung up the phone and placed it down on the desk. Whatever happened next, she felt more confident in her standing. She was back in control. Justine Taylor had almost destroyed everything she'd worked so hard for, and she'd never forget that. But it was true what they said. Keep your friends close and your enemies closer.

She smiled to herself before switching off the shredder and heading up the stairs to her bedroom. It would be strange not having Seb around, but she was better off without him. She didn't need him. She didn't need anyone. She was Rebecca Burton-Webb. No one got the better of her. No one.

THE END

Enjoy psychological & domestic thrillers?
You'll love...

THE PACT

"We had a pact and I broke it. That's why she hates me. That's why she's tracked me down. That's why she wants to make me pay..."

Get your copy by clicking here

WANT TO READ MY BOOKS FOR FREE?

To show my appreciation to you for buying this book I'd like to invite you to join my exclusive Readers Club where you'll get the chance to read all my upcoming books for free, and before anyone else.

To join the club please click below:

www.mihattersley.com/readers/

Can you help?

Enjoyed this book? You can make a big difference

Honest reviews of my books help bring them to the attention of other readers. If you've enjoyed this book I would be so grateful if you could spend just five minutes leaving a comment (it can be as short as you like) on the book's Amazon page.

Also by M. I. Hattersley

THE DEMAND

Your phone rings. A distorted voice tells you they've taken your daughter. They will kill her unless you carry out their demand. You have two days...

CLICK HERE TO GET YOUR COPY

THE EX

Your ex's former lovers are all dying in mysterious circumstances - and you could be next on the list...

A new psychological thriller with an ending you won't see coming.

CLICK HERE TO GET YOUR COPY

About the Author

M I Hattersley is a bestselling author of psychological & domestic thrillers and crime fiction.

He lives with his wife and young daughter in Derbyshire, UK